The DAMAGED BRIDE

The Shadow Brides Book 2

SARA MCCLAFLIN

First Edition

ASIN: B0FFY3XYHT

ISBN (trade): 979-8-9991778-2-7

Book Cover: Pia

Editing: Brandy Gibson

Social Media Coordinator: Tawny Gratto

Social Media Group Moderator: Ashley Sullivan

PA: Sarah Toon

Marketing & PR: Wildfire Marketing Solutions

This book is for anyone who was told their boundaries were hurting someone else.
For anyone asked to reopen doors for the sake of peace, forgiveness, or someone else's comfort.
This story does not believe that refusal is cruelty.
It does not believe reconciliation is owed.
Set your boundaries.
Fuck anyone who thinks they're entitled to cross them.

CHAPTER ONE

Opal

I should be packing for Paris or Venice. Maybe Milan.

Instead, I'm packing to marry an asshole. Not that I need him to be lovable, I just need him to be useful.

However, a job is a job—and this one pays obscenely well.

Love isn't required for this arrangement— fear works just as well.

The knock barely finishes before my bedroom fills with people. It's all coordinated at this point. Not to mention the fact that they all tend to show up at any point in time anyway. It's fine, I trust my team with my life.

I don't have to turn around to know who just came in.

All women. All Rosebud. Good. I don't have time for explanations, and they don't need reassurance.

"So," Karrie says lightly, like we're discussing brunch. KarrieSantos—who can smell dirty money from three accounts away—lifts her coffee. "You're packing like you will be back tonight. Not like you're getting married and moving somewhere else."

"I'll be back," I say. "Just not... uncomplicated."

Lena's eyes flick to the ring box on the dresser. She handles Rosebud's tech and all our invisible problems. She doesn't comment. She never does until she's already five steps ahead.

I exhale. "Before anyone asks—yes. It's real. I'm a Bride."

No one is shocked. It's a running joke around here that I would be eventually.

"Of course you are," Katherine mutters—our physical contingency plan. "Because normal exits aren't your thing."

"The Society wanted me to go to training," I add. "A month. It's retreat style. Talia had to do it before marrying Stellan."

Noor tilts her head—Rosebud's pattern reader, the one who hears meaning before it's spoken. "And you said no."

"I don't do training," I say. "I don't disappear. I won't leave this firm without a leader while someone else decides what I'm allowed to be."

Lena finally looks up. "They agreed?"

"They needed me more than they needed compliance." That's the risk you take when you hire a weapon instead of a rule follower.

I zip the suitcase and turn to face them. My team. My infrastructure. The reason I can become a bride and still have a business.

"I'm still running Rosebud," I say. "Nothing pauses

because I'm wearing a ring. You'll have more authority. Use it. Don't ask me unless it can't be contained."

Karrie lifts her coffee. "So... same as usual."

A small smirk graces my face. "Exactly."

I grab my coat. "I'm working Dante Valera's case personally. Yes, *that* Valera. Yes, he's the fiancé. No, that doesn't make him special."

Noor watches me like she's already running outcomes. "If he becomes a liability?"

"He already is," I say.

I reach into my bag and drop a slim black folder onto the bed.

Lena picks it up without asking. The screen glow dies as she opens it. Karrie sets her coffee down. Katherine shifts closer, eyes flicking once to the door, then back to me.

That's trust. I don't say it out loud, but this team needs to know everything.

"Private material is surfacing inside Obsidian," I say as I shrug. "Someone wants him off balance."

Lena scrolls faster. Noor's focus tightens.

"There's chatter starting to circle him," I continue. "The kind that doesn't need proof to stick. It's early. That's the problem."

Karrie grimaces. "So this isn't external."

"No," I say. "It's too precise."

Katherine's jaw sets. "Inside job."

"Or someone wearing an inside face."

I tap the ring box on the dresser. "Rosebud can trace the perimeter," I say. "Money, systems, behavior." I meet

Noor's eyes. "What it can't do is live in his house." Understanding moves through the room without a word. "He doesn't need an investigator," I say. "He needs someone who belongs there long enough to notice what doesn't."

Lena closes the folder. "You're the access point."

"I'm the blind spot." I pull on my coat. "You run the firm," I say. "Same rules as always. Fix what breaks. This case is our priority, all others are secondary. If you have information, call me immediately. Otherwise, text me letting me know it's urgent."

Karrie lifts her coffee again, this time without a smile. "Anything's possible."

"Exactly." I open the door. "Rosebud never wobbles," I say. "It adapts to anything."

Then I'm gone in a flash.

The driver is sitting in front of my building and opens the door before I ask.

The car doesn't pull around back. That's the first thing I notice. He slows at the curb instead of the service drive, neon washing over the windshield, Obsidian's façade gleaming like it always does—expensive, controlled, pretending nothing ugly ever happens inside.

Interesting.

I glance at my reflection in the tinted glass and reach into my bag.

The rings go on last, one on each hand. The Society's taste runs theatrical when it wants to make a point. I don't fight it. If they want a spectacle, I'll give them one.

The car stops. The driver opens my door and steps

back without a word. Professional. Dante's people always are.

I step onto the sidewalk in heels that click just loud enough to announce intent.

Obsidian's front entrance is all glass and velvet rope, security is perfectly positioned to discourage curiosity and reward confidence. I walk straight toward it like I belong there.

I guess I technically do.

"Ma'am," one of the guards says, stepping into my path. He's being polite as he was paid to be... but not with me. "The club doesn't open until—"

I stop close enough that he has to decide whether to step back or stand his ground.

Without a word, I lift my left hand. The ring catches the light. Platinum. Obnoxious. Impossible to miss.

His eyes flick to it before he can stop himself.

"Go ahead," I say mildly. "Call it in."

He hesitates. His partner is already reaching for an earpiece.

I smile. "I'd hate for Dante to hear I was delayed at the door," I add. "He's very particular about his optics."

That does it. The second guard straightens. "Name?"

I don't miss a beat. "Mrs. Opal Valera."

The guard steps aside immediately. Not toward the hall. Toward the door. "Welcome to Obsidian," he says, tightly.

Inside, the club unfolds around me. It feels like catching a predator mid step. The music plays low, a sultry jazz loop with no one to seduce. Overhead, the lights are up—not flashing or pulsing, but clinical looking.

It's the first thing that feels wrong. Obsidian isn't meant to be seen this way.

The dance floor yawns wide and empty. Curved velvet booths line the outer edge like shadows out of uniform. Low tables sit untouched—no lipstick on the rims, no ice melting in forgotten glasses.

Everything's too visible. Too bare.

The walls are obsidian black, backlit in places with a muted amber glow—but under full lights, they look less seductive and more like stone masks chipped at the edges. It feels like walking backstage at something built to entertain. Like seeing an amusement park with the lights on—no illusion, just exposed wires and empty smiles.

Good.

A male bar manager near the bar clocks the rings and freezes. Someone whispers wondering who I am drifting across me.

I take my time crossing the floor. Obsidian isn't just a club. It's a performance that only works if everyone knows their marks.

I don't look for Dante. There's no need, I can *feel* him here.The room bends subtly in his direction—attention drifting, conversations thinning, the kind of gravitational pull that doesn't need noise to function. I track it out of habit, not interest.

Then I see the bartender.

She's leaning in close. Too close. Not quite touching him—just hovering in that practiced way that suggests access without having to ask for permission. Comfortable.

Despite the bristle in my spine, I don't react. I need to

get a feel for the situation, see just who she is. We need this to be as real as possible.

Dante stands at the bar. Black suit, open collar, all clean lines and restraint. Tall enough to loom without effort. Stillness like a coiled decision. His face is all intelligence and curated charm—high cheekbones, dark lashes, a mouth made for persuasion. Warm brown eyes flecked with amber that read indulgent until they don't.

He's beautiful in the way weapons are beautiful.

The bartender laughs again, the sound like nails on a chalkboard. I can't take it.

I don't announce myself. I don't hesitate. And I sure as hell don't ask.

I take his face in my hands and kiss him.

It's not tentative. It's not sweet. It's possession rendered physical—mouth to mouth, heat and pressure, my body aligning with his like this was always the plan.

For half a second, Dante is perfectly still. Then he responds.

Not leading. Not overtaking. Meeting me stroke for stroke, tension snapping tight between us. His hand comes up to my waist on instinct alone—and stops there. Waiting.

Good.

I break the kiss first.

The bartender is frozen.

"Darling," I say lightly, thumb brushing Dante's jaw like a wife would do. "You left your ring at home."

Dante's gaze locks on mine, dark now, furious and alert and very aware that I just took control of the room without asking.

His hand closes around my wrist. Possessive in the way men get when they realize the ground just shifted under them.

"Office," he says, low and so goddamn controlled.

It makes me want to slap the perfect calm off his face.

That voice grates every nerve I have. He's never had to raise his voice or say please. He's used to being above everyone and expects to be bowed down to.

He walks ahead like he knows I'll follow. He's not wrong. But I still fantasize about driving my heel into the back of his knee just to remind him he's not a god.

Not to me.

I look at his hand. Before moving my gaze to his face.

"I was already walking," I say. "You didn't need the dramatics."

His grip tightens half a degree. Not enough to bruise. But enough to sting. "I didn't ask."

"No," I agree. "You grabbed."

That earns me a warning look, but he doesn't let go. He drags me through Obsidian like the place is allergic to resistance. Doors open before we reach them. People flatten themselves out of the way.

Good instincts.

The office door shuts hard behind us.

He releases me and turns in the same motion, crowding my space like that's still his advantage.

"What the fuck was that?" He snaps.

I roll my wrist once. "An introduction."

"You kissed me."

He doesn't shout it. He doesn't even raise his voice.

He just says it, like the words themselves should be enough to rewind time.

"Yes." I don't bother softening it. There's nothing to soften. He kissed me back

"In front of my staff." He drags a hand down his face now. Clearly he's frustrated.

"Yes." I lift a brow. I thought this guy was supposed to be articulate in high pressure situations. If he can't think on his toes, then I'm not sure what I can do with him.

"In front of clients." This time he stops moving altogether, shoulders squared, eyes fixed on me, trying to pin me in place.

"Also yes."

"You don't get to do that," he says at last. A rule he's said a thousand times and never had questioned. He hasn't met the new me. I don't take well to being told what to do.

I tip my head, studying him the way I would a faulty lock. "I already did."

His lips press together. He takes a step closer, testing distance, reclaiming space out of habit. "That doesn't mean you get to do it again."

"I didn't say I would."

"You didn't have to." His tone hardens. "You implied it."

"I implied nothing." My voice stays level. Flat enough to be undeniable. "You inferred."

"Jesus fucking Christ." The curse slips out. My tone surprised even him. "We're married now," I say. "There is a certain way you need to act. So tone down the attitude."

He stares at me. His mouth opens like he's ready to tear into me. But then he closes it.

Then it opens again, slower this time. "You think this is funny?"

I take a second before answering. Not because I'm searching for words, but because I'm watching him recalibrate. The tension in his shoulders. The way his hands flex like they want something to grab and throw.

"No," I say. "I think it's efficient."

He laughs once. There's no humor in it. "That was a goddamn spectacle."

"It was a controlled narrative." I step past him as I say it, forcing him to turn if he wants to keep me in his line of sight.

"You blindsided me." His voice follows, clipped, irritated. He pivots, tracking me. He doesn't like being the one repositioning.

"I established visibility." I stop near his desk, fingertips brushing the edge.

"You undermined me." He's closer now, not crowding, but near enough that the heat of his frustration bleeds into the space.

That finally earns him a reaction. Not much. Just the corner of my mouth lifting as I look at him again. "You were doing just fine undermining yourself."

One second I'm standing at the edge of his desk, fingers resting against polished wood. The next, his hands are there—planting hard on either side of me, arms locking me in place as he leans forward, crowding every inch of space I just claimed.

The desk presses into the backs of my thighs. Solid.

I don't flinch.

His presence slams down like a wall. He doesn't touch me beyond the barrier of his arms, but it's worse this way. His jaw is tight, eyes dark, breath controlled just enough to tell me this is costing him effort.

"The hell does that mean?"

Now he's willing to listening.

"It means," I say, moving his arm and stepping past him, "that if you're being leaked, surveilled, and framed—and you are—you don't get to play mysterious bachelor king anymore."

I turn back to him.

"You need credibility. You need a fixed point. You need someone people won't question. You just don't like that the wife you need is me."

His eyes flash. "You're enjoying this."

"No," I say honestly. "I'm working."

"This is my life."

"And now," I reply, "it's my case."

He laughs once. Nothing about him says humor. "You think a ring makes you untouchable?"

"No," I say. "Being indispensable does."

"You don't know how this world works."

"I built a parallel one," I say. "And it eats yours for breakfast."

"You used my name out there," he says finally, voice low and tight, like he's been holding something back.

"I married you," I reply without hesitation.

"That doesn't give you control," he snaps, a hand bracing against the desk as he leans in.

"No," I say evenly. "It gives me access."

"You don't get to walk into my club and take over," he adds, jaw set, eyes burning like he is still trying to wrap his mind around my resistance.

"I didn't take over," I say. "I announced myself."

"That bartender—"

"—was a liability," I cut in. "Unvetted proximity. Too familiar. Too visible."

"She works for me."

"So does the rest of your staff," I say. "And one of them is leaking your life to the public."

His nostrils flare. "You don't know that."

"I know you didn't stop it."

"That doesn't mean—"

"It means," I interrupt, voice flat, "that you need oversight. And optics. And someone who isn't emotionally attached to your bullshit."

His black hair is slicked back and his amber eyes are staring at me like he's trying to decide whether to strangle me or fuck me or throw something expensive.

"You don't get to rewrite my rules." He is annoying me at this point. So used to ordering. Not used to taking commands.

"I don't need to," I say. "I'm operating in the space where your 'rules' have failed. I *get* to fix your mess, and you *get* to have the benefit of that."

"This doesn't happen again," he says.

"It will," I reply immediately.

"When?"

"When it's useful."

"You answer to me."

I hate that our conversations are like a tennis match. I hate that he can keep up with my snap.

I step closer. My turn to crowd him. Time to take him out of his comfort zone. "No," I say. "You will answer to me. By the time this is done, you'll get your life back. I'll get to move on with mine. Plus the giant check helps too."

"You think that gives you power?"

"I know it does."

He swears again. Louder this time. "You're not here to make my life harder."

"I'll do whatever I have to in order to get the job done," I say, voice stripped clean of warmth. "If that means pissing you off, I'll live."

"You're here to fix this goddamn mess."

"And I will."

"How?"

"By controlling the narrative," I say. "By forcing visibility where there's secrecy. By giving your enemies a distraction they can't ignore."

He scoffs. "You?"

"Me."

He shakes his head. "You're unbelievable."

"You hired me."

"I hired the society," he scoffs.

"And they hired me. With me comes Rosebud. Take it or leave it."

He opens his mouth to say something. But I have no interest in whatever it is he feels the need let fall out of his mouth

I turn for the door.

"You don't walk away from me," he snaps, finding his voice again.

I pause with my hand on the handle.

"Adjust, Mr. Vàlera," I say calmly. "I'm not going anywhere."

I leave him there—standing in the middle of his office, mouth opening and closing like he's still trying to find a version of this conversation where he wins.

He won't.

We both know it.

CHAPTER TWO
Dante

I catch her before she reaches the door, my hand closing around her waist and hauling her back into my office.

No fucking way she gets the last word.

I reach past her and slam the door shut myself.

"We need to go over some ground rules," I say, keeping my voice level even as my pulse snaps under my skin.

She doesn't look rattled. Of course she doesn't.

"This should be interesting," she says, tone maddeningly calm as she crosses her arms over her chest. A chest I do *not* need to be looking at right now.

I'm used to obedience. It usually arrives before the begging.

Opal offers neither.

I don't take that insolence well.

"What rules are you talking about?" she asks, her patience already halfway gone. "Because if you think this is going to be one sided, you're mistaken."

I know I blink at her like an idiot, for a second I feel like one.

"I have rules too," she adds calmly. "If we're doing this, we're doing all of them. Not just yours."

Breathe, Dante. Don't lose control.

Every instinct I have wants to call the Society and ask them what the hell they were thinking when they chose *this* bride for me.

She's infuriating because she doesn't modulate herself for the room, doesn't soften or recalibrate to gain advantage. She speaks the way people do when they've already accepted the consequences and decided they're worth it.

Loyalty, as most people understand it, clearly doesn't factor into her calculations.

She betrayed Stellan Rothwell without hesitation, without the usual signs of panic or regret. There was no flinch, no collapse, no attempt to disappear once the fallout hit. Instead, she stayed visible, built something of her own, and turned exile into leverage—founding a company that handles problems for people with serious money and even worse secrets.

That tells me exactly how she is. She operates without allegiance, without a banner to hide behind, and without any need to frame herself as a savior.

No visible soul to bargain with.

"We're doing mine first," I say, taking the lead back from her.

She turns back toward me, and the room tilts into something less predictable. I have her focus now, whether she intended to give it or not.

"Nothing happens inside Obsidian without my knowledge," I say.

"Control issue," she replies.

"Territory," I correct.

She knows exactly what I mean. Her business is her territory too.

"And before you continue," she says evenly, "understand this—if you're laying down lines, I'm drawing mine right back."

I hold her gaze.

Good.

"You don't lie to me," I say. "Not directly. Not creatively."

"If I think it matters," she says, "you'll know."

Reasonable on the surface. Slippery underneath. She's giving herself room to decide later what truth costs.

"You don't use the marriage to maneuver my staff or my guests," I say.

Her mouth curves, just barely. "I don't need an audience."

No. She doesn't. She's the kind of woman who doesn't raise her voice because she's never had to compete for anything. She has always been the best.

"If you want something from me," I say, "you ask for it."

"I don't beg."

"I didn't say beg," I shoot back, giving her a smug look.

She doesn't wait for me to say anything more. "My turn," she says, taking the floor. "You don't interfere with my work unless I invite you," she continues. "You don't slow it down, redirect it, or try to supervise it."

"Agreed," I say.

"You don't threaten Rosebud," she says. "You don't apply pressure, you don't bargain with it, and you don't let it take the hit for something else."

We'll see about that. I'm not one to bend my rules for anyone.

"You don't punish me for decisions you'd make yourself," she says.

"That's situational," I tell her.

"So am I," she replies.

I almost laugh.

"And you don't confuse proximity with possession," she finishes. "Being close to me doesn't make me yours."

She doesn't hesitate, which tells me this rule was decided long before she walked into the room.

"If you want sex," she says, "it's me. Only me. I'm not interested in managing risk that isn't mine."

I still, irritation flaring before I can suppress it. She didn't ask, didn't angle, didn't leave space for negotiation. She presented it like a known fact and waited for me to catch up.

"No rotating doors," she continues, completely unruffled. "No impulse indulgences. No stress relief elsewhere."

"That sounds like ownership," I say. I lean back in my chair, completely relaxed.

"It's hygiene," she replies. "I don't need surprises. I don't need complications. And I don't need STDs."

I search her face for provocation. Don't find it.

"Before you get ideas," she adds, "it doesn't mean anything. Sex is sex. I don't want meaning. I don't care about exclusivity everywhere—just there."

I pause longer than I intend to.

"So if I cross that line," I say, "I close every other door?"

"Yes," she replies without a second thought.

"And you don't pretend that means more than it does," I shoot back.

"I don't."

I nod, accepting it without comment. Comment would imply negotiation.

"We break these," I say, "there are consequences."

Her eyes never leave mine. "So make sure you recognize that and weight the risks before you fuck me over, lover boy."

She steps back then. I watch her turn to go again, already aware of the problem she's just created.

She's reduced sex to logistics. Stripped it of power. And somehow made it more dangerous than anything else she's said.

I tell myself this is manageable.

I'm lying.

However, that fact doesn't stop me from stepping closer anyway, close enough to feel the heat she pretends isn't there. She doesn't move. Doesn't adjust. Doesn't give me the satisfaction of retreat or invitation.

Nothing about her posture changes.

"Anything else?" I ask.

It's a test. A narrow one. She looks at me for a beat, then shakes her head once.

She stays where she is, like the idea of retreat never occurred to her. I turn away and pick up the phone.

The line connects immediately.

"Valera," Brenna, the Society of the Shadow Brides Chief of Security, says.

"Get me Mirelle," I reply. The line clicks as it's transferred.

"Dante," Mirelle says. "You sound displeased."

"That's one word for it." I don't look at Opal when I speak next. "Of everyone in your catalog," I say, "of every woman you could have chosen, you sent me her."

"She is uniquely qualified," Mirelle says.

"That's not what I asked."

I can hear the woman's smirk through the phone. "Mr. Valera, you did not ask a question."

I turn then, just enough to meet Opal's eyes. She watches me without reaction, like this isn't the first time someone has argued over her existence.

"You know exactly who she is to Rothwell," I continue. "You know what she represents. You know the history. You still decided to put her in my life."

"We decided she was appropriate," Mirelle says calmly.

"Appropriate," I repeat. "You could have picked anyone else."

I watch her out of the corner of my eye. I don't trust her as far as I can throw her.

"That is precisely why we did not."

My jaw tightens.

"She's volatile," I say. "Unaligned. She operates

without permission and without remorse. That's not a bride. That's a liability."

"She is independent," Mirelle corrects. "Which is why she cannot be redirected once placed. She's a *partner*, Mr. Valera."

"You don't send a woman like that into my house unless you want something to break."

"Yes," Mirelle says. "We do."

I exhale slowly through my nose. I'm frustrated.

"You didn't choose her for compatibility," I say. "You chose her because she doesn't bend."

"We chose her because she survives," Mirelle replies. "You don't need someone pliable, Dante. You need someone who won't disappear the first time you apply pressure. You are... you afterall."

"I didn't ask for a mirror."

"No," Mirelle says. "You asked for a fix to your problems. We gave you that."

I look at Opal again. She hasn't moved, hasn't adjusted, hasn't even acknowledged anything. As if it is someone else's problem. Not hers.

"You could have warned me," I say.

"We could have," Mirelle agrees. "You would have objected."

"Yes," I say. "This isn't what I agreed to."

"It is exactly what you agreed to," Mirelle replies. "You simply didn't think we would be this precise."

I close my eyes for half a second. "You sent me the one woman I really want to kill," I say.

Stellan is one of the only friends I have. That says a

lot because I don't have friends. Opal did everything she could to make sure he had no leg to stand on.

That alone makes me want to kill her.

"Yes," she says softly. "That was the point."

The connection ends without warning. When I lower the phone, Opal is still there, untouched by the exchange. It's honestly impressive.

"Anyone else," I say to her, not bothering to tone down my irritation, "would have been easier."

Something tightens briefly at the corner of her mouth before it smooths away. "I'm aware," she replies.

I sit on the edge of my desk. I don't crowd her. I don't retreat. I put myself just high enough to shift the balance and wait to see if she resents it—or rises to it.

"So this is you reclaiming the room," she says, walking around with a calm demeanor that grates at my nerves.

"Call it posture."

She almost smiles, almost. "You're very attached to furniture."

I huff a breath that might be a laugh. "You're very comfortable pushing," I say.

"I push where it matters."

"You don't scare easily," I say.

"I scare selectively."

I tilt my head, studying her. "You're enjoying this."

Her eyes flick to mine. "I enjoy clarity."

I stay on the desk while she steps into the space between my knees. She's close enough that I register the heat of her before I register the intention. Her movements are slow, like we've done this countless times and she already knows I won't stop her.

She tilts her head, just slightly, eyes on my mouth now instead of my eyes.

"You're thinking about kissing me," she says.

I don't lie. "I'm thinking about the consequences if I do." My voice is huskier than I intended.

Her gaze flicks back up. She's amused by everything. It's infuriating.

I lean forward a fraction. Not enough to close the distance, but just enough to test her—to see if she'll back down. "For you," I say, "I make exceptions to those consequences."

"Careful," she says, smiling like the Cheshire Cat. "That's how men confuse curiosity with permission."

She lifts her hand—not to touch me, just close enough that I feel it there. A ghost of contact. A threat waiting to happen. Our mouths are inches apart now. I can smell her. It isn't meant to entice. It's meant to be noticed.

"If I wanted to kiss you," she says quietly, "I would."

"And you don't," I reply, my voice is barely a whisper now.

"I didn't say that."

The silence between us tightens. Pulls. I can feel it—how easy it would be to close the gap, how badly I want to prove I'm the one deciding where this goes.

She leans in just enough that her breath brushes my mouth. Then she stops. Pulls back. Steps away like the tension was all in my head.

"There," she says. "That's what restraint looks like."

She doesn't wait for a response. Instead, she simply walks away from me.

From behind, she's all lines and intention. The cut of her dress follows her spine cleanly, fabric skimming instead of clinging, as if it knows better than to beg for attention. It moves with her, not against her. The hem hits mid calf, revealing just enough leg to be eye catching.

Her back is straight, her shoulders are relaxed, there's no hesitation in her stride. She's stunning.

The heels are clicking against the floor. I track the way her hips shift—not exaggerated, not coy. The kind of movement that comes from knowing exactly how much space you occupy and refusing to apologize for it.

She doesn't look back.

Now I'm left with the image of her walking away, the pull of it settling low and unwelcome, sharpening into something I don't usually allow myself to linger on. Attraction isn't the problem.

The door closes behind her, and I stay where I am, jaw tight, already aware of the truth. I don't like admitting I wasn't watching her leave.

I reach for the phone. "Lucrezia," I say when she answers. "My office. Now."

She's there in minutes, just as she always is. She shuts the door behind her and takes in the room in one pass—the desk, the chair, the air.

"Opal Greer is on-site," I say. No preamble. "She's here to fix what's broken."

Lucrezia's expression shifts. Interest, not surprise. "The bride."

"The investigator," I correct. "Same woman."

That gets me a look, sharp and curious. She doesn't interrupt.

"I want Obsidian locked down," I continue. "Full internal freeze. Staff access restricted to essentials only. Server permissions rerouted through Rosebud. Everything."

"All of it?" she asks.

"All of it," I confirm. "If Opal asks for access, she gets it. No delays. No approvals. If she wants a door opened, it opens."

Lucrezia nods once, already moving the pieces in her head. "And housing?"

I don't hesitate. "She's not going back to wherever she came from."

"The apartment in Onyx?" Lucrezia asks. "The one you had prepped for the bride?"

"Yes."

She studies me for a beat. "Not the house?"

"No," I say flatly. "Never the house." That space is mine. Unshared. Unnegotiated. I don't bring unknown variables into my walls.

Lucrezia accepts that without comment. She always does. "I'll move her," she says. "Discreetly."

"And keep her close," I add. "I want her inside the perimeter, not orbiting it."

A pause. Then, carefully she asks. "You trust her?"

I meet her gaze. "I trust her competence."

Lucrezia doesn't press. She turns for the door, already issuing orders into her comm. "You know," she says, almost lightly, "you just handed a lot of power to someone who doesn't wait to be told."

I allow myself a thin smile. "That's why she's here. Oh and don't forget to give her my business number. She probably won't use it, but I want to contact her when I need her."

CHAPTER THREE

Dante

Opal Greer isn't just a complication. She's a precedent, and precedents are how men lose ground without realizing it.

I've spent years keeping men from realizing how fragile their power actually is. Anticipating pressure points, rerouting attention, deciding which failures stay private and which ones never surface at all. Opal doesn't redirect outcomes. She forces them. From the outside, it always looks inevitable—boards collapsing in sequence, charges surfacing as if by coincidence, reputations failing under their own mistakes. Nothing ever traces back to her directly. That's the point.

Stellan Rothwell should have been untouchable.

He wasn't careless or indulgent. Rothwell Strategic was built to absorb pressure, redirect attention, and neutralize fallout long before it reached daylight. I've seen weaker operations survive on less discipline.

Opal Greer didn't come at him head on. She adjusted

variables, introduced scrutiny, and let the system do what systems always do when they're cornered. Let PR and media take hold. The rumors swirl on their own while she stays out of the spotlight.

She didn't expose everything, because that would have been crude. She released only what was necessary, timed precisely so the wrong people began pulling threads they didn't understand until the entire structure unraveled in their hands.

What followed was inevitable.

It ended in arrests, frozen assets, and a carefully staged display of accountability meant to reassure people who needed to believe the system still worked.

I move to the bar built into the back wall of my office and pour myself a drink I don't need. The motion gives my hands something to do while my thoughts go where I usually keep them locked.

Stellan—brilliant, controlled, infuriatingly precise—was left standing in the mess, forced to rebuild. I watched him do it because I knew what that kind of recalibration costs. I've been rebuilding since I was seventeen.

Opal is entering my every thought.

I open her contact on my phone several times a day to see if maybe she reached out.

The screen ends up staring back at me with no new messages. Only the old ones.

OPAL

Dante, this is my phone number.

I think about my parents. A mother who was too weak to fight and a father who was too evil to care. I went to their funeral for no other reason than I had to. A plane crash made an open casket impossible. Not that I bothered to stay in touch after I moved out.

I push that thought away. I don't want to think about them. Not right now.

There were no siblings to scatter afterward. No extended family circling with concern or inheritance disputes. Just a house emptied in stages and a city that forgot my last name faster than I expected. I learned early that survival isn't about grief. It's about replacement. You fill the absence or it fills you.

Massimo Bianchi entered my life when I was still deciding what kind of man I intended to become.

He didn't offer sympathy. He didn't ask questions he already knew the answers to. He treated me like someone worth investing in, not rescuing, and that distinction mattered more than anything he could have given me. Massimo taught me how to read rooms that didn't want to be read and how to turn warmth into authority without losing the edge beneath it. He corrected me when I miscalculated and backed me when others tested the perimeter.

He never tried to replace my father. He simply showed up consistently enough that the role took shape on its own.

Alessio came later, already dangerous in the way men are when they don't need to prove it. Where Massimo taught me how to hold power openly, Alessio reminded me why restraint matters. He watches everything. He forgets nothing. He doesn't mistake familiarity for safety, not even with me.

They're not allies. They're not assets. They're the closest thing I have to a family.

Massimo and Alessio aren't principled men pretending at darkness when it suits them. They're as stripped of illusion as I am, just honest about the fact that some people only understand consequence when it's delivered without mercy. They don't romanticize it. They don't apologize for it. They accept what they are and move accordingly.

That's why, when Rafe finally ran out of places to hide, I didn't intervene.

Rafe wore a badge and used it like a shield while he carved fear into Talia's life, piece by piece, believing authority made him untouchable. He thought the uniform would keep him safe.. He thought wrong.

I watched Stellan finish him.

I didn't look away. I didn't step in. I didn't feel a single flicker of regret when it was over. If anything, I felt a sense of satisfaction at seeing a man who had abused power learn, far too late, that it goes both ways. Stellan deserved that moment after everything he and Talia had gone through.

Anyone who calls that soulless has never understood what it costs to live in this world with your eyes open.

Massimo would have done the same thing without hesitation. Alessio would have made sure there were no witnesses and no loose ends. None of us have lost sleep over it.

Which is why Opal Greer unsettles me in a way I don't enjoy examining.

She didn't move against Rothwell Strategic for sport or spectacle. She isolated a pressure point and leaned until the structure gave, unconcerned with who else was standing nearby. At the time, I assumed it was ambition or appetite. The more I look at it now, the more it resembles defense rather than attack.

I've spent years managing the consequences of that kind of intervention. I step in when needed and end the situation when it warrants it.

I take a slow drink and set the glass down. I opened my doors to her. I gave her access. I let her inside my perimeter because I needed what she does better than I needed certainty. I don't regret it. At least not yet. I'm under no delusion that regretting this is out of the question at some point.

But I know better than to pretend this is neutral ground. If Opal Greer decides I'm wrong, she won't hesitate to prove it.

My phone vibrates against the bar. I glance down.

ALESSIO

So. The bride.

I snort softly despite myself and take another sip before answering.

What about her?

Three dots appear. I can barely stand to see what he

has to say. He's been ribbing me about this since he found out.

ALESSIO

I was told that she walked through Obsidian like your wife should. I assumed this was intentional on your part. Although my inside sources tell me it was not. You were caught off guard. I am both impressed and concerned.

I exhale through my nose, more amused than I want to be.

Nothing about Opal Greer is accidental.

ALESSIO

That's not reassuring.

I didn't sign up for this to get reassurance.

ALESSIO

Should I be worried?

I tilt the glass, watching the whiskey catch the light, and let myself smile.

Only if she decides you're in her way.

ALESSIO

Understood. Dinner soon?

Soon.

I lock the phone and set it aside.

I look once more at the door Opal Greer walked through, already knowing this isn't a problem I'll be able to manage from a distance.

I invited her in.

Whatever happens next is on me.

CHAPTER FOUR

Opal

I scroll through my phone without really seeing it, killing time until Dante decides what happens next. For the moment, the control is his. I pushed, he absorbed it, and now I wait because that's how these exchanges work when both sides are deciding the next move.

I open the Shadow Brides manual again, my thumb flicking past sections I already know by heart. They handed it to me in a paper binder, like the world hasn't moved on, so I digitized it the first night. I don't trust information I can't search, annotate, or destroy if necessary.

According to the manual, I'm required to live with my husband. The optics matter. This has to read as a real marriage, not a contractual arrangement disguised for donors, committees, and people who prefer their power sanitized.

There's a problem with that requirement.

I have no idea where Dante Valera actually lives.

I wait for the message, the escort, the instruction that tells me where I'm supposed to go. He'll send someone instead of coming himself. Men like him always do when they're still deciding how much ground they're willing to concede.

There's no chance he's taking me to his real house.

I've done too much research into what my husband has up his sleeve. A month ago, he leased a high rise apartment in Onyx Casino. There was no public justification and no business need that explained it. You don't rent a place like that unless you're planning to keep someone out of your private life. I don't take it personally, because I would have made the same choice in his position.

It does complicate the performance, though. Pretending to be a happily married couple is harder when you're staged in neutral territory, surrounded by expensive walls with no history and no residue to show any joy.

I slip my phone back into my pocket and sit on the bar stool tucked into a corner of the bar, the one positioned to see without being seen. Whoever designed this floor understood the value of peripheral control.

The door to Dante's office opens above me, followed by the soft, unhurried sound of heels on the stairs. I don't look up right away. People who need attention announce themselves. The ones who matter don't.

She stops at the landing. Dressed in black, a matching pantsuit tailored to perfection, paired with designer heels that weren't chosen for comfort, she's obviously important. Her brown hair is pulled back from her face in a way that suggests habit rather than vanity, exposing a heart shaped face finished in full makeup that reads as her loving to be put together.

She reaches the bottom of the stairs and turns toward me. "You're Opal," she says. She's not asking me. She knows everything. Dante doesn't have a personal assistant. Lucrezia, the general manager of Obsidian, would be the closest thing to one. The woman has a reputation almost as notorious as mine.

I angle my body toward her, giving her my attention without offering anything else.

"Lucrezia," she continues, extending a hand that I take firmly. "I run Obsidian when Dante is busy being difficult."

That earns her a fraction of a smile from me. I like her immediately.

"He asked me to take you to the apartment," she adds, already turning toward the corridor that leads out of Obsidian. "Everything you'll need is already in place."

That tells me two things at once. Dante made the call quickly, and he didn't want to be the one to do this himself.

I slide off the stool and fall into step beside her as we move through the back halls, past doors that are usually for employees only. There is a maze of corridors in this club. This place is designed to make people forget where the exits are.

I know he's watching before I ever look for him. Not because I feel anything mystical, but because the space behaves differently when Dante Valera is paying attention.

I don't turn toward the upper level. I don't slow my stride or change my posture to invite acknowledgment. That would turn observation into sensing discomfort, and I have no intention of being vulnerable. If he wants to track my exit, he can do it without my help.

Lucrezia opens the door to a waiting car, holding it just long enough for me to slide in before taking the seat opposite. The driver pulls away smoothly, the Strip bleeding into abstract light beyond the tinted windows.

Only once we're moving does she glance at me again, her expression unreadable but not unfriendly.

"For what it's worth," she says, settling back into the seat, "he doesn't watch people unless they matter."

I meet her gaze without blinking.

She reaches for the leather portfolio resting against her thigh and turns it toward me. The contents are clipped, tabbed, and ordered. I'm intrigued.

"Marriage registration," she says, tapping the first section. "Confidentiality agreements. Non disclosure clauses. Access parameters."

I take the portfolio and begin reading. I am listening to her as I skim.

The language is dense but familiar, written to survive scrutiny from people who make their living signing contracts and running Vegas. Compliance is structured as expectation rather than request. Dante's influence is obvious in the framework even if he never touched the text.

I move through the pages quickly. There are no traps here, no attempts at romance disguised as obligation. This marriage is meant to function, not persuade. Perfect for what I need.

I sign where indicated, initial where required, and return the portfolio to her once I reach the end.

She checks the signatures with a flicker of surprise on her face. "That was efficient," she says. "Most people slow down."

"I don't sign things I don't understand," I reply. "Once I do, there's no reason to hesitate."

Her mouth curves slightly, the expression is genuine. "You're going to do just fine here."

The car slows as the Onyx Hotel rises ahead of us, its black glass reflecting the Strip. The driver opens the door, and Lucrezia steps out first. I follow, smoothing my jacket as I straighten.

The doors glide open without pause. Inside, the casino hums. Dealers move with controlled ease.

She doesn't slow or look around. I match her pace, aware of eyes tracking us without making the mistake of searching for them. We cross the floor toward a private bank of elevators set slightly apart. She taps a card against the panel without breaking stride.

Thankfully, the doors open immediately. It's not that I'm scared of seeing these people, but it's not something I *want* to do. I wasn't exactly the best person in the world for a while there, and the people in this building got the brunt of that.

The ascent is smooth and quiet. When the doors open, we step into a corridor.

She stops at a door and glances back at me. "This is

the apartment," she says. "It was prepared with the expectation that you'd need more than living space."

That gets my attention.

She opens the door and gestures me inside. I cross the threshold without hesitation, already registering the separation from the rest of the building.

I move deeper into the apartment letting my gaze sweep the space the way I always do when I'm somewhere new.

The living area is expansive without being indulgent, all clean lines and muted tones. Nothing shows wear. Nothing suggests habit. The furniture is arranged for sightlines rather than comfort, positioned so no one ever has their back fully turned to the room. The couch faces the windows, not the door. The glass tables are thick and flawless.

It feels staged. A house meant for sale not for living.

The kitchen confirms it. Everything is stocked, pristine, and untouched, the appliances integrated seamlessly into the cabinetry, the counters clear of anything personal.

The bedroom is worse.

The bed is perfectly made, dressed in dark linens that suggest intention without intimacy. The lighting is calibrated—flattering without being warm. Closets line one wall, already filled with clothing that fits my measurements down to the centimeter. Nothing is worn. Nothing is familiar. Everything assumes I will arrive and adapt. The bathroom follows the same logic.

No one lives here.

This isn't a home. It's a holding space, assembled to look convincing without ever becoming real.

It's a beautiful cage.

I turn back toward Lucrezia, who has remained near the entrance, watching without hovering.

"It's fine," I say, because that's true as far as it goes. "But it isn't enough."

She studies me for a moment, then smiles like she's been waiting for that exact assessment. "I thought you might say that."

Crossing the living room she stops at a panel set flush into the wall, indistinguishable from the surrounding surface unless you know to look for it. Her hand moves with practiced ease, pressing a sequence I couldn't have guessed from observation alone.

The panel slides open soundlessly.

The room beyond shifts the entire equation.

I step inside slowly, my fingers brushing the edge of the desk as I take it in. The layout anticipates how I think, how I move when I'm deep in something, how I need information arranged when the stakes are high. Someone went to considerable effort to make sure this would function without friction.

"This is acceptable," I say, smirking, I mean it.

Her smile widens, satisfaction flashing briefly across her face. "Dante insisted," she says. "He doesn't like inefficiency."

I glance back at the apartment beyond the hidden door, already understanding the division. The living space is for appearances. This room is for truth.

"I'll need a secure line," I add. "Redundant power. No cloud access."

"It's already isolated," she replies. "The line is waiting. Your people can come in digitally as soon as you're ready."

I turn back to the desk, already mapping what comes next.

Lucrezia has remained near the doorway. When she sees the screens fully alive and my focus settle into place, she takes that as her cue.

"I'll leave you to it," Lucrezia says, pushing off the wall with an easy confidence. "If you need anything—access, bodies, or problems removed—you call me."

I glance over my shoulder. "You offering all three?"

A flicker of a grin pulls at her mouth. "Only the useful ones."

She turns toward the door, keycard already in hand. "You're cleared through all internal channels," she adds. "No one will interrupt you unless you ask them to."

"I'm asking now," I say, sternly. "Keep them out. I don't want anyone seeing this but me."

Lucrezia pauses, eyes catching mine. She doesn't ask why. I think she's figured me out by now. "Done," she says.

She nods once, satisfied, then slips out, the door closing behind her without a sound.

The chair adjusts under me as I get comfortable, the monitors waking with a quiet hum that feels almost welcoming. This room works the way it should, responsive without fuss, efficient without demanding attention. I slot my phone into the secure dock and initiate the encrypted line, watching the handshake protocols cycle cleanly through.

"Okay," I say as the interface opens up, my voice shifting to more of a friendly tone. "Everyone here?"

Lena's signal locks in first. "Loud and clear," she says. "I ran a sweep on the line while it was connecting. Whoever set this up knew what they were doing."

Karrie comes in next, her screen populating with numbers before she speaks. "You disappear for half a day and suddenly half the city starts acting strange," she says. "I assume that's related."

"It usually is," I say, and feel myself settle further into the chair. This is the first moment since having to see Dante that I'm not performing.

Noor's presence registers without sound at first, her cursor already moving across a secondary feed. "There's a pattern," she says finally. "It's not noticeable for who it is. Someone wants attention without attribution."

"That tracks," I reply. "Flag anything that feels important. This wasn't done in a hurry. We shouldn't rush things too much either."

Katherine's signal pings in last. "I'm on standby," she says. "You good where you are?"

I pause, considering the question in the way I only do with them. "I'm safe," I say. "I'm also being watched."

"That's not at all reassuring," Karrie mutters.

"I didn't say I was worried."

That earns me a loud laugh. With them, I don't have to choose my words so they aren't used against me later. I don't have to leave space for misinterpretation or control the room by withholding. They know me, they trust me. And I trust them just as much.

"I need everything you have on Obsidian," I say, leaning forward now, focus sharpening without tension. "Systems, access logs, mirrored traffic, anything duplicated instead of removed. If it looks like someone was careful, I want it first."

Karrie glances up from her numbers. "Financial pressure is showing up in places that don't make sense yet," she says. "It will."

"It always does," I say.

Noor hums softly, the sound she makes when something clicks into place. "This feels personal," she adds.

I smile despite myself. "That's because it is."

Katherine doesn't interrupt, but I can feel her attention sharpen. "If this turns physical," she says, "I want lead time."

"You'll have it," I reply. "This isn't that kind of mess." *Yet* goes unsaid, but they hear it anyway.

I study the assembled data again, this time without urgency, because the look of it is already familiar.

"This is patterned," I say, scrolling back through the releases and their pacing. "Not just careful, but referential."

Lena looks up from her screen. "Referential how?"

"In methodology," I reply. "In restraint. In the way the damage is distributed instead of concentrated. Whoever is doing this understands that credibility collapses faster than infrastructure when it is done correctly."

Noor's cursor stills. "That sounds intentional."

"I didn't invent this approach," I continue with a huff of a laugh. "I formalized it. I built a framework that demonstrated how to destabilize power without triggering immediate retaliation, how to create sustained erosion instead of visible collapse."

Karrie exhales slowly. "So they're using your work."

"They're using the version of it that's visible," I correct. "The parts that survived case studies and post-mortems. The structure without the context."

Katherine shifts slightly. "Does that concern you?"

"No," I say. "It clarifies the field."

I pull up a comparative overlay, aligning the current leaks with prior destabilization campaigns I've either executed or dismantled. The similarities are too precise to ignore, from the pacing of releases to the choice of implication over exposure.

"This is what you do when the objective is control rather than destruction," I explain. "When you want the target isolated and second guessing rather than publicly ruined."

Lena leans back, considering. "Whoever this is believes they're protected by the rules you established."

"Yes," I say. "They believe staying within those margins keeps them safe."

Noor nods slowly. "And they assume you won't recognize it? I find that hard to believe."

I let the data scroll once more before closing the overlay. "They recognize the architecture," I say. "They do not understand the creator. They know how to open the wound. They do not understand how to finish the process or how to deal with a target when they start to catch on to the offensive measures."

I sit forward again.

"They are disciplined, patient, and informed," I say. "Which means they are also limited by their own assumptions."

That limitation is where this ends.

"All right," I add. "Now we stop analyzing what they have released and start identifying what they are withholding." Because whoever is behind this believes they are operating inside a system I built.

Something about this whole thing doesn't feel like a simple leak, but something that is getting into the very pours of my system, believing they can find something.

That belief is going to cost them.

I didn't design those systems to be fair. I designed them to be effective, and effectiveness has always depended on knowing when to stop following your own rules. The framework exists to control escalation, not to prevent it, and anyone who mistakes that distinction has already lost.

They think they're eroding Dante's credibility. What they're actually doing is narrowing their own margin for error. Every measured release, every calculated implication, every moment of patience tells me exactly how much they fear being seen for what they are. They are careful because they believe care will save them.

It won't.

I built those benchmarks so I would never have to guess how someone like this thinks, and so I would never hesitate when the moment came to dismantle them. I know where the pressure points are because I defined them. I know how long someone can hold control before it slips, because I measured it in other people's failures and recorded the results.

This ends the way all borrowed methods do. The imitator mistakes familiarity for immunity, and the original decides when to stop teaching.

I glance back at the data, already aware that the question is no longer whether I can identify who is doing this, but how much of them I am willing to leave intact when I do.

Because once someone chooses to use my work against me, the outcome is never exposure.

It is removal by whatever means are required—including outcomes most people pretend are off the table. If the only way to end this for good is death, then death becomes part of the solution rather than a complication.

CHAPTER FIVE
Dante

Obsidian is about to open for the night.

Let the absolute chaos begin.

Most believe the best nights to club are Fridays and Saturdays. While that's true, our craziest time is Thursday nights. The night before the drunken mass of weekenders are in, the locals can show up and show out.

Obsidian runs on a rhythm most people never notice. Each day of the week serves a purpose. I don't allow this place to drift. Drifting in an industry such as this, in a city like this one, is how systems fail.

I've kept that pattern for fifteen years. I don't alter structures that keep me alive.

A short knock on my office door before it opens.

"Ready, sir?" Manny, my chief of security, says. "Walkthrough"

I stand, jacket already in my hand. "Show me."

Manny waits just inside my office door, jacket already off, earpiece seated perfectly. He's built like someone who learned early that size only matters if you know how to use it. Former military. Private security before that. His blonde hair is buzzed. His 6 '5 frame is intimidating.

We move together down the stairs, Manny half a step behind me, close enough to speak without raising his voice.

"Anything I need to know?" I ask.

"Yes," he says. "Three things you'll want fixed. Two people you'll want gone. One problem that hasn't been solved yet."

I glance at him. "Start with the people."

He nods. "Already handled. I'll explain while we walk."

That's the rhythm. He talks. I listen. The club adjusts.

"Staff change before open," he says as soon as we're moving towards the bar. "Bartender at east bar. We replaced him. Name was Colin."

I don't know all the names of every staff member or what they look like. Honestly, I hire people to deal with this. I will never care enough to know anything about anyone. Why would I? They'll leave or be fired anyway.

Guess that's why people love or hate me. They love to call me a hardass for a reason.

"What did he do?" I ask.

"He talked," Manny replies. "Mentioned a VIP guest's name to someone who is not part of the group. He wanted to be popular. Instead he got fired."

I don't slow. "When?"

"Last Friday. Lucrezia caught it on audio before it reached the floor."

"And?"

"He was terminated on the spot. Phone wiped. NDA enforced. He signed again under supervision."

"Where is he now?"

Manny doesn't hesitate. "Back in Ohio. His mother's sick. He won't be returning to Vegas."

Good. We may be in the nightlife business, but our priority is to protect our VIP clients that pay for privacy. I don't get involved in their dealings. They protect mine.

"Replacement?" I ask.

"Rosa Alvarez. Twenty nine. Former embassy service in Madrid. Reads six languages. Doesn't drink. Doesn't flirt. Doesn't talk unless spoken to."

"Why her?"

"She doesn't get curious," Manny says. "She notices everything and asks nothing."

We reach the main floor. Lights are still in calibration mode. Our lighting director hasn't finished the final touches. The DJ is setting up. Everything is perfect.

"How many staff tonight?" I ask.

"Two hundred and twelve total," Manny replies. "That includes floor, bar, security, surveillance, runners, and containment."

We pass the central bar. Two guards are standing where patrons will later think they're decorative.

Manny taps his tablet. "All security rotates every forty five minutes," he says. "No one holds a position long enough to get comfortable. Sightlines overlap at all times. Every blind spot is someone else's priority."

"And surveillance?"

"Every room is up and running," Manny replies. "Audio in public spaces. Visual everywhere. VIP rooms are monitored but inaccessible unless you authorize it or Lucrezia flags a breach."

We reach the private corridor. Manny slows just enough to signal importance.

"Any other changes with staff I need to know about?"

"We terminated two more this week," he says. "Server and a runner."

"For?"

"Runner skimmed tips and the server accepted a drink from a guest she didn't recognize. She's lucky that there weren't any drugs. Poor judgement, but we can't have that. Every member of staff needs to be on point at all times."

"Any replacements?"

"Promotions," Manny says. "People who've been waiting. Loyalty rewarded beats talent every time."

We stop outside the VIP area. The glass reflects us back.

"How many people does Obsidian employ as of today?" I ask.

"Seven hundred and forty three," Manny replies. "Full time, part time, contracted. Only about a third ever see this floor. Fewer than fifty understand how the building actually works."

I learned long ago I couldn't be in charge of everything. It's why I have Manny and Lucrezia run it. They just debrief me as things change.

A guard approaches Manny and stops. He looks at me and acknowledges me with a tip of his head.

"VIP list's finalized," he says. "Table seven flagged interest."

Manny nods once. "Logged."

The guard steps away immediately.

"Table seven?" I ask.

Manny doesn't break stride when he tells me about the sort of the VIPs that I honestly hate.

"Legacy money," he murmurs. "Colten Hadings and his friends."

The name registers immediately—familiar in the way recurring problems always are. I keep walking, already thinking about how he is going to make every moment about himself.

"He's twenty one," I say. "A politician's son. That should say everything."

I loathe politicians' kids. They are always so fucking narcissistic. There has only been one that I actually liked. She came with no expectation and just wanted to be safe. Sweetest human ever. Never came back after dealing with Colten Hadings.

Manny nods once in agreement. "Same group he usually brings—louder than last time, more careless. Plus, he's freshly twenty-one. You know how that goes"

"That's what happens when entitlement gets reinforced instead of corrected," I reply.

We pass the booth already assigned to them—close enough to the floor to flatter them, far enough from the service corridors to keep every movement contained. Manny anticipated the need without being prompted.

"I've called his father twice," I continue. "The first time to explain why his son was escorted out. The second time to make it clear that was the last courtesy he was getting."

"And tonight decides whether there's a third," Manny says.

"No," I correct. "Tonight decides whether his name ever opens another door in this city. If Colten fucks up, he loses VIP status. His friends lose access. His family loses the illusion that money substitutes for discipline."

Manny glances at me—not surprised, just confirming what I want. "His father won't appreciate that."

"I'm not here to be appreciated," I say. "Colten isn't dangerous because he's reckless. He's dangerous because he's bored, entitled, and convinced the world exists to absorb his mistakes."

Manny shifts his attention toward the perimeter, already relaying the implications without speaking them aloud.

"Keep them contained," I add. "If they start testing staff or pushing boundaries, they're done for and I will deal with the senator. The kid may think he has connections... but he's never met mine."

"And if they try to test you?" Manny asks.

"They won't," I reply. "They only test people they think need something from them—and I have never needed anything from Colten Hadings or his friends."

We continue walking. Staff straighten as we pass, no one speaks or stares, just a quick glance before busying themselves with whatever duty they're assigned to.

"One more thing," Manny says quietly. "We ran a

stress test on the back halls after last week's breach scare."

"And?"

"Six seconds," he says. "From locked down to isolated. Twelve seconds to full containment. Twenty if we need to make someone disappear without affecting the floor."

I stop.

"And can we do it without noise?" I ask.

"Yes."

"And witnesses?"

"Only the ones who won't remember."

I nod once. Approval granted.

"It's not a person," he says finally.

That gets my attention. I know he's talking about the problem they need me to solve.

We stop near the service corridor, just out of the main sightline. Staff move around us without slowing. Everyone knows better than to hover.

"Then what is it?" I ask.

"Access," Manny replies. "Not a breach. Not yet. More like... pressure."

I turn slightly, enough to face him. "Define that."

"Someone touched a system they shouldn't have been able to see," he says. "Didn't change anything. Didn't pull data. Just reached in far enough to prove they could."

"And you didn't shut it down."

"No," Manny says. "Because whoever it is wanted us to notice. Cutting it immediately tells them they hit a nerve. We need to know what they are looking for."

I consider that as we start moving again.

"When did this happen?" I ask.

"Early this morning. No staff on rotation who shouldn't have been there. No external pings. It came from inside the perimeter."

"That narrows nothing," I say.

"It narrows intent," Manny replies. "They weren't sloppy. They weren't rushed. They didn't try again."

I stop walking.

"And you think they will."

"Yes."

"Tonight?"

Manny hesitates. He doesn't do that often. "Not necessarily," he says. "But Thursday is when people test structures. Friday is when they push them."

I look out over the floor again. The room is still empty, still obedient.

"Who knows?" I ask.

"Me. Lucrezia. Now you," Manny replies. "No one else."

"Good," I say. "What did you change?"

"Nothing visible," he answers. "Internal routing shifted. Every interaction logged. No alerts triggered."

"Those logs don't sit with us," I say. "They go straight to Opal. All of them. Raw, unfiltered, real time. If it touches Obsidian's systems, she sees it before I do."

"We're lucky," he says. "Because whoever did this understands how your inner system works. Now you have someone who can figure out how to understand where it breaks. I'll route everything directly to her. We can't afford to have a delay."

"Good," I say, and start walking once again. "If

someone thinks they're inside my perimeter, I want Opal Greer watching their every movement."

I nod once. I turn to face Manny directly.

"We don't hunt ghosts," I say. "They will be hunted themselves."

Manny's mouth tightens.

"Doors in five," he says.

I start toward the mezzanine. "Let's open," I reply. "If someone thinks they're inside my walls, I want them close enough to make a mistake."

The club has been open for a few hours now. I'm ready to be home. It's been a long day.

Still, I stay where I am, watching the floor from above. Thursday nights always start like this. Even that Colten kid is being obedient.

My earpiece hums once before Manny speaks.

"Dante," Manny says in my ear. "We have a situation."

I don't ask what kind. Manny wouldn't use that word unless it crossed a line we do not negotiate with.

"Tell me exactly what happened," I say, already moving.

"It's Sofia," he replies, out of breath like he's running. "Lower level. West corridor. A guest followed her into the service hall near the private bar. He locked the door behind them. He restrained her. She fought him, but he raped her."

That word. *Rape.* It hits me like a ton of bricks. I

don't wait for another moment before heading right to the stairs.

"She broke away and came straight to security," Manny continues. "She knew what had happened. She asked for the police herself. Medical and the police are with her now. She's shaken, but she's stable."

My grip tightens around the railing as I take the stairs.

Sofia has worked for me for years. Long enough that people forget she didn't always stand behind a polished bar in black with hands that pour drinks that cost more than rent. Long enough that they stop wondering what it took for her to get here.

Single mother. Two kids. No safety net. No margin for error.

She works nights because nights pay better. Because tuition doesn't care how exhausted you are. Because doing what you have to do doesn't stop just because your life looks respectable now. She followed every rule. Did the job. Built something stable out of a past that never gave her a head start.

Her ex husband is an entitled bastard and decided none of her struggles mattered. He wanted their kids to go to one of the best private schools in the state. He took Sofia to court with his fancy lawyers. She now has to pay half on top of the daily needs for the kids and herself.

Some low life asshole decided her body was part of the transaction. Decided Obsidian was another place where money meant he could do whatever he wanted and get away with it.

He was catastrophically fucking wrong.

"The guest had VIP access," Manny adds. "Name is coming through now. Security has him contained. Police are currently questioning him."

Good. That part is done.

By the time I reach the lower level, the perimeter is already in place—casual enough to pass unnoticed. Music still plays. Drinks still pour. The illusion in the club is still a party atmosphere.

"Manny," I say. "Lock the club down. But don't let anyone know what is happening. We don't need a stampede."

He nods once and moves.

I spot her—Sofia—half seated, half folded into herself on the edge of a velvet bench. Her dress is torn at the shoulder, her lipstick smudged. A waiter kneels nearby, uselessly offering a glass of water like it can fix this.

My security lead finds me. "We pulled the guy. Friend of Colten Hadings. Name's—"

"Don't care."

My tone cuts him off. I crouch in front of Sofia, careful not to touch her. "Sofia. It's me."

Her eyes flick to mine. They are wide, glassy, and clear that she is utterly terrified.

"He cornered me," she whispers. "He said he was with Colten—like that was supposed to mean something."

I nod at her keeping my anger at bay. "It means he thought someone would protect him." Her breath stutters. I lean in. "That was his first mistake."

I stand and turn to security. "Where is he?"

"Side room," One of the security men responds.

"Tell him to get comfortable. Also tell Colten..." I pause, slow smile curving. "Tell him his name doesn't open doors here anymore. It closes them. Violently. If he calls daddy, make sure you tell the senator that I know people. He will lose his place if he doesn't put a leash on his son."

"And Sofia?"

I glance back.

"Send her home with a full escort," I say. "Comp her rent for the year. Move her to day shift—night pay. She was hunted in *my* club. That makes her mine. No one lays a hand on her again unless she says yes loud and clear."

My head of security nods. "Understood."

"And once the cops take him," I add, already turning away, "shut Obsidian down for the night. I don't care what it costs us. Let Stellan handle PR. Let him know what's going on. Give him time to spin it."

He hesitates. I know this isn't routine for when something happens. But with the rumors flying and my reputation hanging in the balance, I can't let anything go awry. Better to shut down the club than to have someone use this as another way to start a rumor.

"We can't afford anything else to happen," I finish. "Now, let's go meet our little friend."

I roll my sleeves up past my elbows and walk into the interrogation room without a word. He's lounging in the chair. He doesn't see this being a big deal. He's about to find out how big of a deal it is.

"Colten said you'd be chill," he starts.

I don't raise my voice. I raise my fist. The strike lands square on his nose, bone giving way with a wet pop as blood spills instantly. He screams, stumbling to his feet, palm pressed to his face.

Cops may be around, but they know to turn away.

"What the *fuck*—"

I haul him straight up by his collar and drive my knee into his stomach. He folds like paper.

"You touched her," I say. My voice is deadly and lethal. Enough to make him shake like a leaf.

He stumbles back when I give him a shove. He's coughing and wheezing as he looks down at his hand that's smeared with blood. "She didn't say no—"

I don't like that statement so I slam him into the wall so hard it rattles.

"She *didn't say yes.*"

He swings on instinct. It's sloppy and weak. I block it easily, grab his wrist, twist until I hear the pop. He screams.

"You think because your best friend's daddy wears a flag pin, the world's supposed to cheer for you?" I shove him down, kick him once in the ribs. Controlled force enough to bruise but not break. "You think Obsidian exists so you can hurt girls in the dark and walk out?"

He's crying now. Real tears that match Sofia's. "Please..."

"No." I crouch beside him. "You don't get *please*. You get the police."

I reach into my back pocket, pull out his wallet. I toss it to the guard at the door.

"Get the name. He leaves in cuffs. I want bodycams on. I want charges filed. I want his record permanent."

"Yes, sir."

I look down.

"Tell your boy Colten this room used to cover sins. Now it documents them." The guy sobs into the floor, pathetic.

I adjust my cuffs, then step over him like the mistake he is. Manny is waiting outside the door, face unreadable. He doesn't ask questions.

"Call Lucrezia," I say. "Tell her to bring Opal back to the club and send her up to my office."

He pauses once. Just long enough to smirk at the blood on my knuckles.

"Now," I add.

Manny nods and moves.

I glance back into the room—at the man curled on the floor. He's a mess. But something tells me that there is something about this that is... a problem.

"She needs to see this," I say angrily. "If it's connected, she'll know."

Manny nods and disappears down the hall.

I stay where I am.

The man on the floor moans softly, blood soaking into carpet that cost more than his education. Sirens echo faintly outside.

A boy with inherited arrogance came into my house and assumed I'd clean it up the way I always did with his little friend—quietly, politely, without a problem.

Whatever this is, whoever thinks they're clever

enough to hide behind entitlement and proxies, they've made one miscalculation.

I don't forgive people.

I remove them from the equation.

CHAPTER SIX

Opal

Lucrezia brought me back to Obsidian. Something about that doesn't sit right.

My job isn't to get involved with his club personally. It's to find out who's trying to destroy it. Which means this isn't an operational problem.

Even if it were, Dante still wouldn't have called me—he'd rather die than ask for my help directly. Since Lucrezia is the one pulling me in, whatever happened crossed a line that couldn't be handled by his people alone.

Reputation, then. Or containment. Maybe even optics. The kind of problem you don't fix—you manage. You shrink it until it fits inside a locked room and never leaves again.

This is going to be fun.

It's only ten on a Thursday. This room should be warming up, not stripped down.

Because of the silence, I hear him before I see him. A male voice, already irritated with the answer it's getting.

Complaining at security like this is a misunderstanding. "How long is this gonna take?" He sounds like a whiny little bitch, the sneer curling my lip is involuntary.

The host starts to answer. He cuts her off halfway through the first word.

"Sir," one of the guards says while repositioning himself between the man and the desk, "we're closed for the night."

There's a pause, the kind where *closed* sounds theoretical to him, his expression tightening with offended disbelief.

"Closed," the man mimics. "It's ten o'clock."

"Yes," security says. "And we're closed."

"That doesn't make any sense," he snaps. "This place doesn't close at ten."

"Tonight it does."

He laughs and looks over his shoulder instead of at security, like he expects someone else to handle this for him. One of the men behind him shifts closer, another checks his phone, already bored with the delay. No one steps in. His entourage is not a concern.

He straightens anyway, shoulders rolling back.

"So what," he says, spreading his hands, "we're just standing here? You expect us to leave?"

"We expect you to wait," the host says carefully. "Until you are told otherwise. No one else has a problem with it except for you."

"Unbelievable," he mutters, then looks past her, past security, searching for someone. "Where's Alex?"

Security doesn't hesitate. That's very telling. "Your friend is being held for questioning."

He blinks. "Questioning for what?"

"For his actions toward a member of our staff."

Actions toward a member of our staff. The phrasing triggers my internal PR fixer side immediately. I've spent enough years in crisis rooms and precinct hallways to know when words are being chosen to cover what is going on.

'Actions toward' isn't how you describe a simple incident involving a staff member. It's how you describe something that crossed a line and is being documented without a mess to the club's reputation.

This isn't a drunk friend who mouthed off or got handsy in a way someone plans to excuse later.

Whatever Alex did, it wasn't ambiguous. If it were, he'd already be gone—sent home, warned, banned for a short amount of time. You don't hold someone back unless there's a reason to. You don't call Metro unless you're past internal discipline and into jurisdiction.

I know what this is. Alex didn't cross a line—he obliterated it. Sexual assault, by the sound of it. The realization comes first. The anger joins it after, rising slowly in my chest.

"That's bullshit," he says immediately. "He didn't do anything."

"That determination isn't yours to make," security replies evenly. "He's cooperating."

"Cooperating with who?" he demands.

"With us," the guard says. "And with Metro."

That gets him. His voice spikes. "You called the police?! Over *what*?"

"Over an incident," the host answers, measured. "Involving an employee."

He laughs again, louder now, brittle. "You've got to be kidding me. Alex wouldn't—"

"Lower your voice," security says.

He steps forward instead.

"Do you know who my father is?" he snaps. "You can't just hold people like this."

That's when the name clicks in my head. Not just *who* he is—but where he is from.

Colten Hadings. Senator's son. Same tier of protection I've seen before. Same pedigree. I worked a family like his once, back when I was still inside Rothwell's machine. Gregory Lomier—public facing integrity, private asshole. His son Grayson was worse. Entitled, violent, insulated by the kind of money that silences pretty much everything. Gregory lost everything when the truth finally stuck. Grayson ran away. People like that always do.

Colten is the king of those circles. Same schools. Same parties. Same inherited certainty that the room would bend around him if he pushed hard enough. I remember his name in the periphery—never the headline, never the charge. Another boy protected by proximity, always close enough to trouble to matter, never close enough to be blamed.

Interesting that Dante probably ran in the same circles. Yet he became a very different man.

"Do you know who my father is?" he snaps.

Yes. I do. That's when I step fully into his line of

sight. He finally turns on me, really looks, irritation changing his features into something uglier.

"You don't get to talk to the staff like that," I say, letting the anger in my voice show.

"Who the fuck are you supposed to be?" he snaps. "Because you don't get to talk to *me* like that."

I step closer, close enough that he has to tilt his head to keep eye contact.

"I get to talk to you however the fuck I want," I say. "You're standing in a closed club, screaming at my staff, while your friend is being questioned for assault. You're already out of line. The only question left is how much worse you want to make it."

He laughs, short and disbelieving. "You're out of your mind."

"You're done speaking," I tell him, rolling my eyes. "Now you're listening."

"Do you have any idea who my father is?" he demands.

How many times is this little asshole going to ask that? "I don't give a shit who Daddy Dearest is."

His face tightens, anger flashing hot and fast. "You can't hold people like this," he says. "You can't shut down a place like this. You think you're important because you're standing here?"

I take another step in. Now we're chest to chest.

"I think you're one bad decision away from fucking your life sideways," I say quietly. "You're running out of chances."

He scoffs. "You threatening me?"

"Careful," I say. "You're already in trouble. I'm not threatening you. I'm making a promise."

He looks me up and down, contempt curling his mouth. "Move. I'm done talking to you."

He reaches out. It wasn't a shove, or a grab meant to hurt. It was possessive and dismissive at the same time. Like he was well within his right to touch me, to make me do whatever it is that he wanted me to move.

I pivot and drive my fist straight into his face.

The impact snaps his head back with a wet crack. He stumbles, stunned, hands flying up as blood spills instantly from his nose. He hits the floor hard, shock finally catching up to pain.

Security moves immediately, but I'm already stepping over him.

"You do not touch me," I say, voice shaking with fury now, no effort to hide it. "I always keep my promises."

He groans, trying to sit up.

"That," I continue, pointing down at him, "was the last free lesson you get."

"Who the fuck—" he chokes, spitting blood. "Who are you?"

Lucrezia's voice cuts in from behind me, calm as ice. "That's Mrs. Valera."

He gulps. I see it. The flicker of panic across his features where confidence used to be, the moment his certainty realizes it misread the room. More importantly... he misread me.

"I will make sure Mr. Valera knows what transpired here," Lucrezia adds with a raised brow and writing on her tablet.

I crouch just enough to make sure he hears me.

"You're done," I tell him. "You wait. You shut the fuck up. When you leave tonight, it's because I allowed it —not because your father made a call."

Security hauls him up. He doesn't fight it, he won't so much as look at me now.

The staff around us have gone perfectly still. A few of them straighten without realizing they're doing it. Someone exhales like they've been holding their breath most of the night.

"Dante needs you in his office," Lucrezia says in my ear. She's not asking. This is not time for a suggestion.

I don't take my eyes off the host as I answer. "In a minute."

I turn to address the staff around us. "You did exactly right," I say, giving them my full attention. "Every one of you. Thank you." I notice a few smiles and nods. Only then do I look back at Lucrezia. "Lead the way."

Neither of us speak the entire walk up the stairs. When we get to the office door, Lucrezia doesn't knock, she just pushes it open and steps aside. As soon as I'm through the doorway she closes it behind me.

Dante is already on his feet.

Jacket off. Sleeves rolled. One hand braced on the edge of his desk like he's been holding himself together. Barely. He starts to speak the moment he sees me. "We had an incident—"

I try to pay attention, but seeing him like this ignites a fire in me. I want him. More so, I want to devour him.

"I know," I say.

He stops.

I keep walking, eyes cataloging as I go—the untouched glass, the security tablet left face down, the faint scuff near the desk leg where business is done.

"Your staff rerouted traffic away from the west corridor," I continue, unbuttoning my coat. "Not protocol for a drunk or a fight. Someone was separated quietly. Doors didn't lock until after ten, which tells me you waited on confirmation before containment."

His jaw tightens. Focused now.

"The bar closed, but the music stayed on just long enough to drain the room without spiking it," I add. "That's narrative control, not panic management. And Lucrezia brought me which means it wasn't a standard liability. And you didn't handle it internally because the person involved came with insulation."

I finally look at him.

"A guest crossed a line," I say. "Alex. Colten's friend. Colten draws attention so men like Alex can move unnoticed."

Dante doesn't interrupt. But I can feel his attention sharpen, tracking every movement like he's waiting for a misstep.

"The staff member reported it," I say. "Which means she trusted you to back her. Police were called because this time, burying it would've done more damage than daylight."

"How do you know that?" He asks.

"Because of what didn't happen," I say.

I walk closer to his desk. "No one tried to manage me

when I walked in. No one fed me a version. Lucrezia didn't preface anything. That tells me the decision was already made before I arrived. Also that it had nothing to do with me. Or else they wouldn't have let me in the club. I was expected."

I turn to the computer screen, pulling up security logs, letting the timeline populate as I speak.

"If this had been borderline, the staff member would've been escorted out first, with reassurances and an incident report drafted by legal instead of security, of course. If it had been ambiguous, you would've delayed calling Metro until your attorney arrived, not let officers start interviews on your floor."

I scroll through the laptop trying to find what I am looking for. "But you didn't."

I bring up the footage timestamp. "You isolated the individual immediately. You preserved the scene. You locked down access without emptying the room. That's not damage control—that's evidence preservation."

Dante's expression changes from neutral to one of recognition.

"And then there's the staff," I continue. "They weren't panicked. They were contained and alert. That only happens when someone believes they're protected. That if they speak, they won't be punished for it later."

I glance at him again. "You don't get that kind of trust overnight. You don't get it at all if you've ever asked them to look the other way."

Dante does not say a word. Instead he raises a brow long enough for me to finish.

"So," I finish, fingers resuming their rhythm on the

keys, "I know she reported it because the nuclear system you've built behaved like it does when it is already in motion. I know you backed her because you let it happen without needing to take control."

The data finishes loading. Connections are blooming. I don't look at him when I add, "Men like Alex count on hesitation. On doubt that women like her will never be protected working for a man like you."

I point at the woman in the camera and I finally meet Dante's gaze again. "You took that away from him."

For a long moment, Dante says nothing.

Suddenly, he smiles in a lethal way "What if I hadn't?"

I don't smile back. "Then I would've known that too."

Dante watches the screens populate. After a moment, he nods once. "Do what you need to do."

I don't answer. I'm already doing it.

I move quickly, but there's nothing rushed about it. The first thing I check isn't what Alex has done, but how carefully he's tried to hide it.

People with experience leave depth—layers of obfuscation, shell accounts, patterns that they can't keep track of.

Alex doesn't. His digital footprint is thin and poorly disguised, the kind that comes from someone who has never needed to protect himself because someone else always did it for him.

There are no shell companies, no backdoor transfers, no overlapping access points that suggest planning or insulation.

What's there is blunt and careless, which tells me this

wasn't part of a system or a larger play. It wasn't planned, but it also wasn't new.

There's confidence baked into the mess. He's acted like this before and watched it disappear, likely with a phone call, a lawyer, or a last name doing the work for him. The night has absorbed his behavior before. He expected it to do so again.

A singular event and in no way connected to Dante's bigger problems.

I cross reference him anyway. I always do. Nothing ties back to Obsidian's breach. No mirrored code. No duplicated behavior. No bleed into the larger pattern circling Dante's business.

I lean back slightly.

"This isn't connected," I say. "Alex is *a* problem, sure. But he's not *the* problem."

Dante gives a single nod. Nothing eased. Nothing forgiven.

"The bartender's going to be fine," I say. "You will probably send her home tonight with a full escort. You'll move her to day shift, keep her night shift pay. You'll comp her rent for a year, because she won't sleep for a while and money will be the first thing she worries about. You'll make it clear she doesn't owe you gratitude for any of it."

He, again, lets me continue on without a single interruption.

I pause long enough to reroute permissions and lock down the obvious entry points.

The vulnerabilities are surface level, almost lazy.

Whoever built this system prioritized how it looked over how it functioned. It's expensive security designed to intimidate people who don't know what they're seeing.

I close a backdoor that never should've existed, seal two ports left open out of convenience, and drop in a temporary firewall that will hold against anything short of a deliberate attack. It takes less time than it should.

He paid far too much for this.

The system wasn't built to stop someone competent. It was built to make him feel comfortable.

"She used to sell herself," I continue plainly. "On her terms, when she could. Probably to pay for her deadbeat ex or some fancy school he wanted to send her kids to."

Dante doesn't move, but his voice loses whatever margin for error it had. "Is that a problem?"

I look at him fully. "Why would it be?"

The question isn't defensive. It is rhetorical, though. I don't need him to say anything because the answer is obvious and anything else would be a confession.

"She recognized the behavior immediately," I say. "Men like Alex test first. They probe boundaries, watch for hesitation, wait for the moment someone's guard drops."

Dante steps away from the desk, crossing to the window that overlooks the club floor. He rubs his hand across his face. I know that he is reassessing the assumption that awareness equals protection.

My eyes meet his back when I look up. "She didn't freeze because she didn't understand what was happening. She froze because he trapped her. The fact that she spoke up afterward tells me everything I need to know about her and the way you treat your employees."

He turns around looking straight at me.

"That only happens when someone believes they'll be believed. You will make sure she knows she's safe."

"I will," he says.

"Good," I reply.

He studies me for a moment. "You didn't pull her file."

"No."

"Then how do you know all that?"

I consider not answering him. No sense giving away all of my secrets so quickly. "Because people tell the truth with their bodies long before they trust their mouths," I say finally. "Sofia didn't even realize she was doing it."

He is looking at me in a way I didn't expect. Not appreciation or anything like that. No way that's admiration. More like... awe. He probably never thought I had this side to me. Reading people.

Little did he know I learned a thing or two from Talia Rothwell.

I turn one of the monitors toward him, not showing data—just the paused security footage. Sofia standing near the bar, shoulders squared, weight balanced evenly on both feet. Ready, but not aggressive.

"She never angled her body toward the exit," I continue. "That means she wasn't thinking about escape. She expected to be heard. She also never raised her voice, even when Alex leaned in. Women who haven't learned how men escalate get louder when they're scared. She got quieter." I tap the screen once. "That's control."

I sit back again. "She kept her hands visible the entire time. Palms open. No fidgeting. You learn that when you've had to manage men who think proximity is permission to do whatever the fuck they want to do."

I smile for the first time tonight.

"As for the rest," I keep my voice down, "single mothers don't take night shifts unless they have to. Women who've rebuilt their lives don't gamble it unless they believe the floor won't drop beneath them. They wait for the other shoe to drop. But sometimes people show them they don't have to."

I meet his eyes after doing a once over his body. "She trusted you."

Dante exhales slowly, something unguarded crossing his face for the first time. "That's not intuition," he says.

"No," I reply. "It's pattern recognition."

I turn back to the screen, fingers already moving again.

That's when he understands everything. Not just that I'm ahead of him. But that I always will be.

"Yet," he says, tone smoother now, edged with something he thinks that I can't explain, "you seem very comfortable running my house."

I glance at him over the computer screen. "Someone had to. You were busy proving a point."

"You're not here to manage Obsidian," he says. "You're here to find my problem and neutralize it."

"I am," I say. "This just wasn't it."

"This is my business," he says. "I am the leader. You may think you can stay one step ahead of me, but newsflash—you're not the one in charge."

I smile faintly. "If I were playing against you, you'd be chasing me."

That's when he laughs clearly amused.

"Careful now, Petal." He saunters closer to me, dragging his fingers slowly up my arm, leaving goosebumps in his wake. "I adore a challenge, but I don't like losing."

CHAPTER SEVEN
Dante

Fourteen days. It's been long enough to confirm that my strategy of avoiding her is working, and that it's costing a hell of a lot more than I had anticipated.

My wife is not just inserting herself into my life. She's inserting herself into my being.

At least I don't live in the apartment with her. My own space means I'm not with her 24/7. Avoiding her when she's at my club all the time? That is proving to be more difficult.

The constant questions being asked. Decisions traced back to logic I didn't authorize but can't fault. I know it's her job. That doesn't make it welcome.

She's in my space too. I'm not used to hearing voices when I'm home.

She's temporary. A contract. A solution with an expiration date.

That should be enough. But it isn't. She doesn't push

physically. She doesn't demand more. I don't appreciate that kind of efficiency when it isn't mine.

I hate her.

Not in the dramatic sense. Not irrationally. I hate her because she disrupts order without blinking an eye. Because she moves through my world like she belongs here. She destroyed lives. Yet people seem to have forgiven her.

I hate that she fixes things I would have used as pressure points. I hate that she neutralizes situations before I decide how to handle it. I hate that she looks at my world and sees patterns instead of walls.

This isn't tension. It isn't chemistry. It's an intrusion. That's unacceptable.

I don't allow enemies inside my perimeter unless I know exactly how they snap. So I reach for the one man who understands what it costs to bind yourself to someone you intend to outmaneuver.

It doesn't matter. I see her around town. I watch her when she shops. It's like gravity is constantly pulling her to me. Or me to her.

The line connects on the second ring.

"You've been married for fourteen days," Stellan Rothwell says. "Either you're calling to complain or you're already in trouble."

"I'm calling because you survived it," I reply. "And married her for real. We are in a situation that no one else experienced before."

I hear the faint clink of glass on his end.

"Survived who," he asks, "or survived what?"

"She's dismantling my operation," I say. "With my

people thanking her afterward. She has completely taken over my life."

"That sounds less like dismantling and more like competence." I can hear the smile in his voice, the bastard's enjoying this. Of course, he is.

"She's efficient," I allow. "That's not the issue."

"Oh, but it is."

I look out over the city, lights stacked like promises no one intends to keep. "She doesn't wait to be invited. She just... arrives."

Stellan hums, thoughtful. "And you don't know where to put her."

"I know exactly where to put her," I say. "At a distance."

"That's new," he says mildly. "You usually eliminate variables you can't control."

"She's not a variable. And I can't control her *yet*."

"That's the first lie you've told me tonight," Stellan says.

I don't correct him. "She's not trying to take anything from me," I say. "She's not reaching. Not clinging. She's just operating."

"Worse," he replies. "Those are the ones who change things. Isn't that what you asked for?"

My jaw tightens. "I didn't ask for a philosophy lesson."

"No," he says. "You asked how long you can avoid your wife before it becomes a problem."

I say nothing.

"That depends," Stellan continues, unhurried, "on whether she's noticed."

"She has," I say. "I doubt that that woman has ever not noticed anything."

He smiles. I can hear it. "You're already too late. Come have a drink."

"I'm not in the mood."

"You're never in the mood," he replies. "That's not what this is about."

I consider declining. I'm not good with people. It's probably why I isolate myself.

"The Dutch Wall," he adds. "Beckett's already here."

Of course he is. Stellan doesn't drink alone. Not since he married Talia.

"What time?" I ask.

"Now." The call ends without a goodbye.

I pocket the phone and stare out over the city for a moment longer than necessary. I don't like being corrected. Opal loves to do it anyway.

I straighten my cuffs and reach for my jacket. If they want to drink, I'll drink. If they want to talk about my wife, they'll do it carefully. And if this is Stellan's way of reminding me that avoidance is a luxury with a shelf life, I'll remind him that I decide when something becomes a problem in my life.

Even if, fourteen days in, that decision is already overdue.

The Dutch Wall hasn't changed location, but it has changed its mood.

Frankie's influence is unmistakable. The lighting is warmer now, filtered through smoked glass that keeps its privacy without sacrificing visibility. The old chrome has been replaced with brushed black steel and dark wood that absorbs sound instead of reflecting it. Seating has been reoriented just enough to encourage privacy without isolation, a subtle adjustment that alters how people lean, how long they stay, how much they spend.

Frankie has always understood pressure points. She doesn't redesign spaces to impress. She redesigns them to shape need. The Dutch Wall has always been a place to broker business deals and she knows that.

I spot Stellan and Beckett immediately, seated in a booth near the back.

Roxy appears right when I take a seat across from them, trusty leather jacket zipped halfway. She places a glass in front of me already filled with bourbon, neat.

Beckett looks exactly the way he always does when he's pretending nothing matters. Broad shouldered, relaxed posture, dark brown hair cut just short enough to stay out of his eyes without ever looking styled.

Stellan is the opposite kind of dangerous. Impeccably put together, not a thread out of place, silver begins to show at his temples covering the sides of his dark hair. He doesn't slouch. He doesn't lean.

Beckett tips his glass toward me, grin easy and unapologetic. "So. Married life."

I don't react.

"That's it?" he continues. "Fourteen days married to Opal and that's all I get? No complaints? No visible wounds?"

"I'm still standing," I say. "You can draw your own conclusions."

Stellan exhales through his nose, faintly entertained. "That wasn't the question."

"There's a phase," Stellan continues, unhurried. "Early on. When you're convinced distance equals control, and control equals safety. When you tell yourself it's temporary and therefore manageable."

Beckett grins. "You say that like you didn't rearrange three meetings trying to avoid Talia for a month."

Stellan doesn't deny it. "I say it like someone who did exactly that. And someone who remembers the path it took to true happiness."

He looks back at me, expression composed, voice lighter than the importance of what he's saying. "So yes. We want to know how it's going. Because we've both been where you are."

Beckett snorts. "Not the arranged part," he adds. "But the part where you realize the person you're tied to isn't going to make it easy on you."

Stellan flicks him a look. "That's one way to describe it."

Beckett shrugs, unbothered. "Frankie and I spent the first few months trying to outmaneuver each other. Different goals. Same room. Lots of friction."

Everyone in this city knows their story. It's the kind of thing Vegas loves to mythologize.

Beckett and Frankie got drunk and married, which is already ridiculous enough to be memorable. Two people who should have known better, waking up legally bound in a city built where people try to erase their mistakes the next morning. Most people laugh at that part. Most people assume it ended the way those stories usually do.

It didn't.

Beckett refused the divorce. He just refused to sign.

He wouldn't even flinch at everything. Turns out he wasn't even drunk.

Somewhere between the past and regret, he realized he had already made the worst mistake once—turning her away when she'd offered him something real. He wasn't interested in repeating it.

So he held on. He let her be furious, let her test him, let her decide whether she wanted to stay married to a man who wouldn't chase her but also wouldn't let her go. That standoff lasted longer than anyone expected. Long enough for it to stop being funny and start being annoying.

Eventually, she stayed. Not because he trapped her. Because he proved he could endure her.

That's the part Stellan means when he says they've been here before. This is also the part Beckett doesn't joke about anymore.

"Nothing's gone wrong," I say, changing the subject.

"Uh huh," Beckett replies. "That's usually what men say right before something goes catastrophically wrong."

Stellan takes a slow sip of his drink, eyes never leaving me. "You didn't call to celebrate."

"I didn't call to confess either."

"No," Stellan agrees. "You called because you're irritated."

Beckett smiles wider. "Which is worse. I've seen you fight. Plain old irritation at something outside your control is new."

I shift my glass slightly on the table, keeping my tone level. "This isn't a marriage. It's a contract."

"That's what all the doomed ones say," Beckett

replies cheerfully. "Frankie said pretty much the same thing, actually. How big of a mistake it is. Right before she rearranged my entire life."

"That was your own fault," Stellan says without sympathy. "You married someone smarter than you."

Beckett shrugs. "You did too, idiot."

I don't join in on their jokes. I barely listen anyway.

Stellan sets his glass down. "You don't hate Opal," he says. "You hate what she reminds you of."

I don't react in a way he could see. Inside, I'm fuming. Opal's read me well so far. I don't need it from someone else. I hate being read like a fucking book. "I don't—"

"Don't lie," he cuts me off with a stern voice. "Not here."

Beckett doesn't say a word. He leans back, letting it play out—his eyes full of curiosity now.

Stellan doesn't speak, he doesn't need to. He knows I'll get there on my own—and he'd rather let me waste the time figuring it out than hand me the answer.

"She's not like Michella," I say, noncommittal. "Opal is smarter, and colder in a way that doesn't announce itself. She doesn't posture or perform strength to be seen, and she never lowers herself enough to beg. Everything she does is efficient, precise, and impossible to predict. I built this system to be airtight, and still she finds the cracks. I haven't found her edges yet, and what I hate most is that she knows it."

Michella Carr.

She didn't storm the gates. She slipped in through a

side door and made it feel like I'd invited her. Always agreeable in public, always deferential in private.

She never asked for control. She made me believe it was safer in my hands. Until every choice I made was one she'd already set in motion. One agreement at a time. One suggestion too easy to ignore. Always just outside the blast zone when it finally went to hell.

She studied what I needed and became it. Until I stopped checking her work. Until I started trusting her eyes instead of my own.

She sold information to a competitor. An old man with a legacy complex and a long memory—someone my family buried years ago in business, but never in pride. She married him six months after she walked out. His name was on the paperwork that gutted two of my side holdings. I didn't lose much financially, but that wasn't the point. She didn't do it for gain.

She did it because she felt like she had no future with me and that pissed her off. She was very wrong about that. The day she walked out was the day the ring in my safe was supposed to be on her finger.

When I confronted her, she didn't scream. She didn't cry. She looked at me like I was a child throwing a tantrum over a game he lost. Then she left—no apology, no fear, no sign she ever planned to stay.

Opal has none of her polish. She isn't charming. She doesn't flatter. She doesn't need to be liked, and that makes her more dangerous than Michella ever was. Because Opal doesn't pretend. She just does what needs to be done. If that means taking a shot while your back is turned, she'll take it—but it won't be because your back is turned.

I lift my glass but don't drink. "She gets under my skin without trying. She walks into a room and no one questions why she is there. Not even me."

Beckett watches me now. But he keeps his mouth shut.

"The worst part?" I add. "She has no loyalty. She made a decision to infiltrate a business she didn't understand, on nothing but the word of her mother, and then turned around and stabbed the man who helped her build her career from the ground up in the back."

Stellan doesn't move, but his voice is lethal when it comes. "You mean me.""She didn't hesitate," I say. "Didn't flinch. This woman calculated the angle and took the shot. That kind of disloyalty is instinct. She was built for betrayal. She is only about herself."

Stellan sets his glass down with more care than necessary. "That was my ax to bury. Not yours."

I glance at him, but he doesn't look away.

"I forgave her," he continues. "Talia did too. We didn't do that lightly."

Beckett leans forward, his tone changing from jovial to serious. "You're talking about her like she's a mercenary. But we have all seen mercenaries. They don't look like that when no one's watching."

"She made a call under pressure," Stellan begins. "She was alone, outnumbered, and gambling on instincts to take out who she saw as the enemy."

She had options. She could have looked at her mother like she was crazy. Called her sister to ask. Hell, even look it up. Do some research. Instead she made the decision to trust and not verify.

"You've never met her mother," he says quietly.

I don't answer, but the look I give him is enough.

"Celestine Greer is a different kind of threat," he continues. "She doesn't yell. She doesn't make scenes. She smiles while she rewires your thinking, convinces you the knife in your back is something you put there yourself. She doesn't just manipulate—she erodes. She hates me because I made it, and Maris ended up unhappy in an abusive relationship. She couldn't stand the fact that her daughter wouldn't just tough it out and left. Opal was getting revenge for Maris."

Beckett watches him closely now, but doesn't interrupt.

"She wanted someone to take me apart," Stellan says, matter of fact. "She didn't care who she used to do it. She raised Opal to be her secret weapon, and when she was ready, she pointed her straight at me."

He leans back, unreadable. "So yes, she betrayed me. But she was trained to. By someone who taught her love was a currency and nothing more."

Love as currency. It makes sense. It explains too much —her precision, her distance, the way she never asks for anything she's not already owed. If that's what she was taught, then maybe none of this is personal. Maybe betrayal was never a choice for her. It is all that she ever knew. Somehow, it makes me despise her mother more than she does now.

"If Talia and I can forgive her, and if Frankie trusts her with her life, then maybe the question isn't whether you can trust her. It's whether you're ready to admit she's not the only one carrying a knife," Stellan says. "Maybe it's time you stop holding a grudge on my behalf."

Beckett lifts his glass slightly. "You don't have to trust her, but you do have to work with her. Ask yourself why she gets under your skin so easily. Because it sure as hell isn't just about loyalty."

Michella Carr.

She didn't storm the gates. She slipped in through a side door and made it feel like I'd invited her. Always agreeable in public, always deferential in private.

She never asked for control. She made me believe it was safer in my hands. Until every choice I made was one she'd already set in motion. One agreement at a time. One suggestion too easy to ignore. Always just outside the blast zone when it finally went to hell.

She studied what I needed and became it. Until I stopped checking her work. Until I started trusting her eyes instead of my own.

She sold information to a competitor. An old man with a legacy complex and a long memory—someone my family buried years ago in business, but never in pride. She married him six months after she walked out. His name was on the paperwork that gutted two of my side holdings. I didn't lose much financially. That wasn't the point. She didn't do it for gain.

She did it because she felt like she had no future with me and that pissed her off. She was very wrong about that. The day she walked out was the day the ring in my safe was supposed to be on her finger.

When I confronted her, she didn't scream. She didn't

cry. She looked at me like I was a child throwing a tantrum over a game he lost. Then she left—no apology, no fear, no sign she ever planned to stay.

Opal has none of her polish. She isn't charming. She doesn't flatter. She doesn't need to be liked, and that makes her more dangerous than Michella ever was. Because Opal doesn't pretend. She just does what needs to be done. If that means taking a shot while your back is turned, she'll take it—but it won't be because your back is turned.

"She reminds me of her," I say finally. "Same detachment. Same attitude. But Opal doesn't hide behind anything. She doesn't smile when she pulls the trigger. She just pulls it."

I set my glass down harder than I mean to, splashing the rest of my bourbon on the table. "Michella taught me what betrayal looks like when it's dressed in affection. Opal doesn't bother with the disguise."

Stellan laughs at my expense. "The problem is, you're still talking about her like she showed up uninvited. But you signed the contract. You let her in. You made it real. Now you're moping because you can't seem to keep her in line. That... or she already owns you."

Of course he sees it. Of course he cuts right through it. This isn't about emotion. It never was. It's about losing ground without ever realizing you stepped off solid footing.

"You don't need to love her, Dante," Stellan says, tone clipped. "You don't even need to like her. But you do need to play her game. Because she's not just smarter than you expected... she's loyal to no one, which makes her dangerous to everyone. If she decides you're the enemy, it won't be someone else telling her that. She would never let anyone get into her head again. She will kill you using tactics you use. And no one will blame her."

Stellan thinks he's already calculated the next five moves. He hasn't. But he is right about one thing. I'll keep losing if I let pride dictate my next one.

"You want to be the king? Then stop acting like a man scorned. Handle your wife—or she'll handle you."

I drain the rest of my bourbon, letting my thoughts circle in my head until I find one that makes me chuckle. Both of their attentions turn to me.

"I think I'll stay at the club for a while tonight," I say, tilting my glass toward them. "Talk to some guests. Enjoy a drink in the bar."

Beckett shakes his head with a grin.

"If you think you're playing chess, make sure she hasn't already moved the king," Stellan says.

I don't miss the look he gives me. "Let her move the king," I say. "I'll take the queen."

Beckett lets out a whistle. Stellan smiles, he's warned me and knows it won't matter. He's waiting to see how it ends.

No one says anything else.

I raise my empty glass. "To war with an impeccable woman."

CHAPTER EIGHT

Opal

I steady my hand against the cool marble and draw the liquid black line with a single practiced motion. The wing extends just past my lash line—subtle enough that no one will notice the effort, bold enough that they'll notice me. If they dare look me in the eye to begin with.

The lipstick clicks as I twist it up. Bloodstone, they call this shade. My all time favorite. I swipe it across my lips. The brush sweeps hollow shadows beneath my cheekbones. In the mirror, my reflection hardens into something both familiar and foreign.

Two weeks in this penthouse, and Dante's cologne has never touched these drawers. His razor never cluttered this sink. The marriage license is framed in the foyer for show only. He's never here anyway. It's just in case someone decides to visit.

I felt like we needed something since it's not like we have any wedding photos to put up. Or photos at all.

The silk slides cool against my skin as I step into the

dress. The slit slices high up one thigh—dangerous if I sit wrong, which I won't. My spine stands bare, the open back dipping low enough to draw attention.

In the mirror, the full picture comes together. I check the lipstick line of my mouth, smooth my dress, and reach for my perfume.

My heels click against the hardwood. The shoes can make or break the outfit, I always say.

The phone pings right as I'm adjusting the strap. I glance toward the bed where it lights up. The mirror doesn't lie. I look like a woman who doesn't care what anyone thinks. That's the point. Confidence is easier to wear than armor, and tonight, I need both.

My phone lights up again from across the bed. I cross the room, heels clicking against hardwood, and pick it up.

It's probably another tabloid headline about Dante and me. That's been Rosebud's new full time client lately —tracking, logging, cross referencing press cycles to make sure the story that we put out stays relevant.

Rothwell Strategic has been handling the public side, fielding comments like they were planning this marriage since birth. Everything is so perfect it's like they know every single thing anyone is going to say. That's why they're so good at what they do.

I tap the screen, already bracing for the latest spin.

VEGAS VULTURE EXCLUSIVE

From Carr to Greer: How Did Vegas's Newest Power Couple Become a PR Dumpster Fire?

Let's just say what everyone's thinking: Opal Greer is no Michella Carr.

Two weeks ago, Dante Valera—the ice veined king of Obsidian—quietly married the woman who once gutted Stellan Rothwell's inner circle from the inside. It wasn't a wedding. It was a headline. And ever since then, Vegas has been waiting for something to make this whole thing make sense.

It hasn't.

Because while Valera is still putting in appearances (mostly without his blushing bride), Opal Greer is... nowhere. No interviews. No photos. No red carpet smiles. Just a very expensive apartment and rumors thick enough to choke a cocktail waitress.

Meanwhile, Michella Carr's name won't stay out of anyone's mouth.

Carr had pedigree. Carr had poise. She could hold a Society gala in one hand and a man's attention in the other. She wasn't afraid to speak, but she never had to raise her voice. She had that Valera kind of attitude.

Greer couldn't be more different.

Carr elevated the Valera brand. She fit into the empire like she'd been born for it. She didn't have to claw her way in—people held doors open for her.

Greer? She hacked her way through the walls and pretended like it was meant to be.

Carr left Valera with a scar and a legend. Greer looks like she's waiting for the right moment to bury him.

Say what you want about Michella... but at least she meant something.

Greer is starting to look like a placeholder with an agenda.

Comments from fans of The Vulture:

"Carr had class. Greer has clearance."

"At least Michella loved him. This one looks like she's casing the place."

"Dante blinked and married the woman who made his friend bleed. Can someone check if he's under duress?"

Vegas hasn't forgotten Michella. It's still trying to figure out what the hell Opal Greer is doing here.

Is this marriage supposed to be real?

Then why does it feel like a very public punishment?

More soon, darlings. You know we never sleep.

— The Vulture

I don't blink as I scroll.

They really went for it this time.

Low blow comparisons, society whispers disguised as reporting, and that final line… *why does it feel like a public punishment?* Cute.

The part that really gets me is the comments.

The same people who drink the blood of the wealthy at every gala are now acting like I defiled sacred ground by marrying Dante Valera. Like Michella Carr is some patron saint of ruined men, and I'm just the blunt instrument no one invited to the altar.

Fine. Let them miss her. Let them say my name like it's an infection.

I reach for my phone, already planning the statement I'll drop. Not one of Rothwell Strategic's neutral scripts. Something that makes it clear I don't kneel to legacy wives and memories.

We all know that Dante and Michella were together for a long time. That's no secret. The one thing no one knows is how they ended things. That was never released.

I go to write my statement, but the notification dings before I can even open Notes.

RESPONSE TO THE VEGAS VULTURE
Statement issued by Rothwell Strategic
Personally signed by Talia Rothwell

Let's be honest about what this was.

This wasn't reporting. It was projection. A thinly veiled attack dressed up as commentary. You took one woman's desire to stay out of the spotlight and turned it into a personality flaw. You took another's absence and tried to sanctify it.

What you published wasn't journalism. It was insecurity with a byline.

Let's get a few things straight.

Opal Greer doesn't smile for cameras. She doesn't owe you justification for her love and she doesn't require validation for favor.

You don't have to like her. But you will respect the relationship she and Dante Valera have.

Comparing women to one another is the oldest trick in the book. One's grace becomes another's coldness. One's ambition becomes another's arrogance. What you're really saying is that Opal Greer makes you uncomfortable—and that's the part you should be interrogating.

This marriage doesn't need your approval. She doesn't need your praise. But you owe her your accuracy.

Opal Greer is not the villain of this story. She's the reason there's still a story to tell.

Talia Rothwell

Well. The Vulture pissed her off.

Talia Rothwell doesn't sign her name unless it matters. Not to correct the record. Not to play politics. Only when she wants whoever it is to know they fucked with the wrong woman.

I read the statement twice. Then once more for the pleasure of it. It doesn't defend me. It dismantles them. Point by point. Line by line. This is the kind of piece I used to write myself.

I laugh under my breath as I toss the phone onto the bed and smooth my palms down my hips.

They wanted a show. They're getting bait.

Perfect timing, really. My plan for the night was already in motion. But now? Every eye is going to be on me when I walk into Obsidian. And whoever's been sniffing around Dante's empire won't be able to resist looking twice.

Let them stare.

It's easier to draw a target when you're the one everyone is already looking at.

The Obsidian entrance always has security and a velvet rope. It keeps the wrong people out, and shows the power the right people have at being able to walk right in.

My phone rings in my purse and take it out to see a text from Lena.

LENA

> Pretty sure I have some intel that Dante is acting up. Maybe too flirty. But he never put his hands on anyone. Appropriate but weird.

Not that it matters to me. I have access.

I don't slow down. I glide straight through the lobby and into the pulse of the club. Every eye turns.

Good.

Let them look.

They've seen the articles. Read the gossip. Watched me be dissected and compared like some counterfeit castoff. Let them try to square that version of me with the woman walking past their tables now. The one in the black silk slit high and in stilettos made for men to drop to their knees to beg.

Obsidian's VIP section is full tonight, but it's the bar that catches my attention. Or rather, the man at the center of it.

Dante is leaning against the counter in black on black tailoring, collar undone, drink untouched. His sleeves are rolled, forearms tensed. Women orbit him like they've already been caught in his gravity. They lean in too close, toss back their hair too often, laugh a little too loud at things he isn't saying.

We don't interact a ton in person. We've texted here and there. I swear it's not his actual number though. Probably a business one. Dante doesn't trust me.

It's why I'm in Onyx and not at his home. And why he is avoiding me.

He doesn't touch them, but they're already begging for more. Every one of them vying for attention like he hasn't already signed a contract binding him to someone else.

To me.

He hasn't seen me yet. Or maybe he has and just doesn't care. Either way, the reaction isn't going to be his. It's going to be mine.

I keep walking, slow and smooth, like the spotlight was timed to follow me in. The staff nods. The patrons part. The game starts now.

He wants to flirt?

Fine.

But I came here to remind him who the hell he's married to.

I move toward the center of the dance floor. I don't look around for a partner. I slide straight into the rhythm, hips rolling with the beat, arms rising as the silk of my dress kisses my skin.

The lights catch along the slit of the gown as I pivot, exposing my thigh. I turn with the music, slow and smooth, letting the motion wind around me. My hair falls like a curtain over my shoulder when I tilt my head back, chest lifted, mouth parted.

Somewhere around the bar, Dante's watching.

He doesn't like this game.

Which is exactly why I keep playing.

The beat drops and I drop with it, just enough to draw a breath from someone near me. I drag my hands down the sides of my thighs. A man across the floor swears softly. Another one watches like he's praying for courage. The air thickens.

I feel it immediately. Dante Valera is moving. He is parting the crowd as his marches toward me. The moment his hand wraps around my wrist, the world narrows. Fingers locked, pressure firm but not bruising.

I don't fight him. I let him drag me through the crowd, past the bar, up the staircase, through the velvet curtains that no one other than staff is allowed to cross. I try to keep the anger off my face. It's humiliating being dragged around like a child.

He doesn't look at me, but his grip doesn't falter.

The door slams shut behind us. The lock clicks. The skyline bleeds through the glass walls in bruised golds and city fire. His hand leaves mine.

I take two steps forward, slowly, carefully, like I'm handling a wild thing caged too long.

"You looked like you were enjoying yourself," he says, voice bitter, like scotch over ice. "Trying to fuck one of my clients, or were you taking requests?"

I laugh. Not because it's funny, but because he's mad, and mad means cracked.

"You jealous?" I tilt my head, letting the question hang.

"No." He stalks toward me, voice sharp. "I'm furious. You think this is a game?"

"This is Vegas," I say. "Everything's a game."

He's close now. Closer than smart. His voice drops. "That's not why you did it."

I don't give him the satisfaction of a reaction from me. "No. It's not."

His eyes narrow. "Then what the hell was the point?"

I walk backward, toward the window that faces the entire club. My heels echo on the floor. I stop just before the glass, letting the lights glow behind me like a crown.

"You're being hunted," I say. "You have a leak. Eyes on every room. Every file. And whoever they are, they're watching you." I pause, letting that sink in. "Now they're watching me."

He doesn't answer. His fists curl at his sides.

I smile slowly at him. "Congratulations. You're not the only bait anymore."

His jaw twitches. "So that's what this is? Strategy? You dancing like a whore in my club is part of your brilliant plan?"

"You didn't say I couldn't be seen," I reply, lifting my chin. "And I didn't touch anyone. That was all you."

"You wanted my attention," he says darkly.

I hold his stare. "You gave it to me."

The distance vanishes.

His mouth crushes mine, angry and starved.

He shoves me into the glass.

His mouth drags down my neck, lips open, breath hot. He doesn't kiss gently. Tongue, teeth, the slow scrape of stubble against skin that makes my thighs clench.

I hook a leg around his waist, silk rising, heat blooming where we meet. He grinds against me. Without warning, he turns me with his hands on my hips, never fully breaking contact. My palms hit the glass, cold against my skin, the stark difference in comparison with the heat coming from his body behind me, is enough to drive me wild. Not that I want him to know that.

The club sprawls out in front of me, glittering, unaware. I could scream and no one would hear. I could break and he'd be the only one who saw it.

His voice curls low against my ear, rough and dark. "Tell me to stop."

I don't. I arch instead, back bowed, offering more.

I can feel his anger, see it in the white knuckled grip he has on the glass beside my head. I pushed him too far —I know that—but I don't back down. Not now. Not ever.

Dante's voice is a low growl at my ear. "You think you can embarrass me, Opal? You think you can walk into my city, my world, and challenge me?"

I meet his gaze in the reflection of the glass, chin lifted, unflinching. "I won't let you control me, Dante. I won't be another one of your pawns."

He lets out a harsh laugh, all edge and heat. "You think this is about control?" His hand leaves the glass and comes to my throat. He doesn't squeeze, but the promise is there, deliberate and unmistakable. "This is about ownership, Opal. You were mine the moment you stepped into my club pretending to be my loving wife."

He gives me a look I can't quite read. "Before you go jumping to conclusions. That woman you saw me with? She's my mother's best friend's daughter. I've known her since the day she was born. And she is probably the last person in the world I would flirt with."

I swallow, feeling his fingers rest against my pulse. Fear should bloom, but that's the last thing coursing through my veins right now. Instead a sense of adrenaline, sharp and electric, lights me up from the inside out. I'm playing with fire, and I don't care if I burn.

"I won't be owned," I say, even as my body betrays me, leaning into his touch.

His mouth curves, feral. "You say that," he murmurs, "but your body tells a different story." His other hand grips my hip, fingers biting in hard enough to promise a bruise later. Heat seeps through the silk of my dress, possession threaded through every inch of contact.

I gasp when he turns me again, my back meeting the cold glass. He cages me in, hands sliding over fabric, dragging the hem higher along my thighs. Cool air skims my skin. His gaze burns as it tracks downward, pupils blown wide with want and fury, and I feel every inch of it land.

"You want this, Opal," he growls, his hand sliding up my thigh, fingers sinking in like he's claiming all of me. "You want me. You want the danger, the thrill. You want to play with fire."

I glare up at him, breath short and uneven. "You think you know me, Dante? You think you know what I want?"

He laughs. "I know your body better than you know it yourself. I know you crave the adrenaline, the rush. I know you want me to take you. Claim you. Own you."

I shake my head, but my body betrays me again, arching into his touch, drawn to the heat. "You're wrong," I whisper, knowing he hears the lie.

His grin cuts through the dim light. "Liar," he breathes, gripping my chin, forcing my gaze to meet his. "You want this. You want me."

His hand slides from my jaw to the strap of my dress.

One pull—and the fabric gives. I hear it tear, feel it fall. My gasp catches between us as my hands clutch his shoulders, nails digging into his skin, grounding myself as the room spins. Blood roars in my ears. Heat rolls off his body.

Then his mouth crashes onto mine—teeth, tongue, need. I answer with teeth of my own, biting, tasting, fighting for control. It's brutal. It's messy. It's us. This isn't a surrender. It's a collision.

Dante's hands grip my hips as he lifts me off the ground.

I wrap my legs around his waist, my arms looping around his neck, my body pressing against his. I can feel his erection pressing against my core.

I gasp into his mouth, my body grinding against his, seeking the friction, the release.

I swallow, feeling the press of his fingers against my pulse. I feel a thrill, a surge of adrenaline that sets my body alight.

"I won't be owned," I repeat, even as my body betrays me, leaning into his touch.

"You said that already, Opal, but your body tells a different story." I can feel the heat of his palm, could feel the possessive grip that promised pain and pleasure in equal measure.

His right hand glides up my ribs, past the faintest flutter of my heart, and closes around my throat. Not tight. Not yet. The glass is so cold my nipples ache. His body, pressed against my back, is furnace hot. Every point of contact is a dare.

"You want everyone to see, don't you?" Dante's voice

is velvet poured over razors. He wants a reaction. He always does.

I let the silence speak for me. I let him see the corners of my mouth, the subtle twist I know drives him rabid, reflected in the glass. There's a time for clever comebacks, but not when your throat is bracketed by a man who's turned seduction into a martial art.

"Say it," he murmurs. His left hand finds my hip once again, sharp as a vise.

He could snap my neck or drag me off the ledge. It's an even bet which he'd prefer.

I watch my own breath mist on the glass, the outline of my body lit up by the club's burning grid. "Let them see." My voice is hoarse, but it does not tremble. "Let them watch you fuck me."

He laughs—a sound that's more air than voice, amusement laced with hunger. His grip tightens, both hands now, and he rocks his hips forward. The glass shudders. I steady myself, palms flattened, nails scraping microscopic lines into the pane.

His next movement is merciless. His cock splits me open with a single, brutal thrust, hands locking me in place. The impact drives a yelp from my chest, embarrassingly high pitched, and I want to snarl at him for it. I want to snarl at myself for letting him have that satisfaction. But there's no room in my head for shame or anger, only sensation—cold glass, hot skin, the violence of being taken apart and reassembled.

He fucks me slow at first. The kind of rhythm that would drive any woman mad. I know I will have some glorious bruises in the morning. Each time he slams into me, my forehead thumps the glass, fog blooming like a flower around the outline of my skull. His hand never leaves my throat. His other hand snakes up to splay across my chest, fingers sifting under the torn lace bra. He's greedy.

My hands shake, just enough for him to notice. That's all the invitation he needs.

He drags his lips up the side of my neck, pausing when he finds the hollow just beneath my jaw. His teeth graze, then bites. I hiss involuntarily, and my nails gouge the glass.

"Careful," he whispers. "You break it, you pay for it."

"I'll put it on your tab." My own voice, steadier now, goads him. Always escalate. Never yield.

He grins against my skin. I feel his smile as much as I hear it. He rewards my insolence by squeezing harder, by angling his hips so the head of his cock slams a new nerve ending every time. I clench, desperate to regain some agency, but it only makes him groan—a real, primal sound. Power is a see saw. We're both trying to tip it.

My face is flush with the glass now. Anyone who came up here would get the show.

That thought should humiliate me. Instead, it splinters something inside me—something ugly, something that's wanted to be watched since the first time my mother locked me out of the house in nothing but pajamas.

No one can see through the glass. One way mirrors really can do wonders.

He picks up speed, slamming into me with enough force to rattle teeth. Every thrust is punctuated by a small, involuntary sound—a moan, a gasp, a snarl that I can't keep trapped. I want to pretend I don't like it this rough, but that's a lie only Dante would see through. He can taste my need in the air.

His right hand releases my throat and knots in my hair, yanking back so I'm forced to see our reflection—him, sweaty and tailored, and me, unraveling against his hold. He leans in, lips at my ear.

"You're mine tonight," he says. "Tomorrow, you can pretend to hate me again."

I could slap him. I could break his fingers. Instead, I arch back into him, grinding my ass into his pelvis, daring him to lose control. He takes the bait, hand moving from my hair to my mouth, two fingers forcing my lips open. I bite down, hard enough to draw blood if he doesn't move fast.

He doesn't move fast. He likes the pain.

His hand smears across my jaw, my chin, marking me. He releases my hip only to reach around and circle my clit, a rough rub that sparks white static behind my eyes. I nearly collapse, but he props me up with the force of his body, hips pounding, hand relentless.

I come with a silent scream, jaw clamped tight, fingernails scoring the glass. My legs shake so violently I think I might go through the pane, but he holds me close, thrusting until he's finished too—his release a slow, guttural exhale into the top of my head.

For a moment, the only sound is the club below.

My fingers find the edge of my dress where it lies crumpled on the floor. The fabric sticks to my skin as I pull it back into place—ruined, wrinkled, halfway down my thigh. Of course it is.

Dante moves behind me without speaking, the heat of him still lingering on my spine.

Something brushes my shoulders. His jacket. He slides it over my arms without asking. It smells like his cologne. The smell that does not grace the pillows in the apartment.

"I need to talk to you," I say, still trying to catch my breath.

He pauses, one hand still on my shoulder. "Now?"

"Yes."

He huffs a laugh. "I just fucked you against a window, and you want to have a conversation?"

"I can multitask," I murmur, adjusting the lapel of his jacket.

He circles to face me. "Let me guess. This is about business?"

"Michella." Dante's jaw tightens. The heat's still there, but the mood has shifted. "I think we need to be prepared," I say. "For whatever's coming."

I pull his jacket tighter around me, still smelling of him, still warm from his body. A comfort I didn't expect to enjoy.

I don't look at him.

I look past him, to the dance floor, to the glass that still holds the imprint of my front.

We're not done. Not by a long shot. If I'm going to end this, I want to see every possible twist that could be coming.

CHAPTER NINE

Opal

This is how it always goes. We may have had sex, but that doesn't change what I need to do.

He sits on the edge of the desk, looking this certain post fuck way men think they hide well. Shirt wrinkled, hair a mess, still coming down from the post organ glow.. Hair a mess. Still trying to remember who had the upper hand. I let the silence stretch. He can sit with it.

"I don't want this to be a surprise attack," I say.

"You think she's planning something now?" His tone isn't mocking—but it is tired. As if I'm picking a scab he's worked hard to forget.

"I think she's already started," I reply. "You just haven't felt it yet."

His hand drags through his hair. "You don't know her."

"No," I agree. "But, I know women like her. I was raised by one."

I can feel the question on the tip of his tongue.

I finally meet his eyes. "Women who walk into a room with charm and spite tucked into the same smile. You never see the latter—not unless you're the target. People see what they want. And women like her? They always get what they came for."

He looks away, jaw tight. "That's not how it was."

"Maybe not for you." I step closer. "But I've seen what's left of men after women like that are done with them."

He doesn't say anything, and I don't press. Letting men sit in their own silence is sometimes the best way to watch them squirm.

I turn back toward the window, arms folded in his jacket, my bare thighs still cold from the glass.

"Tell me what Michella did to you," I say. "All of it."

He sighs, blowing out a breath as if he can blow all of this away. "She was the first woman who ever made me want to slow down."

"Must've been some trick. Getting a man like you to slow down." I keep my tone light. I'm dying to know how she did it. Mostly I want to know how it all fell apart.

"She was a bit younger. Polished in that way people are when they've never had to chase anything. She made me feel like ambition could be graceful. Like maybe I didn't have to work myself to the bone in order to win."

His mouth twists. "She liked the rough edges on me. Said I made her feel dangerous. But only when it was convenient. When things got real—when Obsidian started needing more than charm and champagne—she started pulling back."

He runs a hand through his hair, sighs again hard. "I

didn't see it at first. I thought she was stressed. Burned out. I thought if I worked harder, gave her more, proved I could build something that would last, she'd stay." He meets my gaze, and for once, there's nothing calculated behind it. "I was going to propose."

That is a different thought. He's being... honest with me. Vulnerable for Dante.

"She left the week I bought the ring," he says. "Didn't even say goodbye. Just disappeared. Next thing I know, she's married to one of my competitors. Sixty, rich, and powerful in all the ways I wasn't yet."

My jaw tightens, but I don't interrupt.

"She sold him information. For profit and to get back at me. I wasn't doing what she wanted anymore. She used everything we built—everything I gave her—to move on like nothing even mattered to begin with."

He stands now, pacing slow. Tension in every line of his body. "When he died, I thought maybe that would be it. She'd vanish. Fade into whatever high society bullshit she'd always belonged to. But she's back."

By the time Dante finishes speaking, I'm already seated at his desk. The chair gives a soft creak beneath me. I rest my fingers on the keyboard and type in his password.

Of course I know it. He's predictable when he's emotional, and careless when he trusts someone not to betray him.

The desktop loads.

I start with guest logs. No Michella Carr. Of course not. She changed her name when she got married. It takes two clicks to find what it was—Velin. She took his name, wore it like a status symbol, then quietly dropped it after the funeral.

Widow, I think, pulling up Onyx's archived bookings.

There she is.

Michella Velin, three separate reservations over the last six weeks. Same suite block. Same concierge liaison. Always a late check in. Always alone. One of the notes says she requested fresh peonies in the room. That used to be her thing.

I dig through payment records. She used her own cards. There's no attempt to hide the trail—she clearly doesn't care if we know she's here. In fact, I think she wants us to know.

Dinner reservations. A spa appointment. A hair consultation with someone who charges four figures. Her driver logs show drop offs at a gallery opening last week and a boutique launch the week before that, Reese Vineyards closing party.

I tap through the reservation schedule again and send myself the folder. Behind me, Dante hasn't said a word. I don't need to look to know he's watching.

"She's here," I say, voice neutral. "Booked under Carr."

I turn slightly, just enough to catch his eyes. "She's been in and out of Obsidian for weeks." He has a look of disbelief on his face. He doesn't like to be unaware of something this important. "She's not sneaking around. She wants us to know she's back."

I close the laptop, the weight of it echoing louder than it should. "As for why—" I stand, meeting his gaze fully. "That part's still up for grabs."

Dante stares at me like I've said something impossible. "She was in Obsidian," he says slowly, each word bogged down by disbelief. "In and out. And I didn't know?"

I nod. "At least five times in the last month. Concierge logs show the same driver. Same suite block. She never checked in herself, always had someone else do it. But it's her."

His jaw tightens. He turns, already reaching for the intercom. "Get Lucrezia and Manny up here. Now."

Ten minutes later, the four of us are crowded into his office. Manny leans against the bar cart, arms crossed. Lucrezia perches on the edge of the leather sofa, legs crossed, tablet in hand, already pulling up reports.

Dante doesn't sit. He paces.

"Five times in a month," he says. "She stayed under her maiden name. No flag in the system. Nothing alerted me. How?"

Manny shakes his head. "We assumed Carr was too obvious. She never used that name after the wedding."

Lucrezia frowns, scanning her tablet. "The bookings were made through a third party VIP coordinator."

Dante finally stops pacing. "Why now? Why come back?" No one answers. He looks at me. "You think it's me?"

I meet his eyes. "I think it's about power. And right now, she is crawling back because you have some. Now you're married and she can't have you."

Dante exhales, low and rough. "Let's find out exactly what she wants. Before she makes a move we can't counter."

I keep digging.

Not socials this time. I'm looking for mentions in the press. Vanity reprints with clickbait headlines.

The kind of glossy, half factual lifestyle junk you'd find on the coffee table of a hotel lounge.

And there it is.

Here Comes the Comeback? Michella Velin Plots a Second Chance Fairytale in Glittering Vegas

By Claribel Saint, Vow & Vanity Magazine

You know her. You remember her. And if you've spent more than five minutes around a monogrammed cocktail napkin in Vegas high society, you've definitely whispered about her.

Michella Velin (née Carr), once the undisputed queen of champagne fueled galas and diamond draped ambition, is back. Not just back in the city—back in the headlines, back in couture, and maybe (just maybe) back in the arms of her most infamous almost husband.

Yes, that almost husband: Dante Valera.

Let's rewind, shall we? Once upon a time, they were the couple that built a legacy instead of a wedding registry. Word is, she designed more of Obsidian's bones than the architects did. She helped mold Vegas's hottest power player into the kingpin he is today. But somewhere between the ambition and the adrenaline, she vanished.

Into a new marriage. A new life. A new last name.

But fairy tales don't end—they reroute.

Following the unfortunate (but very well attended) funeral of her late husband, banking magnate Emett Velin,

Michella has been seen with increasing frequency in familiar territory. Private dinners. Quiet tables. Obsidian elevators. And most recently? An anonymous tipster spotted her touring the Valera Foundation's new rooftop venue at dusk.

Sources tell Vow & Vanity that the vibe was less business, more unfinished business.

She's been heard referring to her late husband's estate as "an interlude," and we're told she's wearing Carr again for "personal reasons." Translation: She's repositioning herself for Act II, and this time, the spotlight wedding is going to happen.

One insider says: "She always said timing was everything. Looks like she thinks it's finally hers."

The kicker? Our editorial team caught an exclusive glimpse of mood boards and dress swatches at one of Michella's favorite bridal ateliers. Labels were blurred out. But the sketches? Dripping in ivory silk and audacity.

Rekindled love? Whatever it is, Michella's not tiptoeing. She's strutting.

And if Dante Valera isn't on one knee yet, he might want to start stretching.

We'll keep our ears to the ground, our flutes full, and our sources talking.

Because in Vegas?

No one stays buried for long.

I click on the browser and head to a newer article. Flashes of ivory silk and engagement rings scroll past. Centerpieces in blush and cream. Headlines full of perfect second chances and curated love.

"There's a retraction," I say, feeling Dante move in behind me.

RETRACTION: Regarding Our Feature "Here Comes the Comeback?"

Posted two weeks after publication of "Here Comes the Comeback? Michella Velin Plots a Second Chance Fairytale in Glittering Vegas"

At Vow & Vanity, we pride ourselves on celebrating love in all its forms—from surprise elopements to rekindled romances. However, in the rush to bring you the most dazzling exclusives, we sometimes publish stories that evolve faster than we can verify them.

Such is the case with our recent article featuring Ms. Michella Velin (formerly Carr) and Mr. Dante Valera, entitled "Here Comes the Comeback?"

At the time of publication, our editorial staff relied on multiple off the record confirmations suggesting a renewed engagement between Mr. Valera and Ms. Velin, citing anonymous sources, prior relationship history, and hotel sightings. Since then, we have received formal clarification from Rothwell Strategic and representatives for both parties.

We wish to make the following corrections:

- *There is no current romantic relationship between Mr. Valera and Ms. Velin.*
- *Mr. Valera is legally married to Ms. Opal Greer, CEO of Rosebud Investigations.*
- *Ms. Velin was not interviewed for the article,*

nor did she contribute or consent to its contents.
- *No wedding is currently planned between Ms. Velin and Mr. Valera.*

We extend our sincere apologies to all parties involved—especially Ms. Greer—for the distress and confusion caused by our reporting. Vow & Vanity does not condone this practice of not verifying information and will take steps internally to ensure greater editorial accountability moving forward.

As always, we remain committed to love, truth, and tasteful celebration.

– The V&V Editorial Team

But they knew what they were doing. The original article had all the markings of a hit—timed perfectly, sourced vaguely, and written to stir the pot without ever getting too close to the lives they're trying to manipulate. They leaned into the narrative that people *wanted* to believe.

And now they're trying to scrub it from existence. They couldn't. Even though they tried to delete it, I still found it.

At the bottom, the comments are open. Of course they are.

@VelvetVegasVows: So we're supposed to believe this "Opal Greer" just *happens* to be married to him now? PR marriage 101.

@TeamMichellaAlways: Opal looks like the kind of

woman who takes what she wants and doesn't care who she cuts to get it. Michella *earned* him. Opal bought him.

@BridezillaWatch: Y'all see how fast they shoved that marriage certificate at us? Something stinks.

@FakeWifeRealScandal: Let's not pretend Opal didn't leak something to get this shut down. She always gets loud when she's guilty.

@DanteFanWife3: You can literally *see* in photos that he looked happier with Michella. His eyes are dead with Opal.

They're mentioning the photos of us leaving Obsidian together. In the club. Those little paparazzi gnats are everywhere.

@DiamondDagger: They keep saying Opal is a "strategist." Yeah. Strategic enough to sleep her way into his last name.

@ValeraVows: This feels like damage control. I give it six months before we hear about a "quiet divorce" and Dante finds his way back to Michella.

@VultureButMakeItVows: Opal might have the ring. But Michella had the history. You can't fake that. No matter how red your lipstick is.

I look lower at the comments and I found ones that are for me. Rothwell is working overtime.

@RedLipClause: Say what you want, but Opal didn't *need* to marry him. She *chose* to. That's power.

@ObsidianEyes: Michella dipped when things got hard. Opal walked straight into the pit with head held high.

@QueenOfSinCity: Y'all mad a woman like Opal doesn't beg. That's the real issue here.

@StrategistInSilk: If Opal wanted to ruin him, she would've done it already. She's not a gold digger. She's selfmade. Learn the difference.

@ValeraVenom: Reminder: Michella left *him*. Opal didn't steal anything—she just stopped letting people like Michella hold the crown.

@BrideOfObsidian: Let them talk. Meanwhile, Opal's unbothered, unmatched, and untouchable in couture.

@GlitterAndGreer: They keep comparing her to Michella like that's a compliment. One quit. The other conquered.

@CEOslayer: If survival looks like Opal, I'd let her step on me too.

"She didn't give the interview," I say, tapping the screen again, though we've all read the line ten times. "Didn't contribute. Didn't consent. Which means someone *wants* her back in the spotlight."

Lucrezia raises an eyebrow. "And she's not exactly dodging the attention."

"She's waiting for a moment to cash in," I add. "And we're not going to let her pick it."

Manny glances at me. "So what's the move?"

I pull up the itinerary again. "She's booked for another stay next week. Same suite, same driver. She's circling."

Dante's jaw tightens, but he doesn't interrupt.

"She wants relevance," I continue. "We give her enough rope to think she has it—then we pull the floor out."

"What does that look like?" Lucrezia asks, tone dry.

I smile. "Like an invitation. An event she won't say no to. One we control."

Dante finally speaks. "You want to bait her."

"I want her where we can see her."

He doesn't argue. He just looks at me like he already knows the fire's coming, and he's going to let me strike the match.

CHAPTER TEN
Dante

I walk out of Obsidian like the fucking walls are closing in. If I don't get out now, I'll say something I can't take back.

The front doors slam shut behind me. My driver's already waiting. I need space. The silence. The illusion of control.

I slide into the back seat and slam the door harder than necessary. "Home," I mutter, and the engine hums to life.

Except it's not home. Not really.

It used to be. A clean lined architectural flex on a hill outside the Strip. Too much glass. Too much white. The kind of place Michella picked because it looked good in magazines, not because either of us ever felt like it was home in it.

Now I can't stand the sight of the place.

I never set foot in the apartment. I avoided it at all costs. Especially when she was there.

I press my fingers to my temple. Michella can stay far away from me.

The "For Sale" sign went up last week. Photos staged. Listing active. There's already a backup offer. I should feel relief. Instead, I feel like I'm driving straight into a past I should've moved on from years ago.

All I can think of is Opal Greer. I should've known better. I should've stopped myself.

Fucking Opal was a mistake. Letting it happen was one thing. Wanting it—craving it, again—is worse. She makes everything feel like a power play and a promise in the same breath. Like it was inevitable. Like I never had a choice.

But I did. I always do.

This time, I chose wrong.

That's when I see her. Parked at the curb like she owns the street. Leaning against her car like she's waiting for an old friend—or lining up a kill.

Michella Carr. Velin. Whatever name she's using now, I know exactly what she's here for. And I'm not in the mood.

The moment I step out of the car, she's coming towards me.

Her coat is unmistakably designer, a floor length ivory cashmere piece cinched at the waist. The collar frames her neck, turned up against the cool air, though nothing about her reads as defensive. Every detail of her appearance is intentional, each piece chosen for the message it sends.

Beneath the coat, a champagne silk dress clings and moves with her body. Her heels are the same as they always were. Impossible to walk in unless you've mastered power disguised as poise. Michella has always worn luxury like a second skin, not to impress but to announce herself without saying a word.

Her hair is platinum and polished, every strand in place despite the wind. Even the elements seem to know better than to dishevel her. Pale green eyes hold mine.

She stares at me like nothing has changed. For a second, it's almost convincing. She still looks like the fantasy I once bought into.

I shake my head. I need to get past that feeling that I always had around her.

I don't look twice. Don't speak. Just slam the door harder than I need to and keep walking.

"Dante," she calls behind me, her voice syrup smooth and unwelcome.

I keep walking. Every step up the stone path makes me more and more annoyed knowing that she's still standing there. Still inserting herself where she doesn't belong. Her presence grates. Her timing's perfect in the worst possible way, as always.

The sound of her heels follows. She's not chasing me. She's making a point. That she's here. That I'll have to acknowledge her eventually.

But I'm in no mood to entertain ghosts.

"What are you doing here, Michella?" My voice is calm, but barely. I'm giving her no invitation.

She smiles. I know that look. She wants me to feel like this is a casual conversation that we've had hundreds of times. "I was in the neighborhood."

I arch a brow. "Try again."

The gate clicks shut behind her.

"You never changed the code," she says, quickly changing the subject.

I keep walking up the steps, not bothering to turn. "Didn't think I needed to protect myself from deja vu."

Her heels click louder as she follows. "Dante."

I stop at the door, hand hovering over the handle, and finally face her. "Say what you came here to say. Then leave, Michella."

The smile she gives me is too practiced to mean anything. "Just wanted to see you." She tilts her head, eyes scanning mine like she's still entitled to the version of me I was when she left. "You used to be happy to see me."

"That version of me died somewhere between your exit and your husband's inheritance."

The smile falters. Only for a second. But I see it. "You're still angry."

"I'm not angry," I say. "I'm busy. So unless you came here to talk about the money you owe me, turn around and use the gate you slithered in through."

She steps closer. "I came to talk," she says again, softer now. "Really talk."

I let out a low breath, my patience fraying. "You don't get to show up, uninvited, and pretend this is some kind of reunion. What do you want, Michella?"

She shrugs, like it's nothing. Like this is all casual. But her eyes don't match the tone. "You," she says.

I laugh, bitter and unamused, the sound scraping the air between us. "You're about ten years and a marriage too late, Michella."

Her eyes scan my face like she's memorizing it again. "It doesn't look real."

"What doesn't?"

"This marriage of yours," she says, almost curious. "No real wedding. The only thing we get is a generic Rothwell statement. No photos. It reads like it was written two days before it dropped. Weird. It's almost like you didn't even know you were getting married."

I say nothing. Because what's there to say? I can't justify it because somewhere inside, I know she's right.

She steps closer, and her perfume follows. I want to cough. It's basically suffocating me. "You expect me to believe that's love?" Her smile is razor sharp. "You, who used to laugh at society marriages and their little performances? Now you're in one?"

"It's not a performance," I snap. Maybe harsher than I mean to.

Her brows lift like I've proven her point. "Then where's the proof, Dante?"

She says my name like it still belongs to her.

"Where's the wedding ring in every headline? The first look photos? The blackout SUVs and five star honeymoon leaks?" She circles me now, graceful and serpentine. "You think I don't know what a real marriage looks like? I was prepared to have one with you. Real marriages don't hide."

"You were prepared to have one with a man you thought would make more money than he had."

"No," she says, suddenly dead serious. "I was prepared to build with you. Until you made it clear I'd have to suffer to do it."

I look at her now. She believes that. Somehow, she's rewritten the ending so she doesn't come out the villain.

"That is where you are very wrong," I say. "Opal doesn't need a ballroom. She doesn't need cameras to be committed. She doesn't need the world to believe it. It's about us... not everyone else."

Michella's mouth presses into a line.

"You think real love needs witnesses. I think it's what you do when no one's watching," I continue on.

The gleam in her green eyes appears once again. She's about to do something I know will piss me off. "Do you love her?"

I hesitate. I know she sees it.

"Thought so," she says. Her voice is cheerful. She believes she has something on me. "Just be careful, darling. You've always been too generous with the women in your life. A bit too trusting some might say."

I don't move. "That's none of your business."

She smiles, the kind that pretends to be understanding but never is. "It is if you're doing this to punish me."

"This isn't about you."

"You're marrying someone like Opal Greer out of nowhere, and I'm supposed to believe it's not a personal attack?"

I tilt my head, jaw tight. "You're assuming a lot."

She steps closer, the heels of her boots clicking against the stone path like she's stalking a win. "I'm not assuming. I'm reading the fine print. The way she walks beside you like she's still figuring out which mask fits best."

I stop her with a look. “Say whatever you want about me, Michella. Leave her out of it.”

Her eyes narrow slightly. “You’re protective. That’s new. Or maybe it’s guilt.”

“You always did have a talent for fiction.”

She doesn’t flinch. “I know what it looks like when you love someone. I know what it looks like when you don’t.”

“I’ve changed.”

“No, Dante. You’ve just gotten better at hiding it.”

There’s a pause—long enough for her to fill it with more poison.

“She’s not right for you,” she says. “She’s reckless. Unstable. The kind of woman who could never make you happy. She’s not built for it.”

“And you were built for it?” I ask, stepping forward now, voice like ice. “You left the second I stopped being convenient. You didn’t just walk away—you sold me out and married the man trying to cut my legs out from under me.”

Her smile falters for half a second. “I made a mistake.”

“No,” I say. “You made a choice. One you never thought I’d recover from.”

She doesn’t try to move closer again. She stands just outside the reach of the porch light, coat cinched tight, lips parted like she’s considering what to say next.

I cross my arms. "You didn’t just leave me. You stripped me down and handed the pieces to a man who wanted to see me crawl."

Her eyes don’t flinch, but I see her breath catch.

"I trusted you," I say, each word carved out of anger. "You gave Velin access to my projections. My contracts. My clients. You let him dismantle the empire we built—brick by brick—just so you could sit pretty next to his bank account."

"I didn't give him anything," she says softly. "Not knowingly."

I let out a hollow laugh. "You really expect me to believe that?"

"I expect you to remember who I was to you," she says, her voice almost breaking. "I would never have helped him take you down, Dante. If I wanted you gone, I would have done it myself."

She says it like a confession wrapped in loyalty. She always knew how to turn regret into a monologue and make it feel like absolution.

I want to rip through it. I want to tell her that sincerity from her mouth is just another illusion. But then she folds her arms tighter around herself, lowers her gaze, and keeps speaking. "Cornelius kept things from me. He was paranoid, obsessed with power. By the time I realized what he'd stolen, it was done." She raises her eyes again. "You have to believe me."

She's good. I'll give her that.

"Convenient timing," I murmur, voice rough.

"He married me because I still had access to you. That's what it was about." Her lip quivers, but she's quick to steady it. "I didn't know until it was too late."

In my head, I scoff. *Really? That's the story she's going with?*

I know that she's trying to convince me that we're still

in love. I can't figure out what she's after, though. She's still insanely rich from her dead husband. It can't be that. So what is it?

I study her, looking for cracks that aren't choreographed. I find none. It doesn't look like she's wearing a mask to me. If she is, I can't tell. The one person I've never been able to consistently read. The thought is horrifying really.

"You know," I say, trying not to sound like I'm making fun of her even if I am, "divorce would've been an option."

She flinches.

"I didn't come here to fix the past," she says. "I came because I made a mistake—and I lost the only person I've ever loved for it."

My jaw tightens as I glance away, breath dragging through teeth I didn't realize were clenched. "I don't think I know how to love. Not really. Never could. Some people just... aren't made for it. I am one of those people."

She doesn't hesitate. She steps forward like she's known I'd say that. Like she's been rehearsing her part this whole time.

"You did love," she says, voice like silk over glass. "You loved me. You just didn't know how to say it."

Her hands lift slowly. She looks like she is defusing a ticking time bomb. They settle on my arms first before moving higher. One brushes the side of my face, the other loops gently around the back of my neck.

"I never stopped," she whispers.

Her mouth brushes mine—soft and familiar. For a second, my body forgets what my mind knows. Then the spell snaps. The past doesn't kiss back. I do. That's the second mistake I've made today.

The heat flickers against my lips—and I wake the hell up.

I shove her back enough to make her stumble a step. "I'm married."

She stares at me, breath hitching. "I don't see a ring."

I pull my hand from my pocket and hold it up.

Her breath catches, and her eyes glass over. One tear slips down the curve of her cheek. Another clings to her lashes before falling, catching the porch light just right. She doesn't wipe them away. The corners of her mouth tremble, barely, the way a hand might hover before a slap.

I used to fall for that. I almost fall for it now.

"Don't," I mutter, one hand half reaching to wipe her tears before I stop myself. "Michella—don't do this."

She makes a sound—somewhere between a sob and a protest. She's about to throw one of her tantrums. I finally see the performance under the pretty. I take a breath and look her straight in the eye.

"I dodged a bullet when you left," I say. "Because if I'd married you, this is what I'd wake up to every goddamn day."

Her tears freeze. Her face hardens. That is the Michella I know… and hate.

I don't wait to see what comes next.

I turn and go.

I've been here since before sunrise. I didn't sleep last night. I couldn't. My mind was on Opal. And Michella. And everything else that's happening.

The calendar's full. That's the first thing I check. Luncheons, VIP suites, three rescheduled meetings, and a flagged security note about last night's east entrance code being used twice after hours.

I scroll faster. I need numbers. Things that don't cry and kiss and say they never stopped loving me.

The door slams open without a knock.

"What the fuck were you thinking?" Opal's voice slices through the office.

I don't look up right away. I finish typing the last note in the booking system, hit enter, and only then do I lift my gaze.

She's in black again, hair still damp from a shower she clearly took in a rush, lipstick untouched.

"Good morning to you too," I say, leaning back in my chair.

"Jesus," she scoffs at me. "Tell me you didn't let her get in your head." I don't answer fast enough. Her laugh comes out bitter. "Unbelievable."

"What do you want me to say?" I snap, standing up to get in her face. "She showed up. I didn't invite her."

"You didn't have to. You talked to her. You let her in. After everything we just discussed—after we literally planned how to handle her—your big move was to go have a nostalgic fucking heart to heart?"

"I didn't plan it—"

"No, you never do," she bites out. "You just react. Now we've got a mess."

I grind my teeth. "She's not involved in this, Opal."

That stops her. She blinks once, slowly, and then her expression ices over like I've said the dumbest thing she's ever heard. "You can't possibly be that naive."

"I know her."

She stares directly into my eyes "You still have feelings for her."

"She didn't know—"

"How do you know that?" she fires back. "What, she cried? Said she missed you? She *kissed* you? Told you that she still cares? That's all it takes for you to forget she sold your life to the highest bidder?"

"She said she didn't know until after they were married."

"Oh my God," she mutters, disgust curling her lip. "You really bought it. You know most people didn't think I was involved either."

I scowl, but don't give her the reaction she wants. "You weren't there."

"No," she says, stepping back. "But the rest of the world was."

That gets my attention.

I narrow my eyes. "What the hell does that mean?"

She cocks her head. "You check the internet lately, Dante?"

I don't answer. She takes that as confirmation.

"You should scroll once in a while. Maybe see what people are saying. Or how fast her little performance got picked up by every tabloid with a gossip column. You think no one saw that kiss at your front porch? There are screenshots. Captions like it's a fucking wedding announcement."

My stomach drops and I give her a wicked smile. "You're jealous."

Her entire face twists. "Fuck you."

She turns on her heel and heads for the door. "Opal—"

"Don't," she warns, without turning around. "I hope you enjoy the attention while you're about to lose everything... again."

The door slams shut behind her.

My phone buzzes, screen lighting up with back to back texts.

TALIA

Handled the morning rush. Articles going viral. We did damage control.

STELLAN

We shut it down. Barely. If you want this solved, Dante, don't be a damn fool.

I sit down hard. Too late.

CHAPTER ELEVEN
Opal

The second I'm outside of the club, I flag a cab. Not the town car. Not Dante's driver. My phone's already out before the door slams shut.

"Rosebud Investigations," I tell the cabbie. "East side."

He nods, pulling into traffic. This morning was an unmitigated PR disaster wrapped in diamond rings and ex lovers playing dress up.

I finally let myself breathe once we hit the edge of the strip.

I open *The Vegas Vulture.*

VEGAS VULTURE EXCLUSIVE

Happily Never After? Dante Valera Caught Kissing His Ex While Married to Opal Greer

They say old habits die hard—but some resurrections should've stayed buried.

Last night, Vegas's most ice veined mogul, Dante Valera, was spotted in an intimate embrace with none other than

Michella Carr, the woman who once nearly wore his ring... and then left him for an older, richer man. This time? She showed up at his gated Summerlin estate.

And he kissed her.

Yes, you read that right.

Caught on a neighbor's security camera—bless those ultra HD doorbell setups—the footage shows Carr reaching for his face, whispering something we'd kill to lip read, and then... Valera leaning in. It's not a peck. It's not a goodbye. It's a moment. The kind that starts wars and ends marriages.

Speaking of marriages...

What happened to Opal Greer?

You remember her. Former Rothwell powerhouse, current Mrs. Valera—at least on paper. The same woman whose wedding no one attended, whose photos don't exist, and who has only been seen when it is convenient for her.

They say she moved into his luxury apartment. We're guessing she didn't sign up for an ex on the front porch.

Sources say Greer stormed out of Valera's office this morning, no smile, no statement. And honestly? Can you blame her?

This isn't a PR misstep. This is a PR catastrophe.

Because you can spin a quiet marriage.

You can't spin infidelity with your ex.

Carr, for her part, looked like she belonged there. Same platinum waves, same velvet tone, same look that made men rewrite bank codes.

Rothwell Strategic didn't waste time. Within hours, they issued a scorching statement condemning "the deliberate and inappropriate behavior of Ms. Michella Velin" and framing the incident as "a blatant attempt to exploit past associations for personal attention." They called the photo "intentionally misleading," and reminded the press that Mr. Valera remains in a committed marriage.

Which leaves us wondering...

Was this a moment of weakness? A misunderstanding?

Or was it exactly what it looked like?

Because when a man kisses his ex on the porch of his marital home, under surveillance, in Las Vegas?

He's not thinking. Or he's thinking with the wrong head.

Whatever this is—damage control better be coming fast.

Because right now, Opal Greer is looking less like a wife and more like a placeholder.

More soon, darlings. You know we never sleep.

— The Vulture

I don't throw my phone. But I want to.

The photo is everywhere—Dante, front porch, mouth pressed to the woman who shouldn't have been anywhere near him. Her hand on his chest. Her eyes closed. His are the same.

I know exactly how they'll spin it. But the headlines aren't what stop me. It's the statement from Rothwell.

RESPONSE TO THE VEGAS VULTURE

Statement issued by Rothwell Strategic

Let's not confuse manipulation with meaning.

Michella Velin showing up unannounced at Dante Valera's private residence was not romance. It was calculated. She knew there were cameras. She counted on it. So did you.

The kiss you plastered across your homepage? One sided. A staged moment she engineered for maximum exposure and minimum truth. She didn't come to reconnect. She came to provoke.

You gave her the spotlight she couldn't earn on her own.

So here are the facts:

Dante Valera is married. His commitment is not performative. His wife is not temporary.

Michella Velin is not a source. She is not a player in this relationship. She is an interruption. One that's now been handled.

You weren't manipulated by the Valera camp. You were manipulated by Michella Velin. Next time, ask yourself who benefits from the narrative before running it.

We pull up in front of my office building. I pay the driver and head in.

When I step into the front of Rosebud HQ, I pause. The reception desk is empty, but voices drift in from the break area. Mari's laughing. She spots me over her coffee cup and lifts a brow.

"Got something fancy waiting in your office," she says. "Lavender roses and a bottle of wine. No note. Niko thought it was one of our clients."

I freeze. "Lavender?"

Karrie nods, already curious. "Yeah. You've got good taste in admirers."

Noor looks up from her corner perch—she's scribbling something in her notebook, always scribbling—but her eyes move to me instantly.

"Lavender roses," she repeats softly, like she's cataloging it. "Uncommon. Specific to memory... or misdirection."

I don't respond. I just turn and keep walking, until I make my way to my office.

Inside, it's waiting for me. A crystal vase of tightly arranged lavender roses on the center of my desk. A bottle of wine beside it—Reese Vineyards. One of the final containers before the vineyard closed. I've only ever seen it twice.

I don't sit. I don't speak.

I just stare at it, that sick feeling crawling up the back of my spine like a warning.

I have a bad feeling about this. I can't dwell on it any longer because a voice calls to me.

Lena's eyes flick up from her screen, her mouth twitching like she wants to warn me but can't do it fast enough. Noor glances toward my door, then away. Mari's not even pretending to focus.

Celestine Greer stands in the middle of my office. Blush coat, pale gloves, pearls strung like a leash. Her steel blonde hair is wound into a perfect bun, not a strand out of place. Her eyes—cool gray—sweep the room like it's already failed inspection.

"Darling," she says, smiling as if she's welcome.

I don't move. "What are you doing here?"

"I came to say hello," she replies, gaze looking over the space with a barely concealed frown. "And to see how your... little business is going."

"It's going." I nod toward the door. "You can, too."

She tsks, like I'm being ungrateful in front of guests. "That's no way to speak to your mother."

"You stopped being my mother when I stopped being useful."

That cracks her smile, but only for a second. "Well," she says, adjusting her gloves, "Maris didn't seem to mind me stopping by. She made coffee. Said I could come visit anytime."

Everything inside me stills. "What?"

She tilts her head, pretending surprise. "Oh. You didn't know she was back?"

"When?" My throat tightens.

"A few weeks ago, I believe." She waves it off like the detail doesn't matter. "She's got those sweet little girls with her. There's still that awful custody situation. But she seems happy."

I stare at her, trying not to show how much it hurts that Maris didn't call me.

"How do you know all this?"

"We've been talking." She shrugs. "She's family."

"So am I."

Her smile thins. "You were."

I take a step forward. "Get out."

"Opal—"

"I said *get out*."

Her eyes narrow. "You've always been dramatic."

"You've always been poison. Congratulations—we're consistent."

Noor appears quietly beside me, holding the door. I don't need to nod. She already knows.

Celestine straightens her coat, dignity crumpling at the edges.

"Well," she says, brushing past me, "at least Maris knows how to be civil."

Celestine turns as the office door opens behind her, lips already curved into something like happiness. Something she never shows me.

"Hello, darling," she says, like this is brunch and not a business.

Maris walks in, calm as glass. "Hi, Mom." That's all. No pause, no kiss on the cheek. She barely glances at her, instead heads heads straight for me.

"Opal," she says, eyes scanning mine. "I was going to come by. I didn't—"

I don't let her finish. "You're back in Vegas?"

She nods, coat still half on. "A few days now."

"And you told her?" I tip my chin to our mother.

"I didn't," Maris says, shooting a glance back at the doorway. "Fletcher did. She showed up at our new house before the moving truck even left."

Celestine clucks her tongue from behind us. She is not invited in this conversation. "I was being supportive."

Maris doesn't turn around. "You were being intrusive."

My jaw tightens. "So you're just here now? Full custody, moved in, new zip code—and you didn't think to let me know?"

Maris exhales. "I didn't want to drag you into it until I had everything settled. It wasn't about not telling you."

"Sure as hell feels like it."

She pulls off her coat slowly, folding it over one arm. "Stellan helped me with the transition. Got me and the girls into a secured building. Fletcher filed an appeal the next day."

I'm not surprised that he filed the appeal. That man can never lose.

I look past her to the hallway, but Celestine's already gone—retreating with the false grace of someone who thinks slamming a door would make *her* look undignified.

Maris sighs, then meets my eyes again. "I didn't mean for you to find out like this."

I believe her. I just don't know if that makes it better.

My sister settles into the armchair across from my desk, smoothing her trousers like she's trying to press everything into place. "We've had split custody since the divorce. Two weeks on, two off. Civil enough—until it wasn't."

My brow lifts. "What changed?"

Maris looks down at her hands. "He started pushing back. First with schedule changes, then with legal filings. Said the girls were unsettled with me. Accused me of creating instability. Of being overly emotional. He used old therapy notes. Emails. Anything he could twist."

The heat rises in my chest. "Of course he did."

She nods, jaw tight. "He tried to paint me as inconsistent. Unfit. Said I was unpredictable, prone to depressive episodes. He even had the audacity to say I was detached during pickups or drunk most of the time. Meanwhile, he was bribing them with last minute trips and shopping sprees. Turning them into bargaining chips."

I move closer, the edge of the desk cold against my palm. "No one called bullshit?"

"Eventually they did," she says. "The judge saw

through it. I got full custody last week." Maris' eyes gleam. "He had supervised visits. Every other weekend. And he was livid."

"What happened, Maris? What finally pushed it to full custody?"

She hesitates. It's the kind of pause that says *if I speak this out loud, it becomes real again.*

"It was during one of his supervised visits," she says. "At a park. When he was supposed to be spending time with them like he claims he wanted to."

I say nothing. I let her talk.

"I wasn't there," she continues. "But the social worker was. She filed the report." She swallows. "Lenore fell. Cut her hand on broken glass by one of the benches. It wasn't deep, but she and Rhea screamed. And he—he didn't even move. He was on his phone. Scrolling through something. Probably looking at porn. Didn't look up until the worker was already running to her."

My stomach tightens.

"She told him to put the phone down. He told her to shut her mouth. Loud enough for parents nearby to turn." Now she's shaking her head, like she still can't believe it. "She said if he'd reacted even a second later, if she hadn't been there—Lenore could've been seriously hurt. He wasn't paying attention. Not even pretending to. And when she pushed back, he said—he said the kid's fine, it's not like she's dying."

I exhale slowly. "The judge saw the report?"

Maris nods. "And the security footage. And the threats after."

I blink. "Threats?"

She leans forward. "He said I was turning my daughters against him. That if I tried to take them away, he'd make sure I regretted it. He didn't even bother hiding it. Texted it."

"Jesus, Maris."

"That's when I packed. I filed for relocation and sole custody the next day. Told the girls we were starting over. They didn't ask questions. They just... followed along. My babies have been through so much. I want them to live a happy life."

"You should've called me," I murmur.

"I didn't want to pull you in until I knew we were safe." She glances toward the door, then back at me. "Stellan helped move us. He made sure everything was airtight before Fletcher could stop it. But he's trying now. Filing emergency petitions. Wanting hearings. Trying to claim I kidnapped them."

"And you're here," I say. "In Vegas. With all of this behind you, and still somehow right on your heels."

Her smile is bitter. "That's what happens when you share children with a man who thinks control is love."

Lena calls out from her desk down the hall. "Opal—you're gonna want to see this."

I'm already moving, Maris on my heels.

Lena doesn't look up when we crowd behind her monitors. Her fingers fly across the keys, pulling up the cloned file tree.

"This is the dupe," she says. "It's clean—too clean. Whoever did this didn't just copy the infrastructure. They rewrote the entire code from the ground up to match with what Obsidian has."

I freeze.

"Open it," I say.

Lena does. What comes up is a nightmare. A living nightmare. Transaction logs. Guest lists. Service codes that translate to things I *know* don't happen at Obsidian —but look damn convincing here. Cage matches. Companion rotations. Discreet substance procurement. It reads like a ledger from hell.

"Fuck," I breathe.

"It gets worse," Lena says. "They backdated everything. Cross referenced real events—actual guest bookings, staff names, internal memos—and laced them through. Just enough fact to make the fiction virtually bulletproof."

Maris leans in, scanning. "These document styles—these were generated from Rothwell templates. Stolen formatting. Same cadence."

"They wanted it to be believable," I say.

Noor appears in the doorway, tablet in hand. "And they succeeded."

She passes it to me. One of the Society's private channels, leaked early to reporters with zero security protocol. The story is already live.

VALERA'S VICE RING?
Insider Dossier Suggests Obsidian's Secrets Are Darker Than We Thought

Underneath is a redacted screenshot of one of the fabricated reports, Dante's name in bold at the top.

I can't feel my hands. But I feel the rage. "They're

not just trying to ruin him," I say. "They're trying to discredit everything he's built, they want him put away."

"Who?" Maris asks.

I can't answer because I have no idea.

Lena speaks quietly. "We may have a traitor."

Because this level of access shouldn't be possible. Not unless someone already had the keys.

I lift my phone. "Call Dante. Tell him we're pulling the original server logs now and scrubbing for anomalies. No interviews. No statements. Not until we've got proof this was planted."

"What do you want me to do?" Noor asks.

I glance up at her. "Build a timeline. Everything from the last four weeks. Obsidian, Rosebud, Society. Compare real events to this file structure. We find the inconsistencies, we find our entry point."

She nods.

Maris squeezes my wrist. "You're not alone."

No. I'm not.

But if this gets out of hand—I might be the only one who can clean it up.

Noor has Stellan and Talia patched in on a secure line. Dante joins seconds later.

"What are we looking at?" Talia asks. Calm, but I hear the anger coiled beneath.

I click into the file Lena decrypted and throw it on the shared screen. "Prostitution ring. Hidden behind Obsidian's private booking tiers. The rest is violence and drugs, but this—this is personal."

Dante scoffs. "It's garbage."

"Of course it is," I respond, though it's more of a snap than anything else.

"You agree?" The way Talia asks that annoys me.

"I know him," I say, voice clipped. "If Dante Valera ever ran an underground fighting ring, it wouldn't be to exploit women. It would be to protect them."

There's a pause on the line.

"Not that he would," I clarify. "But that's the difference. He doesn't prey. He defends. This whole narrative's built on a version of him that doesn't exist. That's why it *feels* fake, even when it looks convincing."

I glance at the screen again—at the neat little lies dressed up in perfect formatting.

"They didn't just get the data wrong. They got the *man* wrong."

Stellan exhales through his nose. "They had access."

"They had a motive," I say. " Whoever built this didn't just want Obsidian ruined—they wanted Dante branded as evil. You don't fabricate a sex ring unless the goal is to kill credibility and shame any alliance tied to him. No one touches a man accused of trafficking. Especially if the details feel plausible."

"Anyone can fake a calendar," Dante mutters. "This is a hit job, not a hack."

"Maybe," I say, voice low. "But someone knew where to hit."

Talia speaks next. "Who do you think it is?"

I have no idea. So I ask the only question that matters. "Dante. Who have you fucked that hates you enough to do all of this?"

He doesn't answer.

So I press. "Someone who knows your habits. Your access windows. Someone who remembers how your business was structured a decade ago. Someone who wants revenge and has the money to buy the right hacker."

"Opal—" he starts.

"Michella," I say, matter of fact.

"No," Dante snaps. "It's not her."

"Don't underestimate her gut," Maris says. "Opal doesn't say things like this lightly. If she's honing in on someone, there's a reason."

"She wouldn't go this far," Dante insists, but this time, it seems that he is hesitating a bit. "She's selfish. I can give you that. But she wouldn't have come to my house to beg for me back if she was planning this all along."

"She's bitter," I say. "Bitter people don't need to be masterminds. They just need a partner who is. *You* didn't give her what she wanted. So *she* needs to go out and get it. A tiger doesn't change it's stripes, Dante. She did this once. Even if you don't believe she did."

Dante exhales.

"I'll handle Michella," he mutters.

"No," I say, instantly. "You've done enough. We will handle it from now on. Your kiss destroyed everything we're trying to fix. You're fucking yourself over. Eventually, it will bite you in the ass so hard no one can save you."

"She kissed me. I didn't kiss her," Dante says, voice flat through the speaker.

"That's your defense?"

"You looked more than frustrated when you stormed out of my office. It's not just that you're trying to protect my reputation here. It looked a lot like jealousy," he says, almost amused.

Interesting. He's switching his tone. I've never seen him joke... ever. This is the exact opposite of Dante Valera. I wonder if he's like this when he gets cornered. Maybe uncomfortable even.

"So you let her kiss you. After you fucked me against the glass in your goddamned office. Classy, Dante," I say, the laugh that follows dry and ugly in my throat.

"Jesus," Maris mutters beside me, pulling the phone from speaker and staring at it like it might bite. "Are you okay?"

I nod at her, hating that my emotions started to show. I was not jealous. I was pissed as fuck.

Lena clears her throat, chiming in from the doorway, holding up a new drive. "Backtrace complete. Found the trigger node."

I meet her eyes. "Was it local?"

She nods once. "Vegas server. Someone in this city set it off."

My fingers curl around the edge of the desk. "Let's flush them out."

Because whoever thinks they can frame Dante forgot who he married.

CHAPTER TWELVE
Dante

I haven't slept. I can't. Not since the call that blew up my life.

Last night, my world dropped out from under me. I've been sitting in this fucking house for hours. I can't do it anymore.

I spend some time watching Opal work. Something about how quickly her brain works, how fast her fingers move puts me in a trance. She hypnotizes me.

Some idiot tagged Obsidian in a thread about high end trafficking rings. Someone else posted a photo of the VIP elevator and asked if it "led to hell." It's gone viral.

A parody account called @PurgatoryInVegas is already gaining traction.

They're calling me the devil with bottle service.

I don't know when I stopped breathing normally. At some point between the fifth "tipster post" and a very confident, very wrong TikTok expose, I started grinding my teeth again. Old habits. Always come back when things start to fall apart.

A ping breaks through the noise of the thoughts rushing through my head.

STELLAN

My office. Talia and Opal are here.

I let the phone fall to the couch and rub a hand down my face.

I tap into the security feed from Obsidian's back end, scan for anything unusual, and type out a message to Manny and Lucrezia.

Handle the floor. VIP rerouting goes into effect today. Tell security no one gets past Level 4 clearance without my sign off. I may not be back tonight. You guys are in charge.

Lucrezia replies with a thumbs up. Manny sends a skull emoji.

I drag myself off the couch, grab my jacket, and head for the car.

I take the elevator straight to the top of Rothwell Strategic. The office space is still empty. Too early for most people to come in.

Stellan's already standing when I walk in, Talia sits beside him. It's the first time I've seen her in person since the wedding. She's the kind of woman who makes the room bend in her favor before she even mutters a word. Impeccably put together in a matte black suit, heels planted, tablet in one hand like she's ready to follow you into war and then take over because you're not moving fast enough towards victory.

"Nice of you to show up," Stellan says dryly.

"I walked in exactly ten minutes after you texted me," I reply. "That's gotta count for something."

Talia gestures to the chair across from her.

"Sit down, Dante," she says. "You're already hemorrhaging reputation. Let's not waste time pretending otherwise."

Opal's doesn't look at me. Her arms are crossed, her jaw tight, and her phone is face down on the table. I can see her hands itching to reach for it. To either throw it at me or break it because of the headlines, I'm not sure which. I wouldn't blame her for either one if I'm being honest. If I saw a picture of her kissing another man, I'd be losing my shit, too.

Talia taps the screen. The video restarts from the beginning.

A calm male voice fills the room. At least I think it's male. There's a filter over it. But it is the kind of voice people trust.

"Vegas runs on illusion," the narrator says. "But every illusion has a basement."

The screen shows Obsidian's exterior at night. A line of women waiting to get in. Dresses too tight. Heels too high. Faces already tense before they even reach the door.

Then there is a cut.

Security footage. Time stamps intact. A woman entering through a staff corridor. Different dress.

Another cut. Same woman leaving two hours later. Mascara smeared. Shoes in her hand. Head down.

"This is not a nightclub," the voice continues. "This is a funnel."

My jaw tightens.

The video breaks into sections, each one neatly labeled, like a presentation meant to convince investors.

In all caps, there are words that come across the screen: **ACCESS SELECTION CONTROL COMPLIANCE and the woman who knew it all.**

A blurred diagram of VIP floors. Private elevators. Restricted suites. The narrator explains how certain guests bypass the main club entirely. No lines. No cameras. No records that matter. Screenshots of texts. Not explicit, but unmistakable. Women being told where to go, what to wear, how to behave. Language framed as opportunity. Exposure. Networking. The words *generous client* appear more than once.

Opal's fingers are still on her keyboard. Her face has gone flat. That scares me more than anger.

The control section is next. This is where it turns ugly.

A reenactment plays. There are actors and they are staged. But cut together with real hallway footage, real timestamps, real floor plans.

A woman tries to leave a room. A man blocks the door. Another voice off camera says her name.

"She's not screaming," the narrator says calmly. "That's the point. This system doesn't rely on force. It relies on people being desperate enough to do anything to survive. Dante Valera is willing to take all of that for his own personal gain."

The screen flashes with words gliding across it. NDAs. Debt. Immigration status. Housing. Reputation.

I feel something cold settle in my chest.

"They're saying I built this," I mutter.

"They're saying you profit from it," Talia corrects. "Which is worse."

The video shifts again to another section. Compliance.

A blurred interview. A silhouette. Voice distorted.

"I didn't think it was like that," the woman says. "At first. They said it was just entertaining. Just keeping them company. And then it wasn't."

Another voice. Another silhouette. "They told me I owed them. That I drank too much. That I signed something."

The narrator doesn't raise his voice. Doesn't editorialize. "Obsidian didn't invent this model," he says. "But it perfected it."

I stand abruptly. The chair scrapes back.

"This is bullshit," I say. "I don't run anything like this. I would burn my own club to the ground first."

"I know," Opal says quietly. "But they don't," she continues. "They don't need it to be true. They just need it to be detailed."

Stellan exhales slowly. "There's more."

Talia scrolls. The final section loads.

The woman who knew.

Michella's face appears. Old photos. Gala shots. Headlines about her return to Vegas. Then the porch image. The kiss.

"She knew how the system worked," the narrator

says. "She was close to the man at the center. Close enough to walk away."

The implication hangs there. Poisonous.

"They're using her as a moral contrast," Opal says. "The woman who escaped versus the women who couldn't."

My hands curl into fists.

"And the drugs?" I ask.

Talia's mouth tightens. "Secondary narrative. Add on accusations. Enough to suggest scale. Less evidence. But it muddies the water."

If I ran away from accusations like this, I would be hunted.

Even if I didn't, I'd still be guilty until proven innocent.

In Vegas, innocence doesn't trend. The guilty ones are way more interesting anyway.

"Time to talk about suspects," Talia starts.

No one fucking speaks. Of course they don't. They're all looking at me like I've got the answer locked in a vault behind my eyes.

I hate the feeling of being around people who think they know better.

"I don't know yet," Opal says. Not once flinching.

I bite down on instinct. "Not good enough."

Opal turns to me in slow motion. "Do you want speed or accuracy, Valera? Because you can't have both."

Beside her, Talia makes a sound that's a half sigh. "Let's start with the obvious."

Goddamn it. I already know where this is going.

"No." I say it without hesitation. My jaw clenches. "Not her."

I knew none of them were going to let that one slide.

Talia lifts a brow, milking the moment. "Funny. That's what Stellan said about Opal. When I suggested you might be behind the Rothwell breach. *'Not her,'* he said. Turns out I was right."

Opal smirks. It's the kind of expression that says she'd eat her own regret for breakfast if it meant spitting truth in your face. "You were. Congratulations. I'd bake you a fucking cake if we weren't trying to get some more intel."

That doesn't seem to bother Talia as she smirks right back. I cut my eyes toward Opal. "You think it's Michella."

Her laugh's the kind that doesn't actually sound amused.

"Of course I fucking think it's Michella," she snaps. "She has motive, she has reach, and she has the kind of face people *want* to believe. Don't pretend you didn't notice the public fell over themselves to paint her as some kind of wounded phoenix. The kiss photo? That wasn't an accident. That was bait."

"She wouldn't—"

"Don't." Opal slices through it like she's done entertaining delusions. "Don't finish that sentence unless you want me to punch you in the ego."

I bristle. Reflex. She sees it. Likes it, maybe.

"She ghosted you, came back like nothing happened, and now she's conveniently at the center of a multi pronged digital smear campaign with access to rooms she shouldn't know exist? *Spare me.*"

I open my mouth again. Nothing comes out. She's not wrong. I just hate hearing it from her.

She swipes across her screen and brings up another name. Another threat. "Colten Hadings is a possibility, too."

I exhale. My patience is already hanging on by a thread. "The trust fund clown?"

"Yeah. Him. Rich. Bored." She doesn't stop there. "And let's not forget—he was with Alex the night Sofia was assaulted. Colten was pissed because she was in his way of getting a fucking drink order. He said that what his friend did was nothing."

Talia scrolls like this is just another Wednesday. "So. Our list is... the Ex with a vengeance or the walking liability."

"She smiled," I say, out of nowhere.

They all look at me. "I don't think she wanted to. But she smiled anyway."

Opal already knows exactly who I'm talking about. She's the only person who probably figured it out. No one else has.

I'm twelve years old and I'm not in my room.

I'm crouched on the second floor landing, knees pulled tight to my chest behind the iron railing, the carpet burning my skin where it presses into my shins. I can feel my heartbeat in my ears. I shouldn't be here. He told me to go upstairs. I didn't move fast enough. I thought if I stayed quiet, he'd forget.

The house smells different tonight.

Not food. Not flowers. Something thick and sweet that makes my throat tight. Perfume layered over alcohol layered over the sour bite of smoke. The lights downstairs are low, tinted warm, like everything has been dipped in honey.

The velvet curtain at the drawing room is open just a crack.

I can see through it.

My mother steps onto the stairs.

She's wearing a dress I've never seen before. Sapphire blue. Shiny. It slides when she moves, clinging to her hips, her legs. The slit goes higher than any dress she owns. The neckline shows skin she usually keeps covered. It looks expensive. It looks wrong.

It doesn't fit her like her clothes do. It fits like something chosen for her.

Her heels click too loud. She pauses halfway down, adjusts her balance. Her hands shake when she smooths the fabric over her thigh. Her nails are perfect. Her hair is pinned tight, every strand locked into place. Her lipstick is red like a line drawn instead of painted.

There are men in the room.

Three of them.

One is laughing already. Another is sitting with his legs spread, a glass hanging from his fingers, the liquid inside so dark it looks black. The third is standing close to the fireplace, watching her.

My father steps in behind her.

His hand settles on her shoulder. His thumb presses once, slow, like a signal. He smells like cologne and power. His suit is perfect. His smile is easy.

"Gentlemen," he says, like he's proud. Like he's

presenting something beautiful. "Elena understands discretion."

I don't know what the word means exactly.

But I know it's bad.

My mother looks up.

She looks straight at me.

Our eyes lock.

For a second, her face breaks. Just a crack. Her mouth trembles. Her eyes widen. She sees me seeing.

Then it's gone.

She straightens her spine. Pulls her shoulders back. Her lips curve upward. The smile snaps into place so fast it scares me. Teeth white. Jaw tight. Eyes empty. Like she's turned herself off.

Like this is something she knows how to do.

The man with the dark drink stands and puts his hand on her waist. His fingers spread. Confident. Like she belongs there.

She doesn't move away. She lets him pull her closer.

My father's hand leaves her shoulder.

The curtain closes.

I realize I can't breathe.

I slide backward until my back hits the wall. My hands are shaking so hard they knock against the railing. I press them into my mouth to keep quiet. Downstairs, voices murmur. Glass clinks. Someone laughs again.

I crawl back to my room on my hands and knees like if I stay low enough, none of this will follow me. I lock the door. I sit on the floor with my back against it, staring at the crack of light spilling across the floor.

I don't sleep.

I don't sleep the next night.

Or the one after that.

Because now I know what happens in this house.

It's not just my father having affairs.

It's not affairs at all.

My mother's not angry. She's not fighting. She's not leaving.

She's smiling.

She's involved.

I understand that the people who raised me aren't trying to protect me from the world.

They're protecting the world from me by keeping me locked away in their little ivory tower.

Seven years later, I'm standing barefoot in a motel room on the Strip, staring out at a sky that's too bright for the news I just got.

The phone call came six minutes ago. The plane crashed somewhere outside Marseille. Private jet. Engine failure. No survivors.

No headlines yet. Just a text from a number I was told to answer no matter what. It said, "your parents are dead."

The words have no comfort packed inside.

I remember the last time I saw my mother.

Her smile was softer that night. She'd been drinking wine in the kitchen barefoot, humming something I didn't recognize. My father had called her from the next room, and she flinched. Just once. Then smiled again. Just like before.

Like a habit.

Like muscle memory.

I didn't say goodbye.

Now I don't have to.

I press my palms flat to my thighs and wait for the grief to hit.

But it doesn't. There's no sob. No collapse. Just a sense of blankness, like something's been scooped out from the center of my chest. A hole where mourning should go.

I think of the house. The curtain. The blue dress. The men with their hands on her. The way he said her name.

I think of the hand that bruised my neck once because I asked the wrong question in front of the wrong person. The way he always smiled when he hurt you. The way she always looked away.

Then I think... good.

I think it again, slower.

Good.

And then I feel it—the terrifying, unshakable truth of it. They're gone.

That doesn't upset me. It sets me free.

I come back to the room like I've been underwater.

Opal's still watching the screen, but I can feel the shift in her focus. She's listening now. So is Talia. Stellan is curious as well.

I steady my breath and say what we've all been circling. "We need to start with Michella. Really start."

That gets their attention. Opal glances at me, skeptical. "You're saying she's behind it now?"

"She didn't just show up to stir shit between you and me," I say. "She came to make a mess we can't sweep under the rug."

"She's not subtle," Opal mutters, arms crossed again. "But she's smart enough to weaponize attention."

Talia exhales a sound that's almost a laugh. "Well, damn. Growth."

"I'm not interested in growth," I say. "I'm interested in if Michella Carr came back to rebuild something, I want to know what it is. Who's funding her. Who she's speaking to. What she's covering for."

"She's not working alone," Opal says, tone low. "Not a chance."

That's when Stellan finally speaks. "She never does."

We all look at him.

He's still leaning against the far wall, hands in his pockets, like this is all beneath him—because to Stellan Rothwell, it probably is. Ex drama he has no time for anymore.

"She never works without cover," he continues. "Not when I knew her. Not now. If she's surfaced, it's because someone gave her permission."

"Who?" Opal asks.

"That's the question." He straightens, finally stepping forward. "But she's not the threat. Not really."

Talia raises an eyebrow. "You disagree with Dante?"

"I think you're both right," Stellan says. "She came back to stir chaos. But the person who sent her?" He glances at me. "That's the one we need to figure out."

"You're starting to sound like Talia," Opal says, arms crossed, like she already regrets saying it out loud.

"Terrifying, isn't it?" Talia murmurs, not looking up from her tablet.

"I prefer effective," Stellan replies, voice flat.

A jagged alert rips through the feed.

Opal's fingers are already moving. She drags the

window open, and her posture shifts—shoulders tensing, spine straightening.

"What is it?" I ask, already knowing I'm not gonna like the answer.

Talia's gaze lifts, sharp. "Michella?"

"Yeah," Opal mutters. "She's talking."

VEGAS VULTURE EXCLUSIVE

"I Walked Away to Protect Him": Michella Carr Breaks Her Silence on Dante Valera, His Marriage, and the Woman Now in His Bed

In an exclusive statement given to The Vulture, Michella Carr—the once undisputed queen of Obsidian's inner circle—has broken her silence. And just like the first time she stepped into Vegas society, she's doing it with a whisper that cuts deeper than a scream.

"I didn't leave Dante because I stopped loving him," Carr tells us. *"I left because I saw what he was becoming. What the people around him wanted from him. I couldn't watch him be turned into someone he's not."*

Carr claims she returned not for attention, but for accountability. While she never mentions her successor by name, the warning couldn't be clearer.

"The new one… the fixer?" she says. *"She's not just from Rosebud. She's Society. Like Talia Rothwell was. Trained to seduce, to gather intel, to destabilize. I've seen it before. I know what that kind of woman can do—and who sends them."*

When asked if she believed Dante Valera was in danger, Carr didn't hesitate.

"I think he's already been compromised. He wouldn't have

married someone like that otherwise. I know him. He doesn't let just anyone in. If he did this, it's because something went wrong"

The kicker?

"Maybe I made mistakes," Carr adds. *"But I never used love as a weapon. I walked away to protect him. And I came back because I couldn't stay quiet knowing what's happening to him now."*

This isn't a woman fighting to be seen. This is a woman fighting to be heard.

And Vegas? It's already listening.

Something ugly's about to break the surface. More soon, darlings. You know we never sleep.

— The Vulture

Stellan folds his hands, voice low. "Do you want us to respond?"

Opal's already pulling out her phone. "No. We don't respond. We hit."

She scrolls fast, finds what she's looking for, presses the call button. "Julia? It's me."

She pauses for a minute whoever is on the other end to speak. "Yeah, I need to file an intent to sue for libel, slander, and targeted harassment. Name's Michella Carr. No, I don't need the disclaimers."

Talia raises an eyebrow. "Friend of yours?"

"Met her, Julia Carter, when I did volunteer work in Croatia," Opal mutters, tucking the phone between shoulder and cheek while she paces. "She speaks five languages and treats cease and desist like foreplay. She'll have it filed in an hour."

Stellan almost smiles. "Good."

We don't even get a full sixty minutes before the blowback hits.

Lucrezia pings me from Obsidian's media tracker.

@MichellaCarrOfficial: "So apparently I'm being sued... for telling the truth? If someone's so innocent, why are their lawyers working overtime to shut me up? Sounds like fear to me. I'm not scared of you, Opal. And you know why."

The caption's paired with a dimly lit black and white photo of her near tears. She's holding a journal. The implication's clear.

Comments are already rolling in, and our system's flagging them in real time.

"She wouldn't lie. She's trying to protect Dante." "Why would anyone sue unless they had something to hide?" "Opal Greer is giving predator energy." "Carr is class. Opal is a contract." "This feels like erasure."

"Jesus," I mutter, watching the numbers spike.

"She's not playing to win," Opal says, her voice flat, sharp as glass. "She's playing to wound."

"She's trying to martyr herself," Talia adds. "And if this hits mainstream, it'll work."

"She's not a victim," I snap. "She's a goddamn arsonist."

Opal finally looks up. "And now I'm going to bury her."

@TheRealOpalValera: I didn't want this to escalate. You made public claims that are false—and harmful. Dante asked you privately to stop. You didn't. So I responded legally. This isn't about fear. It's about accountability. You're not telling the truth. I won't let you build a platform on trying to hurt me.

I watch Opal's post go live.

Stellan mutters, "Jesus."

Talia's already tracking analytics on her screen. "It's gaining traction."

She closes the app. Doesn't even watch it take off.

"That's it?" I ask.

She looks up. The neutral look in her eyes is blazing. If I were anyone else, I'd be scared of what she is cooking up in her mind.

"No," she says. "That's just my opening move."

CHAPTER THIRTEEN

Opal

I'm in my element.

All six monitors glow in front of me—each one running something different, each one demanding my attention.

Since that collab with Vortex Security, Malcolm Huntington set me up with the crème de la crème of systems.

His wife, Lila, organized the whole thing—keys, codes, redundancies I wouldn't have thought of in a hundred years. They're the smartest couple alive.

They're getting a thank you visit when this whole Dante shitshow is behind me. Assuming I'm not in jail by then. Maybe I'll bring wine. Or a flamethrower. Depends how it ends.

The numbers aren't sitting right.

I don't know exactly what I'm looking for. Not yet.

The instinct is there, though—a persistent itch beneath the surface of the data, like a thread pulling at the edge of a memory I can't quite name. It's not panic, and it's not intuition either. It's pattern recognition, buried somewhere deep in my spine. Something in this system doesn't sit right, and I know better than to ignore that kind of thought.

All six monitors are lit up, arranged in a semi circle around me like a private theater. Each one running a different sector of logs, behavior maps, and ghost files pulled from Obsidian's network.

On the surface, everything looks functioning. There's no obvious breach signature, no explosive data pulls or credential skims. The anomalies are small—too small. A few transient pings, odd access patterns, temporary paths that resolve before they're flagged by the system's internal tripwires.

Harmless, if you're just skimming.

But I'm not.

I isolate one of the flags and drop the sequence into a sandbox environment. No overlays. No guards. Just the raw bones of what was executed that night. I let the loop play out, eyes narrowed as the code unwraps itself line by line.

What I see shouldn't bother me. It's clean, simple, efficient. It doesn't escalate, doesn't damage anything. It threads its way through the system like a needle, skimming surface level structures and retreating just as easily. There's no deeper infiltration. Nothing gets taken.

But that's exactly what makes it so dangerous.

Whoever wrote this didn't want to break in. They wanted to be noticed.

I watch it again. Slower this time. I follow the way

the commands delay at just the right moments. How they pause, then move like a blip in time. Like buffering.

The realization hits like a switch flipping. Not slow, not creeping—just *on*. One second I'm watching code crawl across the screen, the next, it's lit up from the inside, like someone snapped on a floodlight in my mind. Every line, every pause, every carefully staggered delay suddenly makes sense.

The cadence, the logic stacks, the deliberate misdirection, the architecture, language, right down to the nested fallback protocols. Whoever wrote this didn't break in. They didn't need to.

Because I've seen this structure before.

The person who wrote this code didn't just understand my framework. They mimicked it perfectly.

I sit back in my chair, the breath leaving my lungs too fast, too tight. They didn't steal anything. They built a crime scene with my fingerprints on it and waited for me to walk in. Whoever did this doesn't want to ruin the system. They want to ruin the people inside it.

They want to ruin me.

This isn't similar to what I built for my plan to destroy Stellan. It's not inspired by it or based on something I left behind. It *is* it. Down to the sequence lengths, the pacing of the timers, the decoy logic in the fallback paths—it's my code. My plan. The exact one I deployed during the Rothwell takedown.

I wrote it alone, in a blackout apartment tucked above an old wine shop in the Vineyards outside of Vegas. No lights, no sound. Just the glow of three separate firewalled servers running through a burner laptop I wiped and destroyed the moment I finished. I didn't save the blueprint. I didn't share the process. I didn't even speak it aloud. That version of me—the one who built something designed to dismantle giants and erase the evidence afterward—was supposed to stay gone forever.

But now it's back. Pulled from the grave and dropped right in front of me like it never disappeared.

It's a fucking message. The pressure spikes behind my eyes. My pulse is a snare drum.

I stare at the pattern again, just long enough to feel the bile rise. I shut everything down.

They want to see what I'll do next. Good thing they won't have to wait long. I grab my bag, shove the drives inside, and head for the door without looking back.

The elevator barely finishes its climb before I'm out. My apartment door is already unlocked. That alone is enough to put me on edge.

He's here.

Dante's standing in the middle of my living room. It may technically be his apartment, but I think of it as mine. He has never stepped foot in this apartment since we've been married.

He's in the jacket I've seen hanging here more than once—always left behind like a maybe. A silent promise.

Now he's wearing it. Now he's real.

"We need to talk," he says.

I drop my bag by the door and kick it closed with my heel.

"Yeah," I say, unzipping my jacket without looking at him. "We do."

But not yet. Not like this. Not when my skin's still

buzzing with rage and betrayal, and an impossible need to reclaim something.

I turn to him, eyes narrowed. "But I need something else first."

He watches me cross the room, grab his shirt, and pull his mouth down to mine.

If he wants to be in my space, he's going to feel exactly what it means when I've been pushed too far.

I press my mouth to his and I bite. He lets me. Not like he has a choice in the matter.

I don't pretend I'm kissing him out of need. I want violence, the pushback. I want him to give as good as he takes. But tonight he lets me dictate everything, hands still at his sides until I force his mouth wider.

I break it off, licking blood from his lower lip. "You're supposed to stop me."

He licks it, too, eyes darkening. "I never will."

It's infuriating. I want to rip him open, see what makes him crack.

So I shove him, hard, back toward the couch. He takes it, never breaking eye contact. He waits for me to close the gap, for the rules to be rewritten.

I want a reaction. I want a scene.

I want to own something for once in this miserable, zero sum city.

I straddle him, driving his shoulders into the couch-back. My thighs clamp around his ribs. His hands go to my hips, possessive but not resisting—only following my lead, waiting to see how far I'll take it.

I drag my mouth down his neck. I leave marks, little memory traces for tomorrow's guilt. He tilts his chin, exposing his throat. I press my tongue to the pulse there. Interesting... so he's not immune.

I bite the tendon above his collarbone. He grunts, hands tightening on me. This time, when I move against him, I feel the response of his body.

He moves one hand to my jaw, thumb pressing beneath my chin. "Is this how you're going to take it?"

I nod. He's not challenging me, he's confirming terms.

He drags my dress up around my hips. His hand goes under, between my thighs, pushing two fingers into me. I am ready for more. I'm in charge now.

I lower onto his cock inch by inch, my thighs trembling with restraint, watching his brown eyes the entire time. His pupils dilate until only a thin ring of carmel remains, unblinking, eyes burning holes through my skin and into whatever's left of my soul.

He fills me completely, his thick length stretching me to the edge of discomfort. My lips part but I swallow the moan before it escapes.

I set the pace, rhythm like a boxer's fist against canvas. I ride him mercilessly, using his body the way I use physical pain... as tangible, undeniable proof I'm still present in this world when everything else feels like drowning.

His hands grip my ass, fingers pressing into flesh, trying to steer my movements, but I capture his wrists and pin them above his head. If he wants control, he'll have to fight me for it.

He doesn't. He matches my punishing tempo, meets every downward thrust with one of his own, the corded muscles in his neck straining, but never once tries to flip the script. The understanding in his eyes tells me he knows this is the only way I can fuck him tonight.

We don't talk. I pant against his mouth, tasting whiskey and mint, then trail down to his throat where his pulse hammers against my lips, then into the heat radiating above his half unbuttoned shirt. Sweat beads under my tits and trickles down my spine. My hair comes undone from its careful arrangement, falling around us like a curtain.

He bites my shoulder once—just enough to make me hiss through clenched teeth, the sweet sting not enough to change our momentum.

I fuck him like I'm running towards the last bridge to safety.

It builds fast, coiling tight at the base of my spine. I know the signs—the telltale tightening, the quickening breath—I'm about to come, and I don't want to do it alone.

"Don't you dare," I say, breathless.

He tilts his head back, watches me. "What?"

"Come first."

He smirks, wicked and white toothed. "Wouldn't dream of it."

But he's close. I can tell. The rigid set of his jaw, the way his fingers dig into my ass—almost painful.

I want to scream, but I don't. I take it all in, let it shred through me. When it hits, it's bright and mean and there is nothing left to hide behind. I let him see it.

He comes right after, his body shuddering under mine, his face a mask of pleasure.

I don't move. I breathe into his neck, feeling the hammer of his heart through both our skins.

When I finally slide off him, I pull my dress down and wipe my mouth with the back of my hand.

He refastens his pants, rolls his sleeves up to his elbows, and reclines into my couch like a king deposed.

"Feel better?" He asks.

I don't answer the question. But I do feel better. Now I know we need to talk. "I found something," I say finally, staring straight ahead.

Dante shifts, standing up as well. "What kind of something?"

I turn to face him. "It's not a breach. It's not infiltration. It's replication."

He frowns, confused. "I don't—"

"My design," I cut in. "My fucking strategy. It's mine, Dante. The way this whole thing is being orchestrated—from the data trails to the public drops to the psychological pacing—it's mine. The sequence, the decoys, even the time stamps. I built this system years ago when I was tearing through Rothwell's backdoors. Someone's not breaking in. They're playing it back."

I start pacing, because if I don't move, I'll scream.

"This isn't a hack. It's a rerun. Someone took my original codebase and bent it just enough to frame me with my own fingerprints."

His brow furrows. "So they're not imitating you. They're using you."

"Exactly," I snap. "And the way they're moving? They knew how I'd respond. They knew what I'd trace right away and what I wouldn't catch until it was too late."

Dante tries to stop me from pacing, but I just dodge him.

I take a breath, steadying myself now that the fire's been funneled into a tornado. Purpose always cools me down faster than regret.

I glance back at him, still standing near the couch, jaw tight, arms crossed like he's trying not to reach for me again.

"What did you want to talk about?" I ask, trying not to clip my voice. "Before I jumped you."

He exhales—almost laughs, but not quite. It's more of a release valve, like he's been holding that tension since he walked in.

"It can wait," he says.

I shake my head. "No. You came here for a reason. And now I've dumped a fucking bomb at your feet, so... your turn."

"I've been thinking about all of it. The video, the posts, the smear campaign." His jaw flexes. "It didn't just feel personal. Not really. Not like someone was trying to ruin *me*."

I watch him carefully now. The way he pauses. The way his fingers tighten against his wrist. "It felt bigger," he says. "Like there's something underneath it all, something they don't want us to see because if we *did*—we'd know exactly what we are to them."

I tilt my head, heart ticking up. "What are we?"

"A threat," he says simply. "Not just as individuals. But *us*. Together. Whatever this is, whatever it could be—they don't want it." I'm frozen, staring at him, then he adds, "I want you with me tomorrow night."

"Obsidian?" I ask.

He nods, slower this time. "Saturday. Obsidian runs hot—every table filled, every room booked, every member of staff that wants to is. pulling double duty."

He doesn't stop. "That's when the elite and the normal clientele come together on the dancefloor. The VIP clients. The legacy families. The normal corporate employees. Even college kids."

His mouth flattens into something close to a grimace. "If someone wants to make a move—big or subtle—that's when they'll do it."

He takes a step toward me. "I've been watching the footage. Tracking floor access. Colten comes in every Thursday and Saturday without fail. That's not a coincidence."

I raise an eyebrow, but he keeps going. "He's never alone. The same cluster of names keeps popping up. They're low key on the guest list because they're coming with him. High end movement once they're inside. None of them would ever have VIP status without him."

His voice drops. "I've got a hunch. Something's going to move. And I need your brain. I need you next to me," he says, gaze locked on mine.

It's not a question. It's not even a request.

It's a tell.

He's serious. Whatever instinct is firing in his head, it's loud enough that he wants *me* in the room when shit hits the fan.

I nod once, slowly. "Okay."

But when I turn away from him, my brain doesn't follow. It starts running. Pattern matching. Clicking back through every file I've kept open in my head since this started.

Colten Hadings.

He doesn't care about reputation because his ego is too big to fail.

But it's not just him.

Alex Knight.

The two of them together? That's not just a bad combination. That's a closed circuit of privilege and immunity. They cover for each other. Laugh when things go too far. Pretend like consequence is something other people invented for sport.

Both of them were there the night Sofia was raped. Alex is the one that raped her.

I remember her face. The bruise on her jaw. The way she kept folding the edge of her sleeve, over and over, like if she stopped, she'd shatter.

Colten called it a misunderstanding. Alex didn't say anything at all in the interrogation room.

I don't believe in coincidences anymore. I sure as hell don't believe in men who think they can get away with everything just because daddy pays for it.

They're hiding something.

And on Saturday, I'm going to find out what.

CHAPTER FOURTEEN
Dante

Obsidian isn't loud when it's closed. I like it that way. Classical music playing over the speakers, everyone doing their own thing.

It is a nice reprieve from the music that is usually blaring through the speakers during opening hours.

Manny walks beside me. He doesn't ask if I want the briefing. He just walks beside me and starts. "New panic switches were installed last night. Pressure sensitive, wired to remote off sites. Updated mirror tint reacts to movement spikes and body heat. Floor sensors too. If someone runs, we'll know. All of it is officially operational with no areas bare."

I nod once.

"Hallways got five angle feeds now. Faster detection, no latency. Staff headsets got upgraded too. Each one's tied to a silent SOS—bypasses comms, goes straight to security."

Lucrezia steps out from the mezzanine access, hands

folded over a velvet case. "She's here," she says, voice flat. "Thought you'd want this."

She opens the box. The earpiece inside is matte black, custom coded—only four exist. Mine. Manny's. Lucrezia's. Now hers. I take it without speaking.

By the time I step into my office, she's already there—standing at the desk, with her arms crossed.

Her gaze lifts, cool and unbothered. "I saw the new lighting in the VIP corridor. You swapped out the overheads for directional wash lights. Feels warmer, but it isn't. Makes it easier to see who's watching who. Especially since there are people who come here that need to know who is around them at all times."

Of course she noticed.

"There's more," I say, closing the door behind me. "Mirrors got upgraded. Motion tinting, layered reflections. No blind spots. Panic channels are embedded in the floor."

She tilts her head, one brow lifting. "Let me guess. Triggered by heart rate, blood pressure, and your personal signal. Very on brand."

"And now yours," I say, slipping the door lock into place with a soft click.

She doesn't react, she just trails one finger across the edge of the desk like she's testing for fingerprints that don't belong. "You moved the furniture," she says finally. "Not much—maybe two feet. Just enough to center the couch on the mezzanine door. Better line of sight. Worse for comfort. So you're expecting someone you don't want to sit."

Her gaze lifts again—this time to the wall behind me.

"And that painting's new. Or at least new to this room. Color's too warm for your usual palette. Meant to disarm the eye, but the lines are off center. You want people unsettled without knowing why."

I shouldn't be surprised about how right she is.

"What's the event?" She asks.

I take the chair behind the desk. She doesn't move.

"Colten Hadings and Alex Knight are on tonight's list," I tell her.

That earns a flicker of surprise, something that I'm not used to seeing on he. "Alex? Didn't think he was allowed in the club."

"He isn't," I say. "But he's coming anyway. I want him contained before he knows we're watching."

"And Colten?"

"Drunk, entitled, and too loud to notice the net closing around him."

She watches me now, expression flattening as the picture takes shape. "You want me in the VIP lounge? While Colten is preoccupied."

"I want eyes everywhere."

She shakes her head, just once. "No," she says. "You want someone Alex doesn't know. Someone with no behavioral flags in the system. Someone who can get close without triggering his internal alarms. Someone that he can try to attack."

She sits on my lap, smirking. "You want bait."

I hold her gaze. "That's not what I said."

"But it's what you meant," she cuts back. "I'm new to him. You've got two predators walking in, and I'm the variable one won't see coming."

"You shouldn't have to be."

She is one scary woman. But I can't help but feel proud of her. She is not someone you want to be on the bad side of.

She shrugs. "Maybe not. But it's the smart play."

We both know I don't argue with logic. Not when it sounds like that.

I reach to the corner of my desk and hand her the matte black earpiece. She takes it without hesitation.

"Lucrezia," she calls, not bothering to raise her voice.

She's already on her way in. Of course.

"I need something VIP worthy," Opal says, pulling the hem of her jacket down. "Nothing too obvious. Just enough to make a man like Alex Knight lower his guard."

At the threshold, Lucrezia glances over her shoulder, lips curling into a knowing smile.

She rubs her hands together once. "Oh, I've been waiting for this."

Opal laughs. "Just don't put me in sequins," she says, already disappearing down the hall.

I don't watch the door after it closes.

But I do watch when it opens again.

She steps back into the room ten minutes later like the fucking queen.

She's in a black mini dress that hits mid thigh. The neckline is high, but the back is bare, framed by two thin silver chain straps that rest against her skin in a cross formation. The fabric clings in all the right places, smooth and minimal, revealing more in motion than it does standing still. She pulled her hair tight at the nape of her neck, exposing the line of her throat and the curve of her spine. No jewelry. She doesn't need anything else.

She stops in front of the desk, one brow lifted.

"Well?" she asks, voice dry. "Do I pass inspection?"

I clear my throat before I speak, but not fast enough to hide it.

"You look good," I say, and it comes out lower than I meant. *You mean I have to let this woman out of my sight? Let someone else watch her, thinking that they'll have her?* I'm not sure how I'm going to survive the night, if I'm honest.

I'm about to say something I can't take back when Manny's voice clicks through the comms. "Colten Hadings just got here. Alex Knight's with him. Three women on their arm. Alex hasn't looked at a single one."

Figures.

I glance toward the bar through the one way glass of the overlook. Colten's already talking too loud. Alex lags behind, scanning the room like he's already bored.

"Lucrezia," I say. She's at my side in seconds, poised and waiting. "Bar. Colten's tab is open. Make him feel important."

She nods once and glides away, her stilettos silent on the floor.

Beside me, Opal leans in just enough for her breath to brush my shoulder. "That's my cue."

From the overlook, I watch them settle in.

Colten takes the booth like he's expecting a throne. The women they bring are exactly the kind of loud distraction he thinks makes him look important. Alex, quieter, more calculated, nurses a top shelf pour while his eyes scan the room.

He doesn't look at the women. Not once. No. He's watching the floor. Watching movement. Watching *her*. Opal is incredible, there's no doubt about it.

His glass empties. Refills. Colten's talking, laughing, ordering bottles like the bill doesn't touch him. But Alex is slipping extremely fast.

The more he drinks, the more his gaze drifts. down the hall he was last in, across the floor. They drift, but never far from my wife.

She's working the room like she's been doing this for years. Gliding between booths, subtle and poised. Close enough to bait, never close enough to catch.

Until she is.

Alex lifts his glass when she passes. He makes a comment I can't hear. She doesn't stop. That just eggs him on.

He slides from the booth, steps too loose, smile too wide. Follows her through the section.

When she stops near the bar, he closes in behind her, caging her in. I want to rage when I see his hand on her lower back. My vision goes red when he leans in and whispers something in her ear.

She doesn't flinch, and he laughs. Then he lifts his hand—thumb sliding along the back of her neck like they've touched before.

The overlook doors hiss open as I hit the stairs, two at a time.

He palms her waist, his hand moves lower.

I press the comm. "Manny."

Before he can answer, Alex says it. Loud enough for the table to hear. Loud enough for me to hear. "You playing hard to get, baby? Or just hard to break?"

That's it. The look on her face when she traces him is pure beauty to my eyes. it's no more than two seconds before he crashes to the ground. Hard. Good, I hope it fucking hurt.

Her left hand clamps around his wrist while her right catches his shoulder, pivoting her weight just enough to twist his balance out from under him. One quick shift of her hips and she drives him backward into the floor. His head snaps back against the marble. His arm's pinned. She doesn't even break stride.

Colten jumps up, eyes blown wide. "What the fuck—?"

Opal's standing over Alex like he just crawled out of the gutter. She glances at Colten, dead calm.

"Hi, Colten. Didn't know you were bringing trash *in* instead of taking it *out*."

Alex groans, dazed. Colten grabs Alex by the arm, eyes wide. "You absolute dipshit."

He looks up at us—at me, at Opal—and straightens his jacket like that'll help. "Dante," he says, trying for calm. "You want to explain what the hell this is?"

I don't move. Opal answers for both of us. "Leave Alex with us," she says, cool and clear. "And we'll forget he's your friend. You don't get banned." Colten's mouth twitches, making his face shift from jokester to someone who is about to fight to the death for his boy. "Or," she adds, still composed, "we call the police. You both get banned. Permanently."

He looks at Alex, who's still swaying. "Really, dude?" Alex mutters, disbelief thick.

Colten sighs, rolls his eyes and straightens. With a shrug he says, "He's all yours."

He turned on him. For himself. Not that I'm surprised. His own desires matter more than anyone else anyway.

He claps Alex on the back—hard—and smirks as he strolls back to the booth, the women trailing after him like he wasn't two seconds from being erased.

Manny moves to haul him up. That's when Alex Knight explodes.

"This is such fucking bullshit!" he yells, yanking his arm out of Manny's grip. "You're all pretending you don't know what this place is? *Really*? That's the game?"

Alex's voice climbs as we both stay silent. "Colten told me everything! You think I just showed up for drinks and velvet? *He said you ran girls through this place.* Said if you dropped the right cash, they'd take you upstairs, no questions asked! That Obsidian was the *real* Strip—just cleaner, classier, and easier to bury!"

Manny grabs him again, firmer now. Alex thrashes against the hold like a rabid animal.

"I know what I saw," he spits, eyes wild. "Colten's been here with different girls *every time.* Said you don't even check IDs if the family name's heavy enough. Said the Mirror Room's where the good shit happens—where the girls get *trained* to behave—"

A crash echoes from the booth near us. Colten slams a glass down on the table and storms toward us from where he was just sitting.

"You little *fuck!*" he roars, shoving past a server. "Are you *seriously* saying my name in that deranged rat mouth of yours? Are you *high?*"

He's unraveling. Red in the face, hair mussed, all that expensive confidence slipping right off him.

Alex is still yelling. "You *told* me—"

"I told you *nothing!*" Colten snaps. "Don't you dare pin this on me, you limp dicked embarrassment!"

"You said I'd get access!"

"You said you'd keep your *mouth shut!*"

"Both of you need to shut up," Opal mutters, turning toward them.

I'm two seconds from signaling Manny to knock Alex out cold.

But Colten keeps going—turns toward me now, eyes wild. "You believe this shit? I bring one idiot and now I'm the one running the smear campaign? Come on, Dante. This guy couldn't find his own dick without GPS. He's tanking everything just to feel important. You have to see what this is."

"You didn't bring him once," Opal says, tone flat as steel.

He glares at her. "Oh, *please.* You think I give him coordinates every time? Guys like Alex sniff out power like pigs in a truffle field."

"Right," Opal snaps. "And you just happen to talk about VIP girls and secret rooms while you let him tag along like a lost boy?"

Colten's face twists. "You think you're so clever, huh? Just because you—"

"I think you're sloppy," she says, cutting him off. "I think you're scared. And I think you're trying to rewrite your own script now that your friend choked on the lines."

"*Fuck you,*" he growls.

I step forward. I've had enough of the little fucking shit. "Careful."

He turns to me, eyes flaring. "Dante—this can't be on me. He misunderstood. I was bullshitting—guys do that. You know how it is. Locker room talk, just—"

"You weren't talking to locker rooms," I say flatly. "You were talking to him."

"I didn't think he'd *believe* me!"

"Then you're dumber than you look."

Colten flushes, opens his mouth, then closes it. He knows better than to argue with that tone. He turns, shoves his hands through his hair, and stalks toward his booth in a storm of curses.

Good. He's done. Now I just have to decide whether or not he's staying in the club tonight. That is until he stops halfway back at his table.The little prick just can't help himself. "You think this is over?" he yells, voice cracking. "I'm not the only one who talks, Dante! People know things. You can't keep it all locked up behind velvet and mirrors!"

Opal steps forward, unbothered as usual. Fuck, she's hot when she's like this. "You should leave before you say something dumber than you already have."

He sneers. "What, you're gonna ban me? Go ahead.

You think I need Obsidian? There are ten clubs on the Strip waiting to buy the dirt I've got."

"No one's buying your shit, Colten," she says. "You're not dangerous. You're just loud."

He scoffs. "You think you run this? Jesus." He turns to point his focus on me, as if my wife isn't standing right there actively addressing him. "You're just pissed because no one listens to you without a leash around your neck." When he says the word *leash* he nods his head at Opal

I step forward, not to block her from him, but to stand beside her. "I'll pretend you didn't just say that."

Colten smirks, but it falters when he grows the balls to look me in the eye.

I keep my voice as I lean into his ear. "You think being married to her makes me weak? You think I got leashed? She's the only reason you and your little *limp dick* friend are still here."He opens his mouth—nothing comes out.

"You think you're dangerous because you throw money at girls and run your mouth in VIP booths? You're a fucking tourist. She's built for this city. She sees everything, survives everything, and still chooses to stand next to me." I tilt my head. "So no, Colten. I'm not leashed. I'm tame. And you? You just made the mistake of saying her name like it meant less than mine." I step back. "She doesn't need my protection. But I give it freely. And now, you've earned the privilege of witnessing that—just not the way you wanted."

A fist flies past my face. It lands with a sickening crack against Colten's jaw. He reels back two steps, clutching his face. By the time he looks up, Opal's already dropped her arm. Dangerous in a way that makes the room feel suddenly too small.

"I should press charges," Colten spits, voice slurred from shock.

Opal doesn't flinch. "You should sit the fuck down."

He stares at her, chest rising like he might try something stupid. "My father—"

She tilts her head. "Your daddy?" A low laugh slips out. "Your daddy means nothing in this room."

He starts to respond, but she cuts him off. "Alex assaulted me tonight. You brought him in. You stood by while he grabbed women like they were party favors. And you knew—*you knew*—what he was like the first time."

She steps forward. One inch. One mile. "So here's what's going to happen," she says. "You're going to walk out of here quietly. We won't press charges. We won't ruin you."

Her gaze flicks down to his shoes, then back to his face.

"But you're banned. Permanently. And if anyone asks why, you get to say it was because you defended a man who assaults women. If you don't want to admit that, feel free to have them give me a call. I'm more than happy to tell them all about how big and brave you are."

I have to stop myself from laughing, this woman is incredible. Colten glares—eyes wet, jaw clenched, humiliated. He looks to me for backup.

"Lucrezia," I say. She steps forward, already waiting. "Escort him out. Now."

Colten backs off, slowly. No fight left. No swagger.

Just shame. Security shadows him all the way to the stairs.

No one moves. Not until the soft sound of metal shifting causes us to turn around—Alex, still cuffed, still smirking like this is some kind of afterparty.

Manny steps forward. He grabs Alex by the arm without a word and starts walking him toward the back.- Past the velvet, through the hush of Obsidian's inner corridors, until we reach the hidden door behind the VIP lounge—a flush black panel most guests never even notice.

My right hand man unlocks it with a biometric tap.

The hallway beyond is darker. Sound echoes in here. Alex, still smirking, doesn't realize he's already in the cage.

"I mean, you can't seriously think I'm the bad guy here," he mutters, breath hitching as Manny shoves him forward. "Clubs like this—this is what people want. Power. Sex. Vibe. Colten said it himself—Obsidian's where you go when you're tired of pretending."

He's sweating now. Stumbling in his designer shoes.

"Pretty sure he said you had a room for this kind of thing. Something behind mirrors. Soundproof. Real selective entry." He grins like it's an inside joke. "You know what I mean."

Opal snorts softly beside me. She gestures toward the black glass door ahead—the one that locks from the inside, the one that doesn't open unless I say so.

"Is this the Mirror Room you were thinking of, Alex?" She asks sweetly.

He looks up. The color drains from his face.

Manny hits the panel. The door slides open.

Alex tries to plant his feet.

Too late.

We walk him in.

Now he'll learn exactly what happens when you treat Obsidian like a joke and my wife like an object.

CHAPTER FIFTEEN
Dante

The Mirror Room wasn't made for comfort.

It was made for truth—stripped bare and soundproofed, of course. There is no music. No distractions. Only pitch black walls, matte floor, and a single pane of two way glass reflecting the version of yourself you don't want to see.

That's the point.

Manny shoves Alex forward. He stumbles. His wrists are already bound, but Manny doesn't stop there. He hauls him toward the restraint bar mounted against the steel support beam—an old fixture, rarely used.

"Hands up," Manny mutters, already clipping the cuffs higher.

Alex laughs. He's nervous. "Jesus, what is this, a sex dungeon? You want me to call you daddy too?"

Manny doesn't answer. Steps back once the cuffs are locked, leaving Alex strung upright—arms over his head, spine tight.

He looks ridiculous. I know what humiliation does to men like him. It makes them talk.

Especially once they realize no one's clapping anymore.

Opal stands to my right, arms folded, watching Alex with the same look she gives a slow loading program. Bored. Unimpressed. Already calculating where she can play with it.

Then her phone buzzes.

She glances down. I see the shift in her face. For a few seconds, her face drops a fraction.

I step in closer. "Talk to me."

"Rosebud," she whispers to me. "Something on your side. Server signature flagged. They're tracking the movement. See if someone is searching for something. Perfect timing since this is when I would've done it. After a meltdown publicly."

I nod once. "Go. Handle it."

She hesitates—only for a beat—then steps into me and kisses me full on the mouth. Slow enough to make a point. Fast enough not to linger.

"I'll see you at home," she murmurs.

I rest my hand at her lower back. Tap once. Letting her know I heard her. "I'll finish it here."

The door shuts behind her with a soft click. I watch her leave and stare at the door long enough to let my expression slip back into the one of calm focus.

Then, I turn back to Alex Knight. He's still hanging there—arms shackled above his head, sweat starting to cling at his collarbones, the flush of alcohol giving way to the first edges of fear. Finally, that smug smile of his is gone. I didn't realize just how fucking stupid he is.I take a step closer. "Talk."

He swallows hard. "Look, man, I didn't mean anything by it. I didn't even know who she was. I thought —Colten said this place was good for letting off steam—"

"You came to my club," I say, low and cold. "Touched my wife. Lied about how things work here. But that's not why you're restrained. That's not why I'm still listening." I lean forward, enough to let him feel the heat of my breath. "You're not important, Alex. But you're a crack in the pattern. That makes you useful."

He blinks, confused. "What pattern?"

"The one that started a few months ago. Leaks. Lies. Whispers in the right ears. Articles with just enough truth to make the rest believable." I get right in his face and I nod slowly, keeping my tone from showing how unhinged I'm about to be if he doesn't start fucking talking. "Someone's trying to ruin me. And you're going to tell me if you know who."

He tries to scoff. But he can't even do that right."Shit, I don't know anything about that. I just came with Colten —he said Obsidian was... the place. That if I wanted to impress the right people, get in deeper, this was the move."

"Deeper into what?" I ask.

He hesitates. "Colten said you had... arrangements. That there were other clubs, other people. Said Rothwell was backing it—that this place was untouchable because of who was protecting it. Said if I played my cards right, I'd be invited to the Mirror Room."

I glance at Manny, then back to him. "You're here now. Isn't it everything you hoped for?"

He laughs—high and nervous. "Man, I thought this was a sex room or some shit."

"It very well could be," I say, walking a slow circle around him. "But you have to be into the dark stuff, you know, hard core pain play and the like. You see, this is not the sort of place where you survive if you tell lies. Unfortunately for you, the truth is the only safe word that matters in here."

Alex twists to follow me with his eyes. "I didn't know it was serious. I just thought—Colten said the rumors were already out there, that people were starting to believe it, that you were going to take the fall either way—"

"What people?" I snap.

He hesitates. Breath catching. "There's... a guy. Not someone I know well. Just a name Colten mentioned—Davis? Daniels? Something like that. Said he used to work your security detail. Got cut loose and decided to talk."

I look at Manny, his jaw tightens.

Alex rushes ahead. "Colten said he wasn't the only one, okay? Said there was a woman too. Someone who used to run events—got fired last year. Said she's got dirt. Real shit."

I stop in front of him again. Dead still.

"Names," I say. "Or I start removing one finger at a time until you remember."

Alex flinches. He tries to laugh it off, but his mouth twitches too hard for it to mean anything. He's unraveling by the second. "Okay—okay, Jesus, fuck." He licks his lips. "Colten mentioned a name once. Not a real one. A handle. QuietArchitect. Said they were building something. A network or a brand, some weird influencer shit."

Manny straightens at that.

"A brand?" I echo.

Alex nods too fast. "Yeah. Like, this person's whole thing is exposure. Leaking private files. Destroying the reputations of the 'elite.' Said they already torched a political fixer in L.A. Made it look like a suicide. Then a tech investor in Chicago—ruined his startup with a leak, the guy said none of it was true."

"And now it's me," I say softly.

Alex looks up at me, confused. "Colten said the Architect was sniffing around Obsidian. That someone close to you sold floor schematics. Old staff names. Access codes. That you were slipping. Getting lazy."

My blood cools to glass. "Who else knows this?"

"I don't know! Colten just said the Architect picks targets when they get arrogant. When they stop watching their own shadows."

"And why you?"

"I don't fucking know!" Alex snaps. "He said bringing me was a test run. See who bites. See if someone upstairs would react. It's bait. I'm bait."

No. He's proof. Proof someone's testing my defenses—seeding stories, waiting for the infection to spread.

I pull my comm. "Lucrezia."

"Talk to me." The no nonsense tone of her voice is a comfort.

"Lock it all down. Everyone with historical clearance —current or not—goes into audit protocol. I want firewall penetration reports, building access history, comm traffic, everything. Anyone flagged for suspicion gets black bagged and pulled in tonight."

"You got it."

I end the call. Look back at Alex. "You think this is about *me?* I'm just the echo, man. The shit already happened."

I say nothing. Let him dig.

He tips his head back, smirking through split lips. "You really don't get it yet, do you? Whoever's behind this hates you so much they're willing to talk. To deal with your wrath if it is a lie just to hit your ego. Just to destroy you. Even willing to face death. Now who would you know is capable of that? Maybe your so-called wife. Ever cross your mind it could be her? That Opal Greer destroyed one man once and maybe she's working through all his little friends too?"

My hands curl into fists at my sides. "You really shouldn't have said her name," I murmur.

Alex blinks, some scrap of smugness still clinging to his face. "Touch a nerve?"

I don't answer. I nod once at Manny. The first punch hits Alex square in the gut—hard enough to knock the breath out of his lungs. He folds forward, dangling from the restraints as he coughs violently. Blood spatters on the floor.

"You think this is just about a girl?" He wheezes, voice thin. "It's bigger than her—bigger than you—"

Manny's second strike is faster. A backhand across his jaw that cracks loud in the room. His head jerks sideways, neck straining against the cuffs.

"You were the delivery system," I say quietly, stepping forward. "The poison in the bottle."

He groans, chin slick with blood. "I didn't touch her."

I crouch, eye level now. "Oh but you did. Then you whispered in her ear," I say. "That's worse."

I drive my fist into his ribs. I hear the breath leave him, feel something give beneath my knuckles. He screams.

"Let's make something clear," I continue, rising slowly. "You walked into my house and tried to shatter it with rumors you barely understood." I nod again. Manny grabs Alex's hair, wrenches his head back. "You talked about *trafficking*," I say. "About control. About obedience."

A slow breath. "You want to see what obedience really looks like?"

I land a punch to his temple—enough to daze, not knock him out. He slumps, blinking furiously, fighting to stay upright.

"That's lesson one," I murmur. "Truth is leverage. Lies are ammunition. And you handed both to me."

Alex laughs, dazed. "This won't fix it. You beat me to hell and you're still bleeding on the inside. You can't outrun the story."

I crouch again, eyes cold. "I'm not running," I say. "I'm editing."

I swing once again. He's bleeding from the lip. Spitting more than talking.

"I don't want to die," Alex gasps, wild eyed, wrists flexing hard against the restraints. "I didn't know—I didn't *know*—"

"You knew enough to run your mouth," I say flatly. "You knew enough to grab my wife. You knew enough to piss on my name in public."

I open the velvet case. One tool at a time. I don't rush. The scalpel gleams under the low light. The pliers shine like promise. The solder tip glows orange at the end. The needle set is laid out like a silver confession.

Alex starts to shake.

"You don't have to do this," he chokes. "I'm a legacy—my father—"

"Your father doesn't run Vegas," I say, crouching in front of him. "And legacy doesn't mean immunity. It means you're a target."

I lift the pliers. Let him see it. Let him feel the moment tighten. His chest heaves. He shakes his head, violently, like the words might fly loose if he moves hard enough.

"I didn't start it," he blurts. "It wasn't me, I swear—it was Colten. *Colten told me what to say.* He handed me the scripts, the footage—said people were ready to believe it if I played it right—"

"What scripts?" I ask, voice low.

"The Obsidian shit," Alex gasps. "The VIP trafficking rumors. The code trail. Said it would stir things up—just noise, just scandal. Said you'd clean it up like you always do."

I tilt my head. "Why you?"

"Because I'm disposable!" he screams, full on sobbing now. "Because I'm the idiot with a trust fund and no one cares if I tank my own name—he said it'd bounce back!"

"And the code?"

His breath stutters. "Encrypted packet. Said it was old Society stuff—leaked from a contractor. But it had a dev tag. Rosebud."

My fingers tighten.

He sees it. His eyes go wide. "I didn't *know* her—Jesus, I swear, I didn't even know what Rosebud was until I Googled it. I was just the face."

"You were the message," I murmur.

He starts crying harder. Ugly, violent sobs that shake his whole body.

"You don't have to do this," he pleads. "We can work something out—I'll disappear—I'll flip on Colten—*please*—"

That's when it happens. He goes still. A warm, spreading stain blooms across his thigh. It trickles down to the floor. The smell hits second. He's pissed himself.

Manny doesn't flinch. I don't blink.

Lifting the scalpel, I say, "You're not dying today."

I lower the blade.

He's still trembling, soaked in humiliation and his own piss, eyes locked on the scalpel like it's counting down the seconds he has left. "How do you know about the Society?"

His eyes snap to mine. For a second, I can see him calculating—what to say, how much to admit.

"Colten," he blurts. "He told me. Said if I really

wanted to matter, I needed to understand how Vegas works—how *you* work."

"Why does that matter to him?" I ask.

Alex swallows hard. "He said you're untouchable because the Society backs you. Said you built Obsidian as a front—one that makes the Society money while it launders power. Said *everyone* in the inner circle has dirt on each other, and no one blinks as long as the cash flows."

"Is that what you believe?"

"I don't know what I believe," he snaps, then deflates instantly. "I just—Colten said if I threw gasoline on the rumors, I'd get visibility. Sympathy. That even if I got banned, someone would come scoop me up for the story. And he *wanted* it messy. Said he had a plan."

I lean in. "What plan?"

Alex shakes his head like he regrets everything about the last month. Probably the last decade.

"He didn't tell me everything," he mutters. "Just that he needed your name cracked open. That the rumors would lead somewhere if the right people listened. I don't even think it's about you."

I go still.

"He said this wasn't just Vegas," Alex whispers. "Said someone bigger wanted a crack in the armor. That if *you* fell, a dozen other things would collapse behind you."

Manny and I exchange a glance. It's deeper than we thought. But now I have a name. And a link. Colten.

I don't say a word as I leave the Mirror Room. No one tries to stop me. Not Manny. Not the guards. Not even the voices in my comm.

When I step into the apartment, Opal is standing by

the window, wrapped in citylight, a half full glass of bourbon in her hand. Another one waits for me on the bar untouched.

She doesn't say anything.

I cross the room, pick up the second glass, and meet her eyes as I drink.

Opal moves toward the bar and refills her glass. She leans a hip against the counter and looks at me fully.

"So they're using my code to hit your empire," she says. "Which means two possibilities."

I lift a brow. "Go on."

"One..." She lifts a finger. "They got their hands on my system by accident. Maybe Colten bragged to the wrong person. Maybe someone cracked an old Rothwell server, dug through what little was left, pieced it back together, and found something worth selling. That would explain the leaks—because whoever has it doesn't fully understand how to wield it. They're mimicking, not innovating."

I nod. "And two?"

She lifts a second finger. "Someone with *intent* got hold of it. Not for resale. Not for random chaos. For *you.* Which means this isn't about blackmail or disruption—it's personal."

I swirl the bourbon in my glass. "If it's money, they'd hit the other clubs first. Easier marks. Shallower pockets."

"And less surveillance," she adds. "But Obsidian's the crown. Taking you down sends a message."

"To who?"

"That's what I'm trying to figure out." She steps away from the bar, pacing now. "If it's someone from Society, they'd be more subtle. Controlled chaos. Not nightclub brawls and doctored footage."

"So not Society."

She nods. "But they still knew enough to use the Mirror Room as a trigger point. That's targeted."

I set my glass down, watching her move.

"They're trying to collapse me from the inside out," I say. "Erode the staff. Leak the footage. Hint at trafficking. All while using your code to make it look surgical."

"Which would only work if someone believed it." She pauses. "So who benefits from your fall?"

I don't answer right away. The list is short, but powerful. Most of them wouldn't need to use *her*.

She stops pacing and looks at me, eyes clear now. "This isn't random."

"No," I say. "It's orchestration."

She crosses the room again and stands in front of me, her chest almost brushing mine. "So, what's our next move?"

I look down at her hand, still holding the glass. My fingers brush her wrist as I take it from her and set it aside.

I meet her eyes.

"We hunt the Architect."

CHAPTER SIXTEEN
Opal

I wake up and see Dante next to me. In the bed.

He's on his back with one arm thrown across the sheets and the other bent behind his head. His bare chest rising up and down. He looks... peaceful.

It pisses me off.

This feels too normal. I hate it.

This—him in my bed, the sheets still tangled between us—should feel like a red flag. A mistake I already made and somehow didn't learn from. Instead, it just feels warm. Maybe he didn't mean to stay, but never thought about leaving.

One of his legs is kicked out against mine under the blankets. His bare skin hot against mine, too close. His arm, heavy across the space between us, brushes my side like we fell asleep this way.

Maybe we did. I didn't ask him to stay. But he did. And he's still here.

I sit on the edge of the bed and jab two fingers into

his side. He grunts, but doesn't move. I jab harder. "Wake up, Valera."

His eyes crack open—barely. Sleep rough, he mutters, "What?"

Ugh, even his voice is sexy right now. "Why are you in *my* bed?" That gets one eye fully open.

"Where else am I supposed to go? My house sold. Haven't you noticed I've been here?"

I blink. "Yeah. In the other room."

He stretches one arm behind his head, completely unfazed. "Still here, aren't I?"

"That doesn't explain why you're in *this* room."

Now he opens both eyes, fully awake with a lazy. "Because I wanted to be."

I stare at him, waiting.

He shrugs like it's obvious. "Also, it's my penthouse."

"Possession doesn't equal permission."

"Neither does proximity," he says, and now he's propped on one elbow, watching me like I'm the one breaking protocol. "But you didn't stop me."

I throw the blanket off and stalk toward the closet. "Next time you sneak into my bed without warning, I'm tasering you."

Behind me, he groans—more stretch than protest. "You say that like it's not foreplay."

I whip a glance back. "You're talking like you *want* to test that theory."

He doesn't flinch. "What can I say? I like danger."

"You like hearing yourself talk."

He shrugs. How is he so unbothered by all of this? "Only when you're listening this close."

I grab the first shirt I can find—his, of course—and drag it over my head. "I'm not listening. I'm judging."

He swings his legs over the edge of the bed and stands, moving past me to reach for his watch. "You're stealing my clothes now, I see."

I don't want him to know that I steal them whenever I can. Who could blame me. I like the way that he smells.

"It's the first thing I grabbed," I say nonchalantly. "See, I don't leave a mess everywhere... I actually put my shit away."

He huffs a laugh. Weirdly, it sounds real. His hand brushes mine as he grabs his cufflinks. "You always this mouthy in the morning?"

"Only when I wake up to find a six foot smug complex in my sheets."

He turns to face me, cuff still undone. "You could've kicked me out."

"I thought about it."

"Did you?"

I pause. I can't continue to get ready. He is right. I didn't. "...No."

His smile is small. One I really want to wipe off his fucking face. "Didn't think so."

There's heat simmering under the sarcasm now. We don't have time for this. I step away. "We're late."

"We're always late."

"We're not together," I remind him.

He buttons his sleeve with maddening calm. "Tell that to the shape of your ear still branded on my collarbone. And the bruises shaped like my fingers on your hip."

I don't look back when I leave the bedroom. The espresso machine hisses before I touch it. He programmed it.

It's his machine. His penthouse. But the kitchen has been mine since the moment I've moved in. It was clear that he wasn't here... ever.

One night and I'm reminded that control was always an illusion.

Dante heads straight for the coffee like it's a ritual. He doesn't ask where the mugs are. He knows I wouldn't move anything.

I lean against the island, watching him work the espresso machine.."

My phone rings. Mirelle Noire.

I answer right away. "You must be bored."

"Never," she says, smooth as lacquer. "Just curious."

"About?" It occurs to me then that I don't feel the need to walk away. I don't mind having this conversation, whatever it might be, in front of Dante. It's a jarring revelation. One that makes me stop and stare at him for a second.

"I heard about Alex Knight." She pauses for a second, chuckling. "How's the rug in the Mirror Room holding up?"

"Wouldn't know. I wasn't the one scrubbing blood off the floor."

Mirelle laughs—a soft, spectral sound that brings a shiver running down my spine. "You always did have such a practical mouth."

"You always did like knowing things you shouldn't."

"That's why we get along." She waits a beat. "Well. Mostly."

I lean against the island, eyes flicking toward Dante's back as he creates a work of coffee art in a mug. "Did you call for gossip or to warn me about something?"

"A bit of both," she says. "There's a gala. For the foundation."

"Right," I mutter. "The Mirelle Noire Foundation. Why does that matter to me?"

"You're on the guest list."

I go still. "Excuse me?"

"Don't sound so surprised. Stellan and Talia are coming. And you and Dante are marked as in attendance."

I grit my teeth. "By who?"

"Doesn't matter," she says, voice dismissive. "You're part of the machine now, Opal. Learn to wave and smile."

"When is it?"

"Friday."

I glance at the wall clock. "It's Sunday at 8AM."

"Yes," she says. "Try not to embarrass me. See you there."

The line goes dead and I drop the phone on the counter.

"Learn to wave and smile," I mutter. "Bite me, Mirelle."

Across the kitchen, Dante slides his card onto the marble with two fingers.

"Take it," he says simply.

I blink. Then I laugh so hard that I snort and double over. "Cute." I pick it up, turn it once, and flick it back toward him. "I have one. Looks the same. May even have a higher limit than yours."

He catches the card without looking and tucks it back into his wallet. "I doubt it."

"Don't push."

He doesn't. Just turns back to the espresso machine and pours the second shot. This man can go through coffee like water.

"I don't do these kinds of things," I say finally. "Galas. Champagne. Ice sculptures with shrimp circling like bait. I don't—"

"Weren't you raised going to cotillion or something?"

"That doesn't mean I liked it."

He shrugs like it doesn't matter, but the edge of his mouth tips up. "You'll be fine. You already know how to kill a man in heels."

"Not helpful," I mutter.

I open my phone again. Staring at it, I think to myself. This is the part I hate—the part where pride loses to logic. I scroll to Talia's number and press call before I can talk myself out of it.

She picks up on the second ring with a voice filled with far too much joy for this time in the morning. "Opal. I was wondering how long it would take."

"Don't start."

Her voice hums with victory. "Need help?"

"No. Just a favor."

"That sounds suspiciously like help." I can practically see her swiveling in her office chair.

I sigh. "I have to go to a thing. Mirelle's gala. I don't

have anything appropriate. Or the patience to pretend I care about dress codes."

"You called the right girl," she says brightly. "Frankie and I are on our way to Jean Verenne's later. Come with."

I pause. "The place with private guards and six figure zippers?"

"See you there," she says in a sing-song voice, and hangs up.

I stare at the screen and exhale through my nose.

Dante finally turns toward me, coffee in one hand, watching me like he's already guessed the outcome. "You're going?" he asks.

"I'm going," I confirm, finishing the last of my espresso.

He steps closer, voice gravely enough to curl heat against my spine. "Tell her you want something red."

I roll my eyes and shove the cup into the sink. But my pulse ticks harder in my throat.

But I don't say no.

The boutique is like a museum. It's amazing. I tend to stay away from shopping. The Vulture is not kind to women spending money. Especially women that everyone is supposed to hate.

The boutique is all black walls, matte steel racks, and ambient lighting that shifts with your mood if you look too long. No floral wallpaper. No pastel lace. The place smells like leather and expensive attitude.

Not shocking.

Talia and Frankie don't play the same way as everyone else.

A sales associate hands me a glass of champagne—crystal stem, perfectly chilled, like she already knows I'm not here to only browse.

I find them near a row of dresses that look like they could bankrupt a Rothschild.

Frankie's the first to clock me. She gives me a once-over—not judging, just... checking. Making sure I'm real. That I actually came.

"You're on time," she says, eyebrow raised.

"I do know how clocks work," I answer, sipping the champagne. "Even if I avoid most social events like they bite. I always thought that if I showed up late enough times, people would stop inviting me. But alas, here we are."

Talia slides a hanger off the rack, barely sparing me a glance. "This place bites harder than most. But I feel like a dress from here would send the right message... all things considered."

I'm saved from Frankie's scrutiny by the salesgirl leading us to a back lounge—plush velvet seating, silver rimmed trays, and mirrors that don't reflect your flaws unless you know where to look.

Frankie and I were good friends at one point in our lives, she's fiercely loyal to her family, and I fucked up a member of her family. It's understandable that she's still holding a grudge, I know I would be, too. Holding on to a grudge for too long is what put me in this position in the first place, although it was misplaced.

Frankie sits on the plush couch first, then Talia. I stay

standing until I'm sure I won't bolt. I have to make a choice. So I lower myself into the corner seat and set the champagne on the glass table.

It's Talia who starts. "You know we weren't just mad, right?" She says, voice level. "We were hurt and confused. Stellan wouldn't talk about it. You were everything to him. He thought of you like a sister."

Frankie leans forward, elbows on knees. "You blew up the lives of everyone at Rothwell for a need for revenge that didn't even make sense."

"I know," I say quietly. "And I'm sorry. You didn't deserve that. You never did."

Talia's eyes sharpen. "Then why?"

I owe them more than the version I tell myself.

"My mother," I say, and it already tastes wrong. "She didn't just lie—she made it sound like love. Like protecting Maris meant turning on all of you."

I grip the glass harder than I mean to, but I don't let go.

"She told me Stellan stole Maris's business pitch—flipped it into Rothwell, made himself rich off her work. Said Beckett helped cover it up. That the whole team did. She said no one believed Maris. That you called her unstable. That she tried to kill herself because of it."

This is the side that they don't know.

"And while all that was happening—while I was cutting ties with every one of you—Maris married an abusive asshole. She got sold a fairytale while I was chasing a war."

Frankie's lips press into a line. Talia says nothing, but

I can feel her watching me like she's trying to read behind the lines of my mind.

"Now that bastard's fighting for custody," I finish, voice low. "And I spent years thinking the wrong villain won."

Then Frankie sits back and says, "God, you're exhausting."

I let out a short breath that almost becomes a laugh. "You're not wrong."

She takes a long sip of champagne. "I still don't trust you."

"You don't have to," I say, then add, "I think it's clear that I don't blame you. I mean, look how long I held on to that. If anyone can hold onto a grudge, it's me."

Talia stands with her eyebrows raised in a way that tells me that she's... impressed maybe? Brushing invisible lint from her blazer like she didn't just sit through a full emotional dissection, she says, "You're going to need something sharp. Maybe red. You've got a lot to say."

I lift an eyebrow. "That the official dress code?"

Frankie smirks into her glass. "For you? Yeah."

Talia's already scrolling her phone. "And you'll want to be ready."

"Ready for what?" I ask, already wary.

She glances at me, expression unreadable. "Michella Carr made the guest list."

"And she's definitely going to be there," Frankie adds.

"Mirelle says she's working some foundation angle—but she's not coming to network. She's coming to be seen." Talia rolls her eyes as she sets her phone back down. The way these two talk is honestly impressive, it's like they share a brain.

I feel the laugh rise that is venom laced. "Of course she is."

Frankie finishes her champagne. "Better make sure that dress doesn't just say *fuck you.*"

Talia crosses her arms and leans against the polished marble wall. "Make sure it says *try me.*"

"Make it red," Frankie says, setting her empty glass down with finality. "It has to be red. That's your color."

"That's exactly what Dante said," I mutter, before I can think twice.

Talia's eyes snap to mine. "He picked the same color?"

Frankie arches a brow. "Okay—what the hell is this? Are you guys official now?"

"No," I say quickly, maybe too quickly. "God, no."

"Uh huh," Frankie says, unconvinced. She folds her arms, tilting her head with a barely there smirk.

Talia doesn't blink. "But you're living together."

"I'm surviving in his penthouse," I say, pulling in a breath. "Big difference."

They don't let up. I push a hand through my hair, feeling the prickle of heat creep up my neck.

"He's... complicated," I admit. "We're not making this a real thing. He's also spending more and more time around me that is not connected to the case."

"Has he told you he's in love with you, yet?" Frankie asks, eyes narrowing.

I hesitate. "He hasn't said the word. Not like we're around each other enough to fall in love anyway."

"But he's dressing you in red," Talia says, "and it wasn't just a suggestion, but a demand. Because he knows what color looks best on you. He's been watching you, Opal."

Frankie leans forward, pinning me with a look that feels a little too intense to dodge. "How do you feel about that?"

I scoff, but it's thin. "It's a show. We have to make it look real. I figured the society gave him a dossier. I got one on him."

"Uh huh," she says again, dragging the sound out like she's peeling back paint. "Not that real."

Talia's voice drops. "Opal. I got a dossier on Stellan, but it didn't have what color *he* thought looked best on me in it. That took time. He got to know me. My quirks. The ins and outs of my body. What he likes about me. Stop lying to yourself. Tell us how it makes you *feel*. Think about it without your usual walls up."

I look between them. Two women who've seen me at my worst and still let me join them today. Suddenly, lying feels stupid.

"It scares the shit out of me," I admit, exhaling like it costs me something. "When he touches me like that. Like I'm not a weapon or a game piece. Like I'm something he'd fight for."

Frankie says nothing. Talia doesn't blink.

"I don't know what to do with it," I add, softer. "I'm better at sharp edges than soft landings."

Frankie lifts her glass again—this one freshly poured—and tips it toward me. "Well," she says. "Here's to not landing."

"Here's to burning," Talia murmurs.

And I smile, just a little. "Here's to red."

The first dress I try on is an absolute disaster. Too much fabric. Too much shine. It looks like I lost a fight with a sequined curtain and somehow got hugged by a bow.

"No," Frankie says immediately, new champagne glass in hand. "You look like a walking sympathy card."

Talia doesn't even try to joke about it. "Absolutely not."

The second is worse—tight in all the wrong places, the red too loud and too cheap, short and tight like a hooker on lunch break. Not that there's anything wrong with that, it's just not the vibe. And not something I'd ever wear. The neckline dips so low I'd need duct tape and divine intervention to keep it on.

Frankie covers her eyes dramatically. "Oh, good, trauma with cleavage."

"Hard pass," Talia mutters.

The third might be cursed. I swear the zipper hisses at me—like it knows this is a mistake and wants out before I drag it into battle. The fabric clings in patches and gaps in others, like it couldn't decide if it wanted to suffocate me or fall off mid-step.

I catch sight of myself in the mirror and immediately regret it. This one doesn't need a tailor. It needs an exorcist.

We cycle through a dozen. Some too girlish, some too safe, one that makes me look like I'm running for office in the 1980s—shoulder pads, sorrow, and all. Frankie called it "Congressional chic." I called it grounds for exile.

I'm about to fake a phone call and ghost the whole boutique when the stylist returns with one last option—a simple hanger and understated bag, the kind of dress that doesn't need to beg for attention because it already knows it's the one.

I step into the dressing room and pull it on. No zippers fight me. No seams bunch. It slides into place like it was made for me and me alone.

When I walk out, the room goes silent.

Talia stares. Frankie lowers her champagne, her mouth parting. "Holy shit," she breathes.

Even the stylist gives a single, reverent nod. "That's the one."

Talia crosses her arms, eyes narrowed in approval. "Michella Carr's going to choke on her own spit."

Frankie's already grinning. "You're going to own that room."

I look in the mirror—but not too long. Power isn't something you stare at. It's something you carry.

"Bag it," I say, voice steady.

The dress is boxed in black tissue and sealed in matte paper.

When I step outside, the sun is slipping low behind the buildings, turning Vegas gold at the edges. Talia and Frankie are talking beside me. The chaos of the street cacophony are rising around us.

For a second, it almost feels normal.

I never expected to like normal. But maybe it's time I figure out what it means for myself.

Especially with Michella Carr waiting on the other side of it.

CHAPTER SEVENTEEN

Opal

The red dress fits like a dare.

Not bright red—blood red. The kind of color that draws the eye before the mind has time to look away.

It sculpts to my body like it was molded there. No glitter. No lace. It's made of stunning architectural lines that hug my silhouette with every breath I take. The fabric is heavy enough to move like silk and light enough to hint at what is underneath—cut to graze high on the thigh, but slit low enough to whisper of something more. It doesn't sparkle. It absorbs light.

The neckline rides high, straight across my collarbones, sleeveless and sleek—unapologetically modern. But that's just the front. The decoy. The part they'll see first.

Because the back is where the hot begins.

It's open. All of it.

Bare skin from the base of my neck to the curve of my spine, exposed. The dress is held together by one thin clasp at the base of my spine—no zipper, no compromise. Just one pressure point between being dressed and being undone.

It's not made for dancing. Or sitting. It's made for being seen.

Two narrow seams curve around my waist, engineered to cinch without corseting. It's tailored so precisely I don't wear it—it wears me. Every step shifts the hem, just slightly like water flowing over the edge of a cliff. Enough to make people look again. To check what they missed the first time.

When they see the back, they'll realize they never stood a chance.

I hold my hair up with one hand—soft curls pinned tight, but just loose enough to suggest they'd fall apart with the right touch—and glance over my shoulder.

He's already there.

Dante stands in the doorway, black suit, darker eyes, and a bow tie bringing it all together. His gaze drags slow over every inch of me, and when our eyes meet, it's not approval I see. It's possession.

"You're staring," I say, a smirk on my lips.

He doesn't deny it, nor does he move. He's frozen with pure hunger in his eyes. "You're not tied in yet."

I lift a brow. "You offering your services?"

He crosses the room without a word, steps behind me, and takes the thin tie between his fingers. He takes his time making sure I am in the dress and it won't be going anywhere.

"You let them see you like this," he murmurs, close to my ear, "and they'll remember who you belong to."

I smile at our reflection. "That's the point?"

His fingers pause just beneath the clasp. "You'll be the brightest thing in the room."

Heat blooms at the base of my spine. I shouldn't care. Shouldn't want that look in his eyes—the one that says I'm not just part of the plan, I *am* the plan.

I swallow it down and lift my chin. "Well," I say, turning slightly so the clasp clicks into place between us. "Let's give them something to remember."

The car pulls up to the Grand Verdoux—Vegas's second most expensive hotel. Spotlights sweep the curved entryway, glinting off diamond studded gowns and gold accented tuxedos. Paparazzi perch behind velvet ropes, flashes already firing like they're determined not to miss a moment.

Before the driver even cuts the engine, Dante's door opens.

He steps out of the backseat. One nod to the valet, and he's circling the car.

My door opens. His hand extends. I take it.

The crowd hushes when I rise. The red dress drinks in the lights, every curve polished and it's cut is unique. My heels strike the pavement like a countdown. Every step beside Dante screams intentional.

He offers his arm. I loop mine through it.

We walk toward the main entrance, a wall of light and glass ahead. Behind the velvet ropes, someone gasps. Cameras flash in our eyes making it hard to see.

"You ready?" he murmurs without looking at me.

"I was born for this," I whisper back.

The ballroom is too gold. Gold walls. Gold ceilings.

Gold plated people pretending this kind of excess is normal. The kind of place designed to make you forget what real power looks like. Nothing sincere. Only polished surfaces and curated smiles stretched too tight.

I hate it. I've always hated it.

We see Frankie and Beckett alongside Talia and Stellan near the bar. They already have drinks in their hands. Dante's hand never leaves the small of my back as we walk over. The warmth of his skin on mine is a comfort I didn't know I was missing.

"Greer," Frankie says, dragging her eyes over the dress with a grin. "That's not just a statement. That's a declaration of war."

"Valera," Dante corrects beside me. "If we're declaring things, let's get the name right."

I don't respond. I'm too busy scanning.

The room is crowded—too crowded. Staff blends in with guests. The lighting's too bright in some spots, too dim in others. A floral arrangement large enough to hide a body blocks one hallway. It's purposefully disorienting, not that I'd expect anything less from Mirelle.

And the cameras?

They're here. Too many. None of them placed where they should be.

If someone's using my stolen code, this is exactly the kind of venue they'd test it in. High traffic, high noise, high chaos. No one paying attention until it's too late.

I shift closer to Dante. He doesn't say anything, but I know he feels the change in me. I'm not the kind of woman who enjoys parties. Not even this kind of party.

Especially not this kind of party.

I feel her before I see her. Heels click across marble, people start whispering. Then she steps into view. Michella Carr.

She's wearing cream silk, a risky color. It's cut too high to be classy on the thigh, and too low to demand respect on the chest—tight in all the wrong places. I recognize the dress instantly.

It's the cream version of the one I tried on and laughed at. Working girl on lunch break energy. Paired with a fake tan two shades too deep and the kind of highlighter glow that screams desperation.

She thought Dante would like it.

That's the funniest part.

Because I didn't wear that dress. I wore the one that turned every head in the room without having to be basically naked to do it.

She stops in front of us like she's gliding in on a breeze. Champagne flute in one hand, a tilt to her chin that says she still thinks she owns some part of him.

"Dante," she purrs. "It's been too long."

He doesn't smile. Doesn't move. Just a cool nod. "Michella. Still crashing events you weren't invited to?"

She laughs. It's fake. Hollow enough to echo in her throat. "I'm here for the Noire Foundation," she says. "I always support a good cause." Her gaze slides to me, slow and assessing. "You must be the new wife."

I let the pause stretch long enough to sting. Then smile. "Wife, yes. New? Not really. You've just been out of the loop."

Frankie snorts behind her glass. Talia murmurs something I don't catch—but it sounds suspiciously like *bless her heart*.

Michella doesn't flinch. But her grip on the stem of her glass tightens. I see it. She's here to rattle me. Maybe claim something that's no longer hers.

But she wore a knife to a gun fight.

Michella's still smirking, still pretending this is her show. When she turns back to Dante, she sets her glass down on the nearest tray.

"Dance with me," she says, holding out her hand. "For old times' sake."

Dante face tightens, he's trying to hide the disgust that threatening to plaster itself across his face.. "No, Michella."

Her lips part. "No?"

"It's inappropriate."

Her voice lifts, sugar turning sour. "And kissing me on your doorstep wasn't?"

I cut in. "Well, considering you did that just in time for the article to drop the next day, I'd say you're not exactly shy about forcing situations into something they're not."

Her head snaps toward me, eyes narrowing. "God, you're weird," she mutters. "Do you *really* think he's not mine?"

"I *know* he's not," I say easily. "You should've worn red. Might've helped the delusion."

She scoffs. "He kissed me."

"Once. When you cornered him. Not exactly a flex when he shoves you away like unwanted food."

Michella freezes. It's less than a blink—half a second

of silence—but I see it. The flicker of something raw behind her eyes. Anger. Shame. The edge of disbelief like maybe she was hoping I didn't know.

She recovers fast. Too fast. Tosses her hair back and lets out a brittle laugh. "He doesn't need to make it a statement," she says. "Dante's not like that. He always comes back. He gets bored, he gets cold—"

"—and what?" I cut in. "He comes crawling to your door like a stray you left out too long?"

Michella's jaw ticks.

I step in closer, eyes locked on hers. "Must be hard," I murmur, "watching him finally choose something else. Something permanent."

She stares at me.

That's when Dante steps in. "No," he says. "You don't get to change the past to fit your ideal future, Michella. Whatever we had ended. I didn't look back then, and I'm sure as hell not looking now."

She stares at him, waiting for something. When it doesn't come, she turns to me. "You don't scare me."

"Just as you don't scare me," I reply, not even blinking.

Dante shifts at my side. Instead of walking away, he turns to me, effectively dismissing her. "Dance with me."

I blink. "You serious?"

His mouth barely moves. "She doesn't get the last word. You do."

He extends his hand. I take it. The ballroom blurs around us—gold light, polite stares, too many lies under too much polish. But all I feel is the press of his palm at my waist, the steadiness in his hold as we move.

"I like you in red," he murmurs near my ear.

My pulse kicks. "You better."

We dance like no one else is here. But I know Michella watches every second of it.

The music fades. Dante's hand leaves my waist, but his presence doesn't. I can still feel him.

I turn to walk toward the refreshment tables, needing a breath. A second.

That's when I hear the heels once again. Michella slides into step beside me.

"Nice performance," she says smoothly, eyes ahead like we're friends catching up. "Cute. But let me give you some advice, sweetheart. The Society loves a good bride —but they adore a fall from grace even more."

"Then they'll hate how well I balance."

She finally turns her gaze on me. "I wore that dress first, you know. Not the exact one—but close enough that Dante didn't need a reminder."

I tilt my head, slow. "And yet here you are, still trying to remind him."

Her eyes flash, but she covers it. "Just remember who picked the game you're playing. Women like us? We don't get happy endings. We get headlines. You better pray you survive yours."

If she thinks that was a warning... she's about to find out what a real one looks like.

Until I hear the voice. "Hello, dear."

There she is.

Celestine.

My mother.

Her hand curls over Michella's wrist with the same

grip she once used on me—tight, possessive, claiming what was never hers to hold. Her mouth is pulled into a practiced smile. Her tan is too dark, her jewelry too bright.

Money can't bleach the rot out of her core.

I don't have to turn around to feel them approaching —Stellan, Beckett, Dante, Frankie, and Talia. A slow moving wall of power and precision, every step measured and... deadly. The kind of entrance that makes a room freeze.

Frankie's expression hardens the second she sees who's standing across from me. Talia doesn't bother hiding her reaction—she exhales a sound low and lethal, more growl than breath.

Dante's the last to stop—behind me, close enough to feel, but not touching.

Not yet.

Celestine's eyes slide over me with practiced indifference.

"Oh," she says lightly, her voice smoothed down to its most condescending register. "You wore red."

Michella's smile sharpens. "How fitting. Like mother, like daughter."

I stare at them. At the alliance formed between two women. One spent my entire life torturing me. The other is trying to destroy me in real time.

"Funny," I say coldly, lifting my glass to my lips. "You two make sense. One's irrelevant. The other's rotting. Together, you're almost funny."

Celestine's gaze doesn't waver. "I'm simply supporting a dear friend."

"Sure," I say. "And Michella's simply desperate for attention."

Michella's smile twitches. "We're not so different, you and me," she murmurs.

"I hope we're not," I reply. "I'd hate to end up pathetic."

Celestine steps forward, just slightly. "Careful, Opal. These people don't know who you really are."

"They don't know who you raised," I say, voice ice. "Or what you cost."

Dante's hand curls into a fist at his side. Stellan and Beckett flank him. Frankie and Talia edge closer behind me.

But I don't step back.

I let the venom in my soul rise from my toes to my mouth.

"You think showing up here on her arm scares me?" I ask, cocking my head. "You think aligning with a woman who hasn't been relevant since Dante stopped returning her calls is some kind of threat?"

Celestine stiffens. Michella opens her mouth—but Dante speaks first. "That's enough."

He steps forward, placing his body between us. "If you want to play games," he says to Michella, "do it outside. You want to throw your lot in with her?" He looks at Celestine now. "Then you're already forgotten."

Michella glares. "She's not afraid of me. She's afraid of what you'll do when you find out the truth."

"I know everything," Dante says, eyes locked on me.

Michella's voice cuts through the conversation like a serrated knife. "She's not even her daughter, you know."

The crowd nearest to us goes still, every face tilted in polite horror—like they're watching a car crash they'll pretend later not to remember.

"She was adopted," Michella says, stepping forward like she's walking into a spotlight, voice rising just enough to carry. "Out of the kindness of her heart. What does Opal do? Well she uses everything her dear mother gave her to spite Stellan to destroy him."

She turns to Dante, smiling as if she's handing him a favor. "You married a myth, Valera. A fake name and a foster story."

I don't flinch. I don't blink. I just look at her—at *all* of them—and speak the truth she thought would ruin me.

"I know," I say, voice calm. "I've always known."

Michella falters. It's subtle, but I catch it—the tiny shift in her weight, the way her mouth closes before the next jab can form.

"I was ten when I found the first clue. A hospital record that didn't match my birthday. A name that wasn't mine, scribbled on a file Celestine left out while she screamed at a maid for forgetting her champagne."

I take a step forward, getting right in Michella's personal space.

"Thirteen when I found the rest. Hidden in a locked drawer behind designer scarves and forged charity receipts. My adoption papers. The gag order. The checks sent to the birth mother who wanted to change her mind and the threats that shut her up for good."

Dante squeezes my hip as I try not to think too much about the past. Try not to disappear into it.

"She didn't deny it," I go on, my voice harder now.

"She just poured another glass of wine, looked me in the eye, and said I should be grateful. That I was chosen. That I should remember what she gave me—and never forget what she could take away."

A muscle twitches in Michella's cheek. It's the first honest thing I've seen from her all night.

"I wasn't blood. I wasn't Maris. I was the public redemption arc—a pet project with a tragic backstory. The press piece Celestine needed to soften the edges while she locked her *real* daughter away. Except in our town, there is no press. Just useless gossip."

I let the tear fall from my eye. A real one. The first glimpse of the Opal I hide under all of my brains.

"But I'm not ashamed. I didn't inherit my worth. I built it. Without her money. Without her name. Then I rebuilt it again. After she tried to use me to destroy Stellan."

Stellan looks at her for a long beat. Not angry. Not pitying. Just real. "You did almost destroy me," he says, voice even. "But now I see why."

He doesn't look at Celestine, instead he's looking at me. "You were set up. Used. I get that now. Doesn't erase what happened, but it explains it."

Talia folds her arms but doesn't look away. Her tone is firm. "I spent a long time hating you," she says. "And maybe I still do a little." Her gaze softens just a bit. "But I hated the version of you I saw through discovering what you've done. Not the one standing here, taking accountability for everything."

She glances at Celestine, then back. "She broke you, Opal. But you didn't stay broken."

Frankie steps into the conversation, chin tilted, eyes locked on Michella with surgical focus. "Try that shit again. Go on. Let's see if Vegas still thinks you're relevant after tonight."

I don't breathe. Don't blink. Because Beckett is still watching me. Not them. Me. Waiting to see what I am about to do. "You didn't just grow up wealthy," he says, voice calm in a way that breaks something in my chest. "You were used and hurt. Things that make us very aware how little we know about you."

They're not circling me. They're flanking me. They're defending me. That makes me want to cry. My heart is cracking open at it's seems. I believe them.

I stand taller and turn back to Celestine, who hasn't flinched. Not visibly. But I know that look. It's the one she used to give the town gossips when a story didn't go her way. The barely contained crack under polished composure.

I feel him behind me. "She doesn't need your last name," he says, voice deadly. "She's Valera now."

My stomach tightens. His hand comes to rest low on my back once again. A possessive and grounding way that I've not heard from him in a situation like this. Like he's making sure *I* hear him too.

He would usually just let me handle things like this on my own.

"She's mine," he says, eyes on Celestine, "because she chose to be. It took some convincing on my end, but I got her now."

I forget how to swallow.

He leans in so close his breath brushes my jaw. Then

he drops his voice for me alone. "And you haven't even seen what I'll do when you moan my name."

Michella hears it. I know she does, because her breath catches involuntary. Her smile freezes mid performance, like she's been caught in bad lighting. For half a second, she looks stunned. Not angry. Not smug.

Wounded.

"No," she says, too fast. Too loud. "That's—" She laughs, brittle and wrong. A sound that doesn't belong to her. "That's just theater. You always were good at saying things you didn't mean."

But her eyes are shining now. Not tears yet—she won't give that away—but panic flashes there, raw and exposed. She steps forward like she might reach for him, then stops herself when she realizes everyone is watching.

"You can't have feelings for her," Michella says, like she's spitting out something spoiled. "You don't. You don't even *do* feelings, Dante. That was the whole point."

He doesn't flinch, doesn't deny it. He just watches her with that unreadable stare that makes full grown men hide.

It guts her.

"You said I was the only one who could handle you," she pushes, voice rising. "You said *we* made sense. That love wasn't real—it was something that was a waste of time. It was an image. *You* said that." She's not performing now. Not really. She's begging. Dante still hasn't said a word.

Michella turns her focus on me, desperation cracking into hatred. "She's not like us," she sneers. "She doesn't know what it costs to keep a man like you. She'll try to change you. She'll ruin everything you built."

"She won't ruin what I built," he says angrily. "She *is* what I'm building."

Michella stares, hollow and blinking. Like she's still waiting for the punchline.

But Dante's not done. "She doesn't need to *keep* me," he adds. "She already has me. Name, ring, vow. Blood, bone, soul. All of it. Not because she asked for anything." He tilts his head, just slightly. Enough to make Michella freeze. "Because I gave it to her," he says. "Every last fucking piece. I would do it again and again for her."

Michella's mouth opens. Closes. The words don't come. She turns to run, but we all know it's not to salvage her pride. It's because she knows that there was a game. She just never realized she wasn't even in the running for first place.

He straightens like he didn't just rearrange my heart in my chest.

Celestine flinches. She follows Michella without saying another word.

All I can see now is him. He is staring at me. His eyes are telling me that the next move is all mine.

CHAPTER EIGHTEEN

Dante

You don't walk out of a night like that and pretend a bomb wasn't dropped.

The adrenaline hasn't left my system. Neither has the image of Opal in that dress, or the way Michella's face cracked when she realized I meant every word. I don't regret it. But I haven't processed it, either.

There's a lot that we need to talk about. Things that were said. Things I didn't know about my wife.

But there was clarity too. Knowing truly why Opal did what she did.

We don't say anything as we step into the kitchen. The gala was a disaster.

We didn't stay for the dinner, didn't bid on a single item, didn't make the rounds like we were supposed to. Mirelle didn't even blink when we left—too busy collecting compliments and counting cameras. If she wanted us there, she got what she needed the second the photographers snapped their shots. Anything after that was window dressing.

I toss my keys on the counter, strip off my jacket, and head to the bar. I need a drink. I pour two glasses, red and full, and slide one across the island toward her without asking.

I glance at Opal as she leans against the counter, wineglass resting between her fingers, knuckles tight. Her eyes are distant. Her mind is elsewhere. Probably thinking of the night.

I could ask. I could push. But we're both too raw to really get into it right now.

So I drink. Then I say the one thing I know we both agree on. "Well, that was a fucking circus."That gets a humorless breath from her. "You could say that." She swirls her glass but doesn't drink.

"She's always played dirty," she says. "I'm honestly surprised it took her this long to weaponize my origin story."

I blink. "You're not even fazed."

"Oh, I'm fazed," she says, finally sipping. "Just not shocked. Celestine doesn't go for the throat. She goes for the place you already cut yourself. She wants to hurt you in a way where she can't get blood on her hands."

I stare at her, wine forgotten, and shake my head. "That was something else. And the way Michelle and her teamed up? That was rough."

Opal looks at me sideways. "You dated her. Lived with her. Slept next to her. And you're only now realizing she's a monster?"

I glance at Opal. "She wasn't like that with me."

Opal arches a brow, unconvinced.

"She could be self centered, sure. But the claws?" I

shake my head. "That wasn't the woman I lived with. That... desperation. That venom. I don't know what that is."

I pause to think about everything. And swallow my pride admitting that I was blind."Or maybe I didn't want to see it."

Opal gives a short, bitter laugh. "Then congratulations. You're catching up."

I take a step closer, resting my hand against the counter. "You really knew?"

"That I was adopted?" She meets my eyes. "Yeah. I've always known."

It knocks something loose in me. Not shock... but clarity.

It's why she never talked about Celestine unless it was with clench teeth. Why she walks like someone is about to stab her in the back at every moment. It explains that cold precision in her voice whenever she mentions her past. The way she protects herself like she fears for the worst at any moment in time.

She wasn't Celestine's daughter.

Adopted to make her image cleaner. Then repurposed into a precision tool the moment it suited her mother's agenda—aimed straight at Stellan, at Talia, at whoever the fuck Celestine thought deserved to go down.

That's why she hates her. And I can't blame her. Because now I see it. The whole fucked up game. Celestine built a daughter out of spite. She didn't just hunt Stellan for revenge. She did it because she thought it might finally earn her approval.She aimed at him because it's what Celestine wanted. Because for once,

Opal wanted to be seen not as a placeholder, but as a daughter.

I feel like that makes it even worse. The betrayal of having a sliver of hope ripped away.She hoped that giving Celestine what she wanted would be enough. That loyalty would buy love. That selling out someone her mother wanted to might finally make her *belong*.

Now I know why she did what she did. I also know exactly how it feels.

"She made it my story before I even understood what it meant," she goes on. "Celestine had an affair. One that blew up in her face and tarnished everything she'd built. So she found a way to clean it up. Adopted me from a junkie and sold it like she was some kind of saint. A redemption arc in pearls. Maris was the real daughter. I was the good press. The clean up act. The placeholder on the stage."

I grip my glass tighter than I need to. The stem creaks in my hand.

"You deserved better."

Opal raises one brow, amused and annoyed at once. "Don't get sentimental on me, Valera."

"I'm not." I finish my glass. "But I'm not going to pretend that wasn't a fucked up thing to witness."

"She's tried to erase me before," Opal says, eyes hard. "That wasn't new."

"But?"

"She underestimated one thing."

"What's that?"

"I don't go away when there's still work to be done."

There goes our volley again—firing back faster than most people realize.

She shifts, glass in hand, chin high. "I'm going to bed."

"Are you?" My voice comes out a bit rough.

She stops.

I take a slow step forward. "You think you can say all that, walk off, and I'm just supposed to let you?"

She gives me a look that is unreadable. "I didn't realize I needed your permission to sleep."

"You don't," I say. "But I didn't think you were the type to run."

The glass leaves her hand and hits the counter with a soft clink, her eyes never leaving mine. "I'm not running."

I close the rest of the distance. "Good."

My hand catches her waist, pulling her back—just a breath. She inhales. I press her against the wall, one palm flat beside her head, the other gripping her hip.

"You think I didn't notice?" I say, voice low against her ear. "That you kept scanning the room? Watching every exit, every angle? I saw you calculating. Just like you're doing now."

She smirks, but there's a hitch in it. "And what exactly am I calculating?"

"Whether you'll let me touch you." My fingers brush her jaw, trail down her neck—just barely. I feel her swallow.

"You wore that fucking dress," I say, tone turning darker. "In the color I told you to. Walked into that room like a goddamn fantasy. And now you want to act untouched? Like you didn't know exactly what the fuck you were doing to me?" I lean closer, my lips grazing her cheek, just above the corner of her mouth. "I don't believe you."

She exhales—slow, hot, defiant.

I drop my voice even lower. "Tell me to stop."

She doesn't. I tighten my grip on her hip. My mouth finds the edge of her throat.

"You can't, can you?" I murmur. "You want this as bad as I do."

She doesn't answer. She grabs my shirt instead—fists twisting in the fabric—and pulls me in.

My mouth crashes to hers. I lift her in one motion, palms gripping the backs of her thighs, and press her hard against the wall. Her dress rides up. Her legs wrap around my waist. She gasps into my mouth.

"You knew exactly what you were doing in that dress," I breathe against her throat. "You knew you were tempting me."

Her nails dig into my shoulders. "And you like being tempted."

"Fuck yes, I do." I kiss her again. I've been starving for this.

She moans into my mouth, hips shifting against me. I push off the wall, her legs still locked around my waist, and walk us toward the bedroom.

We don't slow down. We don't look away.

She's kissing me like she wants to swallow the part of me that still holds back. Like she knows it's there and she's done pretending not to notice.

I shoulder open the bedroom door. It bangs against the wall, sending the frames shaking.

I don't set her down gently. I drop her onto the bed like a gauntlet and follow her down, pressing my weight into her, dragging my hand along her thigh, up the line of that goddamn red dress.

"You wore this," I growl, voice rough in her ear, "and thought I'd behave?"

She grins—fucking grins—like she knew all along.

My hand is at her waist in a breath, pushing her down into the mattress as I slide over her, catching her wrists and pinning them just above her head. Her breath catches, but she doesn't look away.

"You think you've got me figured out?" I murmur against her jaw. "You haven't even scratched the surface."

I kiss her hard then trail lower, biting the edge of her jaw, her throat, the place just beneath her collarbone that makes her shift beneath me. One hand releases her wrists to drag down her side, slow and possessive, stopping just at the inside of her thigh. I pause there.

She squirms. Her lips part, but I cut her off with my mouth again, this time slower, tasting her like a secret. My hand slides higher, slipping under the hem of what's left between us, fingers grazing heat. When she gasps, I catch it with my teeth.

She's wet already.

Now she can see exactly what kind of fire she started.

Her nails dig into my shoulders as I slide my hand lower, but it's not enough. Not yet.

I pull back to look at her, admire her. Hair wild against the pillow, chest rising fast.

I sit up just enough to yank her dress up over her hips. The tie fights me for half a second before I tear it open. Not careful. Not patient. I don't give a damn if it rips. It was made to be ruined.

She gasps as I strip it down her body, baring inch after inch until she's in nothing but the scraps she wore beneath—delicate and completely useless.

I crush my mouth to hers again, swallowing whatever she was about to say. Her hands are on my shirt now, clawing at the buttons, and I let her try—right up until I lose patience and tear the whole thing over my head, buttons scattering across the floor.

There's nothing slow about this. No restraint left.

My belt hits the floor with a snap. Her bra follows. Then the rest. We're all hands and teeth and heat, locked in a frenzy that's been building all night long.

I lift her, twist, and drop us both back onto the mattress. No more barriers.

The first thrust is annihilation, a splitting of the atom. Intimacy under the shattering edge of violence. Her hips yield to maximize the impact, angling herself to take me as deeply as possible.

I feel her shudder all the way through the mattress, the aftershock rippling up my spine and burning off every rational thought. The sheets draw tight around us, trapping heat, sweat, and the mingled scent of hunger.

She stares up at me with that silvered, undomesticated spark in her gaze—provocation, promise, threat. I meet it, just as electrified.

We hold it for a half second, a breathless standoff, and then all the theater of self control collapses.

We are animals, stripped down to the grist and bone,

every movement a raw negotiation of dominance and need.

I don't fuck her. I orchestrate her, a conductor with an audience of one. I pace myself, merciless, locking her limbs beneath mine and setting a tempo she can never predict. Each drive is a way to say you're mine.

She grabs for anything that she can hold on to, nails scoring the backs of my shoulders, but I catch her wrists, pin them to the pillow again, and tangle them in the damp, writhing silk.

She's trembling now. Inside her, I feel the pulse of her core, desperate to take and to give. I mark my territory with every thrust.

She arches up to meet me, bending at the perfect angle, and I change position to drive deeper, testing her limits until I find the boundary no one else has reached.

My mouth finds her jaw, her throat, mapping every contour with tongue and teeth, feasting on the salt of her skin and the frantic clutch of her breath.

The headboard drums a tattoo against the wall. I listen, hungry for each sound. I want to record them, play them back inside my skull forever.

My breath syncs to hers, ragged and inexorable. "Tell me you want it," I command, my voice a whip smacking against the ground.

She could lie, but she doesn't. Her body tells the truth, convulsing as she holds me tighter. "You already know," she says, barely audible, a thread of surrender.

I laugh, low and mean. "I want to hear you beg for it."

I drive myself harder, piston through her until she's all but sobbing, clawing at the sheets and at her own resolve. Then I stop, cruel as a king, and hold myself inside her—motionless, immutable, the only thing she can feel.

Her eyes flutter open, glazed but aware. I pin her sternum flat with my palm, feeling the thunder of her heart. "You ever wonder," I whisper, "how close you really are to giving up?"

She can't answer. I don't need her to. I shift back, slow enough to torture, watching her tremble. "That's the problem with you, Valera," I say, voice soft as a noose. "You never surrender. You just make me work for it."

When she comes, it's a detonation. She arches off the bed, spine bowed, hands locked in my hair. She screams, not my name but something old and wordless and holy. I ride the aftershocks, grinding her to the edge again and again, until my own restraint shatters and I empty myself into her, teeth bared, vision gone white at the edges.

We lie there, not touching. The sex part... that I know how to do. It's everything else that is the problem. The after.

Women never stay long enough for small talk. Sure Michella and I had a place. But I was building Obsidian and I was there more than I was ever in the home we were supposed to be building.

I like my solitude. I like being alone. But, now Opal is here and I don't know what to do with myself.

I wasn't prepared for her to start speaking. "Maris was the only one who ever gave a damn."

I turn my head slightly, watching her without making it obvious. She's not looking at me. Her eyes are firmly fixed on the ceiling. I shift back, looking at the ceiling as well.

"She was kind. Not a fake kind. Not polite for company kind. Just... good."

It's the first time I've ever heard her describe someone that way. It sounds like it's a foreign word in her mouth.

"She used to sneak into my room. Bring me cake. Brush my hair. She never treated me like a placeholder." She blows out a breath. "I ruined that when I tried to burn Stellan to the ground just to prove I was worth something to the woman who never saw me. And now Maris is paying for it."

She stops, takes another deep breath, but there's no tears. I realize if I don't say something now, I never will.

"I didn't have a Maris," I say quietly.

Opal doesn't move, but I know she's listening. Her breath hitches, only just slightly.

"My parents died in a plane crash when I was nineteen. I was in some shit motel room on the Strip. My father kicked me out the moment I turned eighteen. I was no use to him anymore. I went to the funeral. Had to play pretend for all the people mourning two monsters. A lawyer came up to me with a will in one hand and a list of debts in the other."

I flex my jaw. It aches.

"My father built empires with other people's money. My mother was... useful to him in ways I didn't understand until later." I glance up at the ceiling. "He married her young. She was beautiful... and even more desperate. The perfect victim for him to train her to be what he needed. After he secured her, he tried to turn her into something way worse."

Opal's closer now, even if neither of us has moved.

"I don't know if I have siblings. I probably do." I force a breath. "He pimped her out to ever joe schmoe in vegas and beyond. And she stayed. Because what else was she going to do? She tried to love me the way she thought was possible. She tried to protect me from all of it. If he stopped beating her, I was next in line. But when they died... it was just me. Both a relief and some grief."

I let myself crack open what I've kept sealed. "I built walls because no one was coming. Because I learned early that grit is the only thing no one can take."

I pause with a little emphasis on how I'm feeling. "But lately, I've been learning what happens when you let someone in."

She turns to face me. Her voice is low. Barely above a whisper. "So what now?"

Now. The word is tripping me up because I have no idea what will come next.

I shift, facing her fully for the first time since we got in bed. "Now," I say, "we stop pretending we're not in this together."

CHAPTER NINETEEN

Opal

I wake up and see Dante next to me again. This is becoming a regular occurrence that I'm not sure I enjoy.

It's not the sex. God knows that's not the problem. It's the way he stays afterwards. Sleeps as if he's done it a hundred times before. Wakes up next to me as if it's routine.

I just lie here, staring at the ceiling, and wait for the ache in my chest to pick a side—fight or flight.

My phone buzzes against the nightstand, rattling on the wood. I roll over and look at the screen.

Maris. What could she want this early?

"Who is it?" Dante is wiping his eyes and groaning.

"Maris," I say. "Wonder why she's calling.

"Hello?" I answer, already bracing.

There's no voice at first. All I hear is a faint static of the line, a hitched inhale. Another two or three hitches. Wet, shaky. Like she's trying to keep it together and failing.

I ease my voice, careful not to press. "Maris?"

A strangled noise slips out, raw and unguarded—like the moment she lets herself fall apart. I fist the sheet. Something is terribly wrong.

"They're going to take them, Opal."

My stomach drops. "What? What are you talking about?"

Her voice is already in pieces. Frayed from screaming or sobbing. I can't tell which. "Fletcher showed up." Maris's voice cracks, shredded and trembling.

I sit up, every nerve firing on all cylinders. "What the *fuck* are you talking about?"

"He ambushed the custody review. I didn't even know he was coming." Her words come out clipped and breathless. "He had a new lawyer. Slick bastard in a thousand dollar suit, waving around 'evidence' like it was the fucking Bible. Said I was unfit. Manipulative. That I coerced the girls into fearing him."

"Jesus Christ—"

Wait. A thousand-dollar suit?

I blink, and for a second, all I can think is... *how the hell is Fletcher affording that?*

Last I knew, he could barely scrape rent on a two bedroom and couldn't hold down a job that lasted longer than a bottle of cheap whiskey. That kind of legal muscle doesn't come cheap.

"They played a video, Opal. One of me comforting Lenore after a nightmare—*he* spun it as psychological abuse. Said I was planting ideas. Training her to hate him," she continues on.

My stomach flips. "They brought in screenshots from

my support group. Personal shit. Context ripped to hell. Said I was unstable. Dangerous."

I'm already out of bed, yanking on clothes. "Where are the girls?"

She hesitates.

"Maris. *Where are they?*"

She pauses for a moment and I know that I am about to hate what is about to come next. "With Celestine."

Yeah I really hate Fletcher now.

"She filed for emergency placement. Said it was temporary. Told the judge she'd be neutral. That she'd *help.*" Her voice breaks. "It was a lie. She's working with Fletcher."

"That fucking bitch," I breathe.

"She said if I don't sign over joint custody, she'll testify against me. She'll say I'm a threat. That I've damaged them." Maris chokes on the next part. "Lenore begged the judge to stay with me. Rhea cried. They still took them. Said it wasn't safe."

My jaw clenches so tight it hurts.

"She has my daughters, Opal. She *has them.*" Her voice is a sob wrapped in steel. "She's trying to break me."

"No," I say, fury turning my voice to hardened metal. "She wants to punish you for what I did to her. I embarrassed her. And If I don't fix it, she'll take out what I hold dear."

"What do I do?" Maris asks, her voice is so small, I've never heard her sound so helpless. "I don't have anyone left to fight this."

My jaw clenches. *You have me.*

"I need everything," I say. "Every document. Every

statement. Every lie he told that court and whatever bullshit he waved around like proof. Text it. Email it. I don't care. Just get it to me."

A shaky exhale crackles through the line. "Okay."

I'm already dressed and almost ready to go, grabbing my phone and dragging a sweatshirt over my head.

"There's an attorney," I tell her. "Julia Carver. She's cutthroat, and terrifying when pissed off. If she's in town, she'll take this. And if she takes it... Fletcher doesn't stand a fucking chance."

"You'd do that? Even after I ambushed you with my return?"

I freeze at the edge of the bed. The heartbreak in her voice hurts me more than anything Celestine ever managed. "Yes," I say. "Because you're my sister. Because they're *my* nieces. And because if you lose them, I will hunt everyone and anyone until they are in the fucking ground."

"I'll send everything now," she whispers.

"Good." My voice is iron. "We're not letting them win."

I hang up, jaw locked so tight it aches.

Behind me, the sheets rustle. "What happened?"

I don't answer yet because I'm too busy already dialing.

"Opal." Dante is firmer this time. I hear him sit up, but I can't stop.

"Maris is losing the girls," I say, just as the line begins to ring. "Fletcher's trying to take them."

Dante swears under his breath, but I barely hear it.

Julia picks up on the third ring. "Carver."

"It's Opal." I'm trying to keep my anger in check while talking to her. "I need you."

"How bad?"

"My sister's fucking asshole of an ex ambushed the custody review this morning with some self-important shark in a suit. Claimed Maris is unstable. That she coerced her daughters into saying they're afraid of him. The judge bought it. At least enough to grant temporary placement."

"Where are the kids?" she asks.

My stomach knots. "With Celestine."

A beat of stunned silence goes by before she speaks again. "Your mother?"

"Yeah. My mother," I spit. "Fletcher and Celestine are working together now. Maris told her off last week and I've... pissed her off more than usual. She wants to punish us both. So now the girls are in her house, hearing whatever story about Maris she's feeding them, until the final ruling in seventy two hours."

"I'm in Vegas," Julia says. "Send me everything you have. I'll be there in two hours."

The line goes dead. I exhale and look up to find Dante watching me. He's already halfway out of bed, jaw tight, muscles coiled.

"She's coming," I say. "If Celestine thinks she can use my nieces to get her way, then she has no idea who the hell she just picked a fight with."

It's been seventy two hours, and we're ready for court. Or as ready as anyone can be when the stakes are two little girls and a legacy of damage.

Maris stands next to me in the hallway outside the courtroom, her posture straight but fraying at the edges. She's wearing a navy suit, but her hands keep twisting the strap of her bag like she's holding herself together with thread.

"She's in there already," she says, barely above a whisper. "Celestine. With Fletcher."

My jaw tenses. I know. We saw them walk in twenty minutes ago, flanked by that smug little attorney I recognize as the same one who signed my adoption papers. As soon as I found them, I looked him up. I wanted to know every single person involved in placing me with this monster of a woman. Celestine showed up dressed like a martyr and a millionaire. Pearls. Dove gray. The whole act.

"They can play the part," I say. "We brought the truth."

Maris lets out a soft, broken breath, but doesn't fall apart. Not yet. Because she knows I won't let her.

Julia Carver approaches, tablet in hand. Her dark brown hair is swept into a smooth chignon, hazel eyes ready for battle, just uncanny enough to unsettle. She wears slate tones and precise tailoring, minimal jewelry, not a thread out of place. Everything about her is polished but never fussy or calm. She doesn't need to speak to command attention. She is where all eyes are drawn to.

"They're trying to introduce character statements

from her ex husband's network of friends," Julia says flatly. "We're filing an immediate objection. Most of them were conveniently acquired in the last 48 hours and are riddled with inconsistencies."

Maris swallows. "And the girls?"

"Guardianship transfer is still temporary," Julia replies. "But we've got signed statements from the school counselor, pediatrician, and two neighbors all verifying Fletcher's history of instability. If even one part of their campaign cracks, the whole thing starts to unravel."

The courtroom door creaks open behind us.

We turn as the social worker enters, one hand holding each of the girls'.

Lenore spots her first. "Momma!" she cries, voice cracking wide with emotion.

Her pale brown curls bounce as she tears across the tile, loose ringlets flying into her eyes despite someone's attempt to brush them back. She's wearing a soft cream pinafore over a pale pink dress, white tights wrinkled at the ankles, and one shoe slightly untied. Something small and squishy is clutched in her fist—a plush bat, maybe. She bolts from the social worker's side like she was born to run back into Maris's arms.

"Mommy," Rhea says, more withdrawn but nonetheless excited.

Her voice trembles, but her spine doesn't. Long, dark brown curls are pulled into a tight braid she clearly did herself, not a strand out of place. Her coat is deep plum, buttoned to the throat. Underneath it, a navy cardigan and skirt peek out—prim and proper, her version of armor. A small leather journal is clutched to her chest, something she always has and will never let go of.

Her chin is high, but her eyes—hazel green and so painfully neutral—search Maris's face like she's checking for proof it's really her.

Then she follows, one careful step after another. She is always too controlled and measured. The way older kids get when they've been forced to grow up too fast.

Maris drops to her knees before either of them reach her. Her arms open instinctually. Lenore crashes into her with a sob, her tiny hands fisting into the fabric of Maris's coat. Rhea folds herself in slower, but the moment her mother's arms close around her too, her body sags like she's been holding the weight of the world on a nine year old spine.

"I've got you," Maris whispers into their hair. Over and over. "I've got you, I've got you, I've got you." Her voice breaks. And this time, she doesn't fight it. Her shoulders shake with the sobs she's kept caged for seventy two hours of hell.

Neither girl lets go.

It takes a moment before Lenore peeks up, still sniffling. Her cheeks are blotchy, her curls wild from sleep or crying or both.

"Aunty Opal," she says, reaching blindly with one arm.

Rhea turns next. Her eyes—green with flecks of storm —land on me like she's assessing everything. Then she steps forward and hugs me too. Not a child's hug full of joy, but one of sorrow and fear.

I hold them both, one on each side, and I can't

breathe for a second. Because these girls—these two small, breakable people—are what it's all been for. What it will *always* be for.

Another social worker arrives.

She's kind in the way people get when they've learned how to detach without becoming cruel. Early forties. A canvas tote slung over one shoulder that probably holds crayons and granola bars and a thousand small attempts at normalcy.

Rhea notices her immediately. Her shoulders stiffen, journal pressed tighter to her chest. Lenore doesn't understand yet. She's too busy watching a dust mote spin in a sunbeam near the window, humming under her breath.

"Hi, girls," the social worker says softly, crouching to their level. "My name's Erin. We're going to go play in another room for a little bit, okay?"

Lenore blinks. "Like... with toys?"

"Yes," Erin says. "There's coloring books. And juice."

Lenore turns to Maris, uncertainty blooming across her face. "Momma?"

Maris's hands tremble where they rest on her knees. She forces them still.

"I'll be right here," she says, voice steady through sheer force of will. "You're just going to play while the grown ups talk."

Rhea doesn't ask. She steps forward and hands me her journal.

"Hold this," she says quietly. "In case. Momma might need it."

I press it close to my chest and nod my head at her.

This girl is going to be a force to be reckoned with one day, and I cannot feel more privileged to watch it happen. "I will," I promise.

Rhea nods once. Satisfied. Lenore clutches her plush bat, then reaches back and grabs my fingers without asking permission.

"Don't let them keep us," she whispers.

My throat tightens. "I won't," I say.

The social worker gently shepherds them down the hall. Lenore looks back twice. Rhea only once.

Maris exhales like she's been punched in the lungs.

Julia checks her watch. "They'll stay in the playroom unless the judge asks to speak with them. That's standard."

Maris nods, swallowing hard.

"Let's go," Julia says.

The walk to the courtroom feels longer without the girls. Their absence presses against my ribs with every step, like something essential has been removed and the body hasn't caught up yet.

The doors are already open. Voices spill out. They are low, overlapping, inconsequential. Lawyers murmuring. Papers shuffling. The soft scrape of chairs being moved an inch closer to power.

I don't look at any of it as we walk in.Julia doesn't acknowledge anyone. She angles us down the center aisle with quiet authority.

I keep my gaze fixed ahead. Celestine is already seated.

She's sitting in the row behind Fletcher. Her hands are folded, pearls catching the light, expression neutral with her usual practiced restraint. The picture of concern for her granddaughters. The lie she's perfected over decades. How can she care more for their father than her own flesh and blood? Yet still says she cares about her granddaughters.

Fletcher sits beside his lawyer, stiff and coiled. He doesn't look at Maris. His attorney leans in close, whispering with the urgency of someone paid to be convincing.

Good. Let him be afraid.

Julia pauses just long enough to place a hand at the small of Maris's back. A grounding touch. Permission to breathe.

Then we sit. I fold my hands in my lap and still them by force. Control is the only thing that belongs to me here.

The bailiff moves, "All rise."

I am going to be sick. I push down the bile that is rising in my throat.

The room shifts as one body. The door behind the bench opens and in comes the judge. She's in her mid-fifties if I had to guess. I can tell by the way she looks around the room that she can read each and every person in this space. She's not only going to be looking at the physical evidence, she's going to look at the way we're acting. who is genuine, who is playing a part. Who is lying.

The judge enters.

Mid fifties. Female. She takes in the room in a single, efficient sweep—who's sitting where, who's standing, who looks rehearsed and who looks terrified.

She takes her seat.

"Be seated."

The room obeys. Just like that, there's nowhere left to hide.

The judge adjusts the files in front of her. She doesn't look up right away. Let the paper speak first. She does a bit of reading of all the new evidence that was added.

"This is a continued emergency custody review," she says at last. "Temporary placement was granted seventy two hours ago based on allegations of emotional instability, coercive behavior, and risk of parental alienation."

Her eyes lift. They land on Fletcher. "Those are serious claims," she continues. "And they require serious proof."

She turns to Julia. "Ms. Carver. You may proceed."

Julia steps forward, unhurried. Folder in hand and voice calm enough to be lethal.

"Thank you, Your Honor. We're asking the court to dissolve the temporary placement order and immediately reinstate primary physical custody to Ms. Morland."

Fletcher's attorney rises halfway. "Your Honor—"

"You'll wait," the judge says, eyes still on Julia.

Julia doesn't glance at Fletcher. Not once.

"The emergency order was granted based on three representations," she says. "That my client is emotionally unstable. That she manipulated her children into fearing their father. And that the temporary guardian would act as a neutral party."

She pauses. "All three claims are demonstrably false."

She taps the button on the remote for the tv to switch screens. "Exhibit A: sworn statements from the children's school counselor and pediatrician. Both document long term anxiety patterns linked to Mr. Morland's behavior—missed visitations, raised voice incidents, and emotional withdrawal—not maternal influence."

The judge reads as Julia continues on.

"Exhibit B: visitation logs covering the past eighteen months. Missed exchanges. Last minute cancellations. Extended gaps followed by sudden urgency once custody was challenged."

Fletcher shifts in his seat. Julia keeps going.

"And Exhibit C," she says evenly, "text communications between Mr. Morland and the temporary guardian, Ms. Celestine Greer, coordinating the emergency filing and discussing leverage over my client."

Fletcher's attorney stands. "Your Honor, these messages are being taken out of context—"

"Sit," the judge snaps. "You'll speak when I tell you to."

Julia turns to the next slide. "Ms. Greer explicitly threatens adverse testimony unless Ms. Morland agrees to joint custody. That is coercive conduct. It invalidates the emergency placement."

The judge looks at Celestine. "Ms. Greer," she says, voice clipped. "Is this your phone number?"

"Yes."

"Did you send these messages?"

Celestine smiles thinly. "Out of concern—"

"I didn't ask why."

The smile falters. The judge nods once and turns back to Julia. "Anything further?"

Julia doesn't hesitate.

"No, Your Honor," she says. "Nothing further at this time."

Fletcher's attorney steps forward. "Your Honor, if I may briefly respond—"

The judge nods once. "Briefly."

"Much of what opposing counsel has characterized as missed visitation occurred only after Ms. Morland chose to relocate out of state," he says smoothly. "My client remained in Arizona. The distance made consistent visitation—"

Julia turns her head.

"No," she says calmly.

The attorney stiffens. "Excuse me?"

"That is not accurate," Julia continues, tone even. "And since counsel has chosen to raise it, the record should be corrected."

The judge looks back to her. "Go on."

Julia taps her tablet once.

"Mr. Morland informed Ms. Morland, prior to her relocation, that he had secured employment in Las Vegas," she says. "He encouraged the move so the children could remain in one school district and represented that he would follow within six weeks."

The judge's gaze sharpens. "Is that correct?"

"Yes, Your Honor," Julia replies. "We have emails and text messages confirming it." She hands the clerk a document.

"Mr. Morland did not follow," Julia continues. "Because he lost that job before the move was complete."

Fletcher shifts hard in his seat.

"And he failed to disclose that fact," Julia adds,

"while allowing my client to relocate under false pretenses. He then cited the resulting distance as evidence of obstruction."

Fletcher's attorney opens his mouth. Closes it.

The judge looks directly at Fletcher.

"Mr. Morland," she asks, "did you tell Ms. Morland you had secured employment in Las Vegas prior to her relocation?"

He did. Heard that Stellan was planning on hiring him to help Maris out, but when he found out about the abuse, he took the offer back. He wasn't about to help someone who was so good at hiding his true colors.

"Yes," Fletcher mutters.

"And did you inform her you had lost that job before she moved?" The judge asks.

"No." Fletcher grimaces out.

The judge exhales slowly, writing something down.

"So the mother relocated based on your stated intent to co parent locally," she says. "You did not follow through. And you now argue that the consequences of your own misrepresentation should be held against her."

She looks back at Fletcher's attorney. "That argument is rejected. Anything else?"

"Yes," Julia says. She's about to show everyone why you don't screw with Julia Carver. "We're requesting sanctions."

That's when Fletcher laughs. "That's ridiculous," he says. "This whole thing is a setup."

His attorney hisses his name a little too late.

"Mr. Morland," the judge says, "you are not recognized to speak."

Fletcher stands anyway. Maris flinches. How can anyone not see that she is a victim after this?

I feel it in my spine. This is the moment he doesn't know how to stop.

"She does this," Fletcher snaps, pointing at Maris. "She twists everything. Plays the victim. That's how she poisoned them against me."

"Sit down," the judge orders.

He doesn't.

"She coached them," he insists. "Filled their heads with bullshit. That older one—" He shakes his head. "She's manipulative already. Just like her mother."

The room goes dead silent. The judge stands.

"Bailiff." The bailiff steps forward instantly.

"Escort Mr. Morland back to his seat."

Fletcher jerks his arm away. "This is a fucking joke."

"Sir," the bailiff warns.

Fletcher points again, voice loud now. Too loud. Maris covers her ears.

"You think you've won?" he snarls at Maris. "They'll see it eventually. You always ruin people."

The judge turns to the court reporter. "Strike the last statement," she says calmly. "Note the father's demeanor."

She looks back at Fletcher. "This outburst confirms the court's concerns."

Fletcher's attorney grabs his sleeve. "Sit down. Now."

Fletcher does. But it's over.

The judge faces Julia again. "Based on the evidence presented," she says, "and the father's conduct in this courtroom, the court finds that unsupervised contact presents an emotional risk to the children."

Fletcher's head snaps up. "You can't—"

"Primary physical custody is restored to Ms. Morland effective immediately," the judge continues. "All visitation is suspended pending a full psychological evaluation, anger management assessment, and further order of this court."

Maris gasps. Her knees buckle. I catch her elbow.

The judge doesn't slow down. "Any attempt to contact the children outside approved channels will be considered harassment."

She turns to Fletcher's attorney.

"Given counsel's failure to disclose material conflicts and the submission of misleading emergency evidence, this court orders sanctions."

The attorney stiffens.

"A formal reprimand will be entered," the judge says. "And counsel will pay reasonable attorney's fees incurred as a result of this filing."

Julia inclines her head. Just slightly. "Thank you, Your Honor."

Fletcher slams his hand on the bench. "This is bullshit—"

"That's enough," the judge says. "Another word and you'll be held in contempt."

Silence. Good and peaceful silence.

The gavel strikes. "We are adjourned."

Maris rises and hugs Julia. Fletcher Moreland isn't getting what he wants for probably the first time in his entire life.

Things are going our way for once.

CHAPTER TWENTY

Opal

It's been forty eight hours since the ruling.

Maris insisted on driving herself and the girls home. They needed to spend some time together. Apparently the girls were traumatized during their time with Celestine. Not even a little bit surprised by that. I've been traumatized by her my whole life.

We're now working on coding the anagram we got.

Stellan is already gone—pulled into another meeting, another fire to contain. Dante never left Obsidian after the staff meeting this morning. He has more work that he needs to do.

That leaves the office just to us. Frankie came for lunch, but needed to head back to The Dutch Wall to help with the afternoon shift.

Maris stands near the window at first, arms folded loosely, gaze tracking the Strip far below like she's grounding herself. She's lost in thought, still stuck in the courtroom. Fletcher hasn't left her alone in the last couple of days. She may need to consider a restraining order if she doesn't get rid of him.

Talia moves with more certainty, already approaching the workstation to get started on the next thing we need to work on.

I take Stellan's chair. It's the best angle for looking at the screens.

"We're not starting from scratch," I say, waking the screens with my fingerprint. "We're finishing something that already wants to exist."

Maris turns from the glass. "The anagram."

"The structure behind it," I correct. "The anagram is just the surface."

Talia steps closer, eyes flicking across the data as it loads. "You said the language was wrong," she says. "Not inaccurate. Misplaced."

"Yes," I reply. "Like it was written to be recognized by someone who knows what it's supposed to sound like... but not by someone who actually reads it."

"That's... very specific," Talia says.

"It is," I agree. I glance at Maris. "This is why I brought her in," I say.

Maris stiffens slightly. She still isn't used to being named as an asset instead of a liability. "She doesn't solve puzzles by forcing them," I continue. "She listens to how they were built. Especially when language is involved."

Maris looks back at the screen, not at me. "Because literature isn't about words," she says quietly. "It's about rhythm. What's supposed to be there. And what's missing."

I pull the extracted text back onto the main display. Letters only. No images or numbers.

"We already pulled one configuration," I say. "Now we teach the system how to find the rest."

Maris comes to my side, close enough that I can feel the heat of her arm through her blazer. She scans the strings without touching anything. She never rushes in. That's always been her strength.

"These clusters," she says after a moment. "They repeat, but not identically. They're being protected. Someone wanted them to survive rearrangement."

"Proper nouns," I say.

"And values," Talia adds quietly. "Words someone wouldn't sacrifice. Not names. They are beliefs of some sort."

I glance at her. "Like?"

Maris leans in, close enough now that her breath fogs the edge of the glass. "Wait," she says. "Run it again. Slower."

I adjust the output, letting the reconstructed strings scroll line by line instead of collapsing into data blocks.

She reads silently at first. Then her lips move. Barely.

"'Order is the first necessity,'" she murmurs. "That's not a proverb. That's Carlyle. From *Past and Present*."

Talia looks at her sharply. Maris keeps going.

"'A place for everything, and everything in its place.' That's often misattributed, but it's from early Victorian conduct manuals. Domestic hierarchy disguised as virtue."

I feel a cold satisfaction settle in my chest.

She scrolls again.

"'Character is fate.'" Maris lets out a short breath. "Heraclitus filtered through nineteenth-century moralism. That phrase shows up constantly in finishing school readers. It teaches inevitability. If you suffer, it's because you are wrong."

She stops the scroll with two fingers.

"And this—" Her voice tightens. "'We are afraid to care too much, for fear that the other person does not care at all.'"

I recognize it.

"Austen," I say.

"Yes," Maris replies. "But not *Persuasion*. It's *Mansfield Park*. And not even the whole sentence. Just the restraint. Never the consequence."

Talia's arms fold slowly. "They stripped the rebellion out."

"They always do," Maris says, the smirk on her face brings a smile to mine. She's starting to come back to herself. "They take literature that wrestles with power and reduce it to obedience."

She scrolls again. "Burke," she continues. "But only the parts about continuity. Tradition. Reverence for inheritance. None of the warnings about corruption."

Another line. "Smiles," she says. "*Self Help*. But different. Success framed as moral worth. Failure as personal flaw."

She looks up at me then. "This anagram isn't random," she says. "It's a syllabus."

"A syllabus for what?" Talia asks.

"For teaching people how to exist inside hierarchy without questioning it," Maris replies. "Every quote here reinforces the same belief. Power is natural, resistance is crude, and suffering is a personal failing."

I glance back at the screen.

"And the cadence?" I ask.

"That's the tell," Maris says. "Real literature argues with itself. These excerpts don't. They've been curated to agree. To soothe. To tell you the world is already ordered correctly."

She exhales slowly.

"This is elite conditioning," she says. "The kind taught young. Repeated until it stops sounding like ideology and starts sounding like culture."

I start adjusting the filters, feeding the system new parameters.

"Then we're not just decoding communication," I say. "We're mapping belief."

Maris nods. "And personal belief systems always reuse the same books."

Talia squints her eyes. "Which means they also reuse the same blind spots."

I let the code run again, now listening for cadence instead of content. The screen stutters. Rebuilds.

This time the phrases don't seem like an anagram but something real.

Maris inhales. "Oh," she murmurs.

Talia glances at her. "You hear it too?"

Maris steps closer to the screen, eyes narrowing—not confused, but focused. Like she's tuning an instrument. "This isn't classical anymore," she says.

I glance at her. "Meaning?"

She lifts a finger, tracing a line of text in the air. "Joan

Didion," she says immediately. "Not quoted directly, but the rhythm. The emotional distance. That clean cruelty where observation replaces judgment."

She shifts to the next cluster.

"And this," she continues, "is Zadie Smith. Fragmented identity. Authority questioned through voice instead of plot."

Talia's brow furrows. "That's very specific."

Maris nods. "Because it's taught that way."

She scrolls farther, faster now. "This section borrows from post 9/11 essay culture," she says. "Didion, Sontag, early Atwood nonfiction. Power framed as something you survive by understanding the story it tells about itself." She pauses. "And here—this is Baldwin. Moral clarity without mercy. The insistence that systems rot from the inside, not the edges."

My fingers are still on the desk. "This isn't casual reading," I say quietly.

"No," Maris agrees. "Not for most. Whoever this is enjoys all types of reading apparently." She straightens, turning to look at me fully now. "Someone was trained to think this way," she continues. "To analyze power through narrative fracture. To believe language *creates* reality, not just describes it."

Talia folds her arms. "So whoever wrote this believes control is linguistic."

"And intimate," Maris adds. "They don't just want obedience. They want belief."

The code finishes its pass. The final output settles into something eerily smooth.

I stare at it. Modern. Confident. Dangerous in its restraint.

"This is the voice of someone who learned that power doesn't announce itself anymore," Maris says softly. "It *curates*."

Because now I see it too. The one piece of the puzzle that I just couldn't see. I don't know the culprit yet. But we are getting really close.

The door opens. I look up towards it. Dante and Stellan walk in together.

"What did we miss?" Dante asks.

I swivel the screen toward them. "Enough to matter."

Stellan steps closer, eyes already scanning the output. "Talk."

"This isn't encryption," I say. "It's literary encoding."

Dante's jaw tightens. "In English."

I don't blink. "It means the leak wasn't written to hide. It was written to be recognized."

Maris straightens beside me. "By someone trained to hear language instead of read it."

Stellan's gaze snaps to her.

"The structure tracks education," I continue. "Classical obedience frameworks first. Institutional theory next. Modern narrative control last."

"Progression," Stellan says.

"Curriculum," Maris corrects.

Dante looks back at the screen. "So this is one person."

"Yes," I say. "Not a group. Not a system."

"And not accidental," Stellan adds.

"No," I confirm. "Deliberate. Personal."

Dante exhales once. "Can you trace it?"

"Not yet," I say. "But we're close."

Maris gestures at a cluster of text. "These modern fragments—Didion, Baldwin, post structural essay theory. Someone who learned power as narrative management."

Stellan goes still. "That narrows the field."

"Drastically," I say. "Elite programs. Controlled access. Society adjacent."

Dante's voice drops. "So whoever's doing this thinks they're invisible."

"They always do," I reply.

Stellan looks at me then. His look is direct and assessing. "Be careful, Opal." I meet his stare. "You may be more dangerous than the men trying to destroy him."

I don't argue. I turn back to the screen. "We're getting really close. I can feel it."

"Fuck," Stellan says. "I think Opal may be more dangerous than any enemy we've ever faced before. I'm glad she's on our side this time."

"Careful," Dante replies dryly. "She hates being *managed*."

I don't look up. I'm already moving pieces.

"What are you doing now?" Dante asks, leaning over my shoulder. The smell of his cologne grounds me, the tension in my shoulders loosens before I realize they were that tight.

"Playing," I say.

Stellan's mouth twitches. "That's never comforting when it's you."

"I'm playing *their* game," I clarify. "They spoke first. I'm just answering."

My fingers fly across the keyboard now, fast and precise. This isn't digging. It's composition. I rearrange cadence, snap phrases into place, bend syntax until meaning follows what this person wants. Letters scatter, reassemble, fracture again. I don't need brute force. I need rhythm. I need recognition. I let the message take shape the way a threat does when it's dressed like intelligence. Implied. Elegant. Impossible to ignore.

Dante leans closer. "Answering how?"

"In literary terms," I say. "They think in references. Authority through citation. Power through implication." I pause, then add, "So I'm sending a message they'll recognize."

Stellan folds his arms. "You're taunting them."

"I'm identifying myself," I correct. "There's a difference."

Dante arches a brow.

"Maybe," I say, fingers still moving. "Maybe a little taunting will be involved."

Maris snorts softly. "You're not even pretending this isn't personal."

"It's not personal," I reply. "It's professional curiosity. They wanted to be clever. I'm just letting them know I noticed."

Stellan shakes his head once, half amused, half wary. "You're leaving a signature."

"Yes," I say. "But only for someone arrogant enough to recognize it." My fingers don't slow as I type.

Maris steps closer, eyes flicking over the new string as it resolves. Her lips part. Then she laughs—soft, surprised, delighted.

“Oh,” she says. “That’s vicious.”

Dante looks at her. “Read it.”

The text resolves into a single paragraph.

I stop typing. On the screen, the message sits pretending to be literature.

The author is not dead. She is watching you misquote her. Power prefers mirrors to witnesses, and those who believe themselves unseen mistake silence for consent. We tell ourselves stories in order to live, but you have mistaken the story for control. Elegance is not innocence. Citation is not camouflage. You were never invisible. You were simply unchallenged.

Dante stares at it for a beat. “What’s it from?”

Maris smiles, slow and delighted, already stepping closer.

“Multiple places,” she says. “That’s the point.”

She taps the screen lightly.

“‘The author is not dead’ is Barthes, reversed. Death of the Author, but she’s resurrecting it on purpose. She’s saying authorship still matters when someone is watching.” She moves down the paragraph. “‘Power prefers mirrors to witnesses’ is pure Foucault. Surveillance theory. Self policing dressed up as elegance.” Her finger shifts again. “Those who believe themselves unseen mistake silence for consent’ is Baldwin. Essays. Moral clarity weaponized.”

She exhales, almost laughing. “‘We tell ourselves stories in order to live’ is Didion, but twisted. She turns survival into accusation.”

She looks up at me now, eyes bright. “And the rest isn’t quoted. It’s synthesis. Atwood’s nonfiction cadence.

Power pretending to be taste. Control calling itself refinement."

Stellan mutters, "Jesus."

Maris nods. "It's a calling card. Whoever's doing this will recognize themselves immediately."

Dante looks at me. "You didn't threaten them."

"No," I say. "I corrected them."

Maris grins. "Anyone who hides behind literature hates being told they read it wrong."

I save the file. "They wanted to feel clever," I say.

"And what happens when they read it?" Dante asks.

I finally lean back in the chair. "They'll panic," I say. "Because now they know the game isn't anonymous anymore."

Stellan shakes his head once, half impressed, half unsettled. "You didn't block them. You didn't trace them."

"No," I say. "I let them feel seen. Then they will answer, make a mistake, and leave it open to being traced."

Maris's smile widens. "Anyone who hides behind literature hates being corrected."

Dante's gaze lingers on me, dark and intent. "You just challenged them to respond."

"Yes," I agree. "And they will."

"Why are you so sure?" Stellan asks.

Because people who think they're clever can't resist proving it.

"Because I didn't threaten them," I say. "I insulted their reading comprehension."

Maris laughs again, full and bright. "God help them."

I stand, shutting the system down.

"They wanted a story," I say. "Now they know they're in one."

Somewhere out there, someone just realized they were never writing alone.

Now we wait to see who can't resist writing back.

CHAPTER TWENTY-ONE

Dante

Rosebud doesn't feel like Obsidian.

That's the first thing I notice standing in the middle of Opal's office.

She doesn't hide herself from everyone else.

Opal's office opens straight into the rest of the floor, glass and sightlines instead of walls. Screens are visible from angles they shouldn't be. People move in and out without needing to open random doors, without asking permission. Nothing here is sealed off from the rest of the room.

It's the opposite of my office in Obsidian.

My office is designed to keep the world out. Velvet, mirrors, controlled lighting, doors that close and stay closed. Everything is curated. Everything contained.

There's no performance here. No velvet, no mirrors, no closed doors hiding me from the rest of the world.

This is where the real work happens.

Opal is at the main workstation, sleeves rolled up, hair pulled back tight. It's the posture of someone who doesn't expect to be interrupted and won't stop if she is. Talia leans against the edge of the desk, arms crossed, attention fixed on the screen. Stellan sits next to her, arm wrapped around her shoulders. Maris sits a few feet away, notebook open, pen resting between her fingers.

The rest of Rosebud is out on a job.

Everyone here is intentional. No one is talking. But it's not a suffocating silence. It's just a fact, respected, that they only talk when they need to. There's no need to fill the silence, there's no need for mindless chatter.

We've been running the protocol Opal built since we arrived. So far, nothing. Which tells me whoever built this understands restraint.

Then one of the secondary monitors flickers. Opal stills. I see it in the way her shoulders tighten before the system even finishes parsing.

"That's new," she says quietly.

She brings it up on the main screen.

A block of text appears. Stripped of identifiers. No metadata. No source trail. Dropped somewhere it shouldn't exist at all.

I read it once. Something about it tickles my brain. I read it again.

Through me the way into the suffering city. Through me the way into eternal pain. Abandon hope, all who enter —for some gates are crossed only once.

Maris's pen starts moving immediately, copying the lines down. Halfway through, she stops.

"...That's not right," she says.

Talia glances over. "Not right how?"

Maris frowns, rereads the text, before she shakes her head. "It's Dante. Inferno. Canto III. But it's wrong."

Opal turns. "Wrong as in inaccurate?"

"Wrong as in altered," Maris says. "It's stitched. Paraphrased. The cadence is off. Whoever wrote this knows the reference, but not the structure."

She underlines the last line twice.

Abandon hope, all who enter—for some gates are crossed only once.

"This part especially. That sentence doesn't exist like this. I don't understand. The author has kept cadence even if the words didn't match... but this is not either."

I don't need the explanation. I already know.

My chest goes tight as I remember why I know that quote.

Michella used to quote Inferno at me. It made her feel smart. Even if she always quoted it slightly wrong. I looked it up one day. It was not the same words. Except these match the ones she would say. I can hear her voice in the phrasing, hear the way she'd linger on abandon hope like it was a promise instead of a warning.

"This isn't the author," I say.

Opal looks at me. "You're sure."

"Yes."

Opal doesn't hesitate. "Michella."

Maris nods once, as if the name simply completes the thought. "The reference isn't meant to communicate. It's meant to *signal*. To someone specific."

Maris's eyes flick to me."You recognize it."

"I do," I reply. "She always quoted it when she wanted to feel powerful. Never when she actually was."

Opal folds her arms. "So the author wants us looking at her."

"Yes," I say. "Because Michella *is* involved."

Talia tilts her head. "But not like this."

"No," I reply. "She's behind some of the media leaks. The stories that hit my reputation first. The kind that rely on getting noticed without fingers pointing."

Maris listens, expression intent. "She wants you back."

"Exactly," I say. "That's her terrain."

Opal's gaze turns to me. "But she didn't steal my code."

"No," I say. "Michella's an idiot, but not a useless one. She has a talent for twisting things just enough to make people feel sorry for her. She knows how to cry at the right time, leak the right half of a story, and let the public finish the lie for her. That's instinct, not intelligence. She doesn't plan outcomes. She reacts and then rides the wave like it was intentional. It works on crowds. It doesn't work on systems. And it definitely doesn't work on Opal."

Opal tilts her head, thoughtful. "So she survives on sympathy and borrowed depth."

"She thrives on it," I say. "Like mold."

Opal snorts before she can stop herself, then looks at me. "You dated mold."

"I was young," I reply, kissing the top of her head. "And distracted by ambition."

Maris makes a quiet choking sound behind us.

Opal's mouth curves. "That's generous."

"I'm being kind," I say. "She never once planned anything through. If a complete shitshow worked in her favor, she would claim it. If it didn't, she cried until someone else fixed it."

Opal glances back at the screen. "So if she tried to touch my work—"

"She'd break it," I say. "Then blame the system."

Maris laughs openly now. "I feel like I just watched a divorce, and I wasn't even there for it."

Opal finally looks at me, eyes amused. "You have terrible taste."

"I improved," I say.

The words knock everyone in the room off their kilter. I don't know where that came from.

Opal holds my gaze, something unreadable flickering behind her eyes.

Maris clears her throat, very deliberately. "Wow. Okay."

I exhale through my nose and look back at the screen. "That wasn't—"

"Necessary?" Opal offers, still amused.

"Planned," I correct.

Her mouth curves. "That happens sometimes."

Maris taps her pen against her notebook, smiling to herself. "I'm going to pretend I didn't just witness character growth in real time."

I ignore her. But I don't take it back either.

Maris exhales slowly. "Okay. I'm just going to say it."

Opal doesn't look at her. "I don't think you should."

"Oh, I absolutely should." Maris tilts her notebook against her knee. "Because if you two get any closer without acknowledging what's happening, one of you is going to trip over it."

Talia hums in agreement. "That's accurate."

I glance at both of them. "We're working."

"Yes," Talia says, calm and unbothered. "And you're also flirting. Poorly, I might add. Opal, blink twice if you need help."

Opal finally turns, brows lifting. "Noted. but we are definitely not flirting poorly. if anything I'd say we're quite good at it."

Maris snorts out a huff of laughter andraises the notebook slightly. "You just bonded over mutual disdain, shared history, and personal growth. That's foreplay in most cultures."

I open my mouth.

"You're aligned," Talia cuts in. "You trust each other. You're finishing each other's thoughts." She pauses. "You're also both pretending that's incidental."

Opal scoffs, turning back to the screen. "This is strategic compatibility."

"Of course it is." Maris smiles sweetly. "And I'm here strictly for the literature."

"This is not—" I start.

"Romantic?" Maris supplies. "No. Obviously not. It just sounds exactly like every couple I've ever known right before they admit it."

Opal glances at me, something warm in her eyes. "Ignore them."

"I intend to."

"You won't," Maris says cheerfully.

Talia folds her arms, satisfied. "Good. Now that we've acknowledged the obvious, can we return to figuring out what the hell is going on here.

Opal turns back to the screen.

She's smiling.

And I don't miss it.

Three days since the author sent us Michella. We've heard nothing since.

Michella is in hiding. It doesn't help that the author sold her out, but I think it was how Opal handled the gala. She made it impossible for Michella to get away with anything.

Opal is working on another case that needs her attention tonight. That leaves me at the club.

I find myself leaving operations in Lucrezia and Manny's capable hands more and more often.

Tonight, Alessio is heading over. We haven't seen each other since I got married. Life has been busy, and he went back to Italy for reasons he never explained.

The Bianchi family is an enigma in Vegas. They may be one of the most powerful families in the underground, but they're also some of the best people. Unless you fuck them over. Or piss them off.

They are protective of family. And I'm lucky enough to be part of that.

Massimo Bianchi has been my surrogate father since I was twelve. He hated my father and never let that be a secret.

The velvet rope lifts. Giving access to Massimo as he opens his arms and pulls me into a hug that's firm and familiar, one hand pressing briefly at the back of my neck the way it always did when I was younger. "You look well," he says.

"I am," I reply. This time, I mean it in a different way.

Alessio steps in right after, grinning, and claps a hand on my shoulder before pulling me into a rougher embrace. "It's good to see you," he says, and there's nothing joking about it.

"Good to see you, too," I say. It surprises me how much I mean that.

Massimo sits first. Alessio stays standing, restless in the way he's always been when something matters. I notice immediately.

Massimo looks at me over the rim of his glass that a waitress set in front of him. Everyone knows what he likes now. "I want to talk to you about something."

I raise a brow. "That sounds ominous."

"It's not," he says. "But it is important."

I glance at Alessio. "Who did you kill?"

Alessio snorts. "No one. Yet."

Massimo ignores him. "Alessio and Lucrezia."

It takes a second to realize he's not stating the obvious. He's asking for something. "What about them?" I ask.

"They want to get married."

Holy shit. Pretty much the last thing I was expecting to hear tonight. I look back at Alessio. He doesn't look away. But he doesn't grin this time. He's not being ridiculous. In fact, he is being serious for once.

I lean back slightly trying to process what's going on.

They've been together for years. It's always been a need to know relationship. Lucrezia has always moved through his world and made friends with the Bianchi family. I never questioned it. They've always been perfect for each other.

But marriage is different.

Marriage means permanence. Something I never thought Alessio would want.

"And you're telling me," I say slowly, "because?"

"Because she's yours," Massimo says simply. "And he's mine. This crosses both lines."

He's not wrong. Lucrezia isn't just staff. She's family. I've been her guardian in every way that matters since she was barely more than eighteen. I've protected her, backed her, trusted her with pieces of my empire I don't hand to anyone lightly.

I don't doubt Alessio. That said, I need to know.

"I need to talk to her," I say.

Alessio nods immediately. "Of course."

I don't waste time and tap the comm in my ear. "Lucrezia."

She answers instantly. "If this is about the east bar inventory, I already fixed it."

"I'm in VIP," I say. "With Massimo and Alessio."

She pauses for a fraction of a section. "...Right now?"

"Yes."

There's a pause. Then a soft, knowing exhale. "On my way."

I love that I do not need to ask her to come up. She just knows exactly what I want by my tone.

Alessio looks... nervous. That tells me everything I need to know. He loves her.

"This isn't an interrogation," I say to him. "But it is a conversation."

"I know," he replies. "I just want her to choose me. In a way that we are not going to be able to hide for much longer."

Good answer.

Lucrezia steps into the VIP area and everything that she tries to harden instantly loosens up.

Her eyes find Alessio instantly. She crosses the room without hesitation and kisses him like it's just another Tuesday morning. Her fingers curl into his jacket like she's anchoring herself there. He exhales, a sound halfway between relief and joy.

When she pulls back, she murmurs something low in his ear. He smiles. Not the one he puts on for the crowd. The real one.

"You called," she says, turning to look at me. This is probably the one time I don't feel slightened by being ignored at first.

"I did. Sit."

She does, but Alessio stays where he is. She reaches for his hand without looking, their fingers lacing together like muscle memory. Massimo watches them with open pride.

"You told me years ago," I say. "About the two of you."

She nods once. "I didn't need permission."

"No," I reply. "You needed trust."

"I had it," she says quietly.

"Yes," I say. "You did."

Marriage is the word no one says, but it's in the room now.

"I know what this changes," Lucrezia says. "Visibility. Risk. Expectation." Alessio tightens his grip on her hand. "I've lived in rooms where love is treated like something that could be exploited in every way. Where trust became a weakness," she continues. "I never let it be one."

I glance at Alessio. "You know who you're standing next to. Someone more powerful and has more balls than you will ever have."

"She doesn't shrink," Alessio says, like it's obvious.

Lucrezia glances at him, amused. "Did you ever think I would?"

He smiles. "Once. Very briefly. Learned my lesson."

She bumps her shoulder into his. "Good."

"She doesn't bend either," he adds.

Lucrezia hums. "Well you love when I bend for you."

Gross. Don't need to know that.

"I do," he says easily. "Saves time when we're in a pinch."

She laughs under her breath, eyes warm now. "I get louder when I'm ignored."

Alessio's gaze drops to her mouth. "I've noticed."

"And more dangerous," she adds, clearly enjoying herself.

"That's my favorite version," he says. "The one that scares everyone else."

Massimo chuckles softly.

I lean back, decision already made. "You don't need my permission," I say. "But you have my blessing."

Something in Lucrezia eases. She stands and kisses my cheek. "Thank you."

Then she turns back to Alessio. He lets go of her hand only long enough to reach into his pocket. He drops to one knee like it's always been his plan.

Lucrezia freezes. For the first time since I've known her, she looks stunned.

"Lucrezia Verraldi," Alessio says quietly, voice rough. "I've chosen you every day for years. I want to choose you where the world can see it now."

He opens his hand. The ring is simple. Yet so elegant. It's perfect for her.

"Marry me."

Her breath leaves her in a soft laugh. "Yes," she says immediately, pulling him up by the collar and kissing him hard. "Obviously yes."

Massimo laughs, wide and unguarded.

I give them three seconds of pure bliss before I clear my throat. "Just so we're clear, you're not stealing her from me."

Lucrezia pauses mid-kiss and looks at me flatly. "Excuse you?"

Alessio doesn't hesitate. "Absolutely not. I value my life."

She snorts.

"She's still my right hand," I continue. "Still runs Obsidian like an army bootcamp."

"I don't answer to you," Lucrezia says sweetly.

"You correct me aggressively," I reply. "Which is worse."

Alessio grins. "She does that at home too."

"That's marriage," Massimo offers.

I point at Alessio. "You're marrying her. You're not relocating her. If she starts living in Italy, I'll burn something of yours that is very expensive."

Alessio lifts his hands. "She's not going anywhere. I wouldn't dare."

Lucrezia leans into him, pleased. "Good answer."

I nod. "Smart man."

She slips her hand into his jacket pocket. "Relax, boss. I'm not leaving."

"I know," I say. "If you did, the building would collapse around us."

She beams. Alessio kisses her temple.

This has been a wonderful night. Until our earpieces go off. The comm in my ear crackles once. Manny's voice cuts through the chatter. "Dante. We've got a problem."

I don't answer yet. I'm waiting for him to tell me what happened.

"Alex," Manny says. "He grabbed Sofia near the west bar. Dragged her toward the service exit."

How the fuck did that little asshole slip by? We didn't plan for a trap. I thought we got rid of him. "How did he get in? Where did he enter from? His face was plastered everywhere on the system. He should've been spotted."

He shouldn't have been able to get within ten feet of the entrance before he was caught.

"South corridor," Manny responds. "Went through the service bar and kitchen to get to where Sofia is. Caught her on break and tried to take her."

"How many people have come across him since entering?"

"Two security and four servers," Manny responds immediately.

"I want them all fired," I say to him.

My phone vibrates in my hand before I even ask for more.

OPAL

Alex. South corridor. Manny's on him.
They have eyes.

Good. She saw it too.

"He didn't make it out," Manny adds. "We've got him."

I stop walking. Lucrezia is already standing.

"Who," Alessio asks.

"Alex Knight," I reply. "He put his hands on Sofia. Again."

Alessio's expression goes flat. Massimo exhales slowly through his nose, the way he does when someone has made a terminal mistake.

Lucrezia doesn't raise her voice. She just reaches for Alessio, pulls him down, and kisses him once.

"I'll handle the club," she says. Already turning. "Lock it down. Staff stays calm. Sofia doesn't leave my sight."

She looks back at the three of us, eyes cold now.

"You take care of Alex," she adds. "Permanently. This time."

No one argues. No one needs clarification.

Massimo adjusts his cufflinks, calm as ever. "Sloppy," he says. "In my son's house."

Alessio rolls his shoulders once, loosening tension the way a man does before violence. "I liked tonight better before this."

"So did Alex," I say, already heading for the private staircase. "He just doesn't know it yet."

My phone buzzes again.

OPAL

I'm keeping tabs on everything. Manny brought him to the room. Figured you want to take care of him. Tell Alessio and Massimo hello for me. Let me know if you need anything. Also, contacted Timothy and let him know you'd need clean up when you're done. He said text him whenever.

I don't reply. I do chuckle though. Weird to see the side of Opal when she's on your side.

Alex dragged a woman out of my club. Tonight, he learns the punishment that goes with that.

Alexander James Knight does not realize how far he has already fallen until the lights of Las Vegas disappear completely.

At first, he assumes this is intimidation. The SUV is blacked out, soundproofed, moving smoothly through traffic that thins into open highway and then into desert. No one speaks. No radio hums. The silence stretches long enough to make his breathing sound intrusive.

He tries anyway. "This is a mistake," he says, voice rough with panic. "I didn't hurt anyone. I swear."

No one answers.

Massimo sits across from him, posture relaxed, hands

folded neatly in his lap as if this were a business meeting he has attended many times before. Alessio faces forward, eyes on the road, expression unreadable. I sit beside Alex, close enough that he can feel my presence without my having to touch him.

When the vehicle turns off the main road and onto gravel, Alex finally goes quiet.

The facility is low, unmarked, and partially buried into the desert rock. There are no windows. The doors open without resistance, admitting us into air that smells faintly of disinfectant and cold stone.

Timothy is waiting when the doors open.

"Scan," he says.

Timothy's eyes flick briefly to Alex. "He's not coming back out."

"Not this time," I reply.

"That's what I thought."

The inner gate unlocks. Timothy steps aside, he knows he doesn't need to lead us to our bunker. We know the way.

"I'll start cleanup when you're done," he says, already turning away.

The gate seals behind us.

The bunker sits lower than the access road, poured concrete disappearing into the desert. Alessio takes the descent smoothly, tires crunching once before silence swallows us whole. Alessio cuts the engine.

Alex is still breathing hard when we pull him from the vehicle. Not struggling now. He learned that lesson earlier. His feet drag against the concrete as we move him forward, the sound dull and final in the enclosed space.

The inner door opens.

Massimo steps aside first, giving Alessio room. I take Alex by the shoulder and steer him forward.

He stumbles once at the threshold.

I don't catch him.

He goes down hard inside the room, palms scraping against steel as he tries to orient himself. The door slides shut behind us with a muted thud, sealing the space completely.

Alex looks around, finally understanding the shape of his error. "You can't do this," he says, his voice breaking. "You don't have the right."

Massimo steps forward first, his tone calm and measured.

"You dragged a woman from a public space," he says. "Not to mention you've already done enough to her. See? You pissed off Dante, and now you're on our bad side too."

Alessio follows, his voice quiet but absolute. "You were not confused," he says. "You were careless. That is worse."

Alex turns to me last. His eyes search my face for something resembling mercy.

"This isn't about anger," I tell him evenly. "It is about correcting a wrong."

Alex sits when I tell him to. The table is bolted to the ground, but I keep my hands on it—palms up, like a piano player waiting for the cue. Alex watches my fingers, maybe hoping for mercy. I don't play that key anymore.

"You know why you're here," I say.

"I genuinely don't." He says it too fast, tries to catch himself and smiles. "If this is about tonight—"

"It isn't just about tonight." I nod. "Now say you're sorry."

He tries to laugh it off, but it crumbles. "For what? I didn't—"

"For thinking you could fuck me," I say, no heat, just the fact of it. "For thinking I wouldn't notice."

His hand twitches on the table. He's running the odds. "It was nothing personal."

"It never is." I stand, and lean over the table. "But this is."

He knows it's coming, the fear is thick enough to taste. He tries to stand and Massimo palms his shoulder, keeping him rooted. Alessio steps closer, not to intervene but to witness.

I move around the table, and for a second I see the boy in Alex's eyes. I hook my hands under his jaw. "Do you know how much trouble you caused me?" I ask, voice soft. "You put my name in the wrong mouths."

His breath comes in wet, ragged bursts. He shakes his head. I squeeze, just a tick, and his eyes bug wide.

"There's a way out of this," he whispers, spit catching on his teeth. "I can fix it, just give me a day, an hour—"

Massimo leans in. "No more hours."

Alex makes a sound, not quite a whimper. "Please—"

I press him back into the chair and hold. I feel the bone under the skin, the jump of his pulse. He tries to fight, but all his life he's been a talker, not a brawler.

He thrashes, tries to scream, and Massimo clamps a hand over his mouth, slamming his head back into the chair. I take the scalpel, twist it so the light dances along the edge. Alex whines behind Massimo's palm.

"Hold him," I say.

Massimo pins his arms. Alessio tips the chair back. I start with the face using no more force than to slice a tomato. Blood comes fast but I'm careful. I don't want him unconscious yet. The lesson needs to write itself into every nerve ending.

"Count backward from a hundred," I tell him, and when Massimo lets go, Alex screams the numbers, each one messier than the last.

I cut him in increments. Starting with a knuckle, the fleshy part of his palm, moving to a calculated line down his forearm.

"Why?" he sobs. "Why—"

He tries to spit the blood filling his mouth at me. But he doesn't have the strength, it dribbles down his chin instead.

I use the handkerchief to mop it up. "You always wanted to be important, Alex. Now you are."

His sobs go animal, then quiet. He slumps in the chair, leaking from a dozen points, face unrecognizable. I nod to Alessio. He takes the tooth from the bag, a memento. I grip Alex's jaw and pry his mouth open, thumb pressed against the tongue. I feel the wet snap as Alessio plucks a molar, tidy and practiced.

I grab my favorite gun as Alex's eyes flutter open one last time, recognition dawning as I press the barrel against his temple. The silencer makes it sound like someone dropping a book. His body jerks once, then stills. Blood pools beneath the chair, spreading in a perfect circle.

The cleanup is a mercy. We lay him on the floor, Alessio neat and reverent, like dressing a child for bed. Massimo wipes the chair, sets it right. The room resets itself, all trace of violence sluiced into the drains set discreetly in the corners. I pocket the tooth, still warm, a souvenir for whoever needs reminding.

We leave the bunker the same way we entered it.

The door seals behind us, locking the body inside with the systems designed to erase it. Timothy will handle the rest. By morning, there will be nothing left that proves Alex Knight was ever here.

Alessio drives. His grip is tight on the wheel, eyes forward as the bunker recedes into the dark. Massimo settles back into his seat, already finished with the night. I don't look behind us.

There's nothing worth checking.

The desert stretches on, vast and indifferent, and when the lights of the Strip finally reappear, the world will still be turning exactly as it should. The club will open. Sofia will be safe. The line will remain intact.

Some problems don't require aftermath.

They just require permanent removal.

CHAPTER TWENTY-TWO

Opal

Dante said he'd be late.

He didn't say why, but he didn't need to. Some things don't require explanation between people who understand the cost of crossing certain lines. Alex Knight crossed one. Dante doesn't leave loose ends.

I don't pace. I don't check my phone every five minutes. I sit on the couch with my legs folded beneath me, laptop closed, TV with the volume on low.

I want to know how it ended.

The lock clicks. When he sees me, he freezes, hand hovering above the catch all bowl by the door.

"You're still up," he says.

"I was waiting," I reply, giving away nothing.

He studies me for a beat, then nods once like he understands exactly what I mean. "I need a shower," he says.

"Okay," I say, already standing. "I'm coming with you."

He peels his shirt over his head, revealing old scars that I haven't seen before. Probably because I never noticed anything about him before. I also didn't care.

I reach for the faucet. The water hisses to life, filling the room with fog nearly instantly.

He steps into the shower first, standing under the spray like he's trying to drown something. I follow, closing the glass door behind us. My skin prickles.

He leans his palms against the wall, head bowed beneath the stream. I move closer, close enough that I feel the tension in his back like wire strung too tight.

"Tell me," I say quietly. "What did you do?"

Dante lifts his head slightly, the water streaking down his face like it's trying to wash away the night. "I cut his face first. I spent some time on his mouth. So he couldn't lie anymore."

I swallow, but stay still. The heat presses against my skin, wrapping around every word.

"He begged," he says, quieter now. "Cried, even. But not for the right reasons. Not for her."

"And then?"

His eyes meet mine, the color dark, unflinching. "Then I made sure he'd never be found. Well I guess Timothy will make sure of it."

He waits—for judgment, maybe. For fear. But I only nod slowly. "Good."

"I didn't do it for justice," he says. "I did it because I couldn't stand the idea of him breathing the same air as you. Or anyone else for that matter."

He catches himself. He did it for me, but doesn't

want me to know that. Also, that I'm seeing this side of him that most would think is a monster.

"I know," I whisper. "That's why I'm not afraid of you."

His hand finds my jaw, thumb dragging across my lower lip with unbearable pressure. "You should be," he murmurs.

"I'm not."

That's all it takes.

He kisses me like punishment. Like he's possessing me.

His mouth crashes into mine. He tastes like fury, like something raw and sacred. I gasp, and he takes advantage —tongue sliding deep, hand tightening in my hair as if he needs the anchor.

He pulls back just enough to speak, lips brushing mine.

"Say it again."

I smile against his mouth, my hand sliding low.

"I'm not afraid of you," I whisper.

His breath hitches—then he growls, low and primal— and kisses me like he plans to ruin the word *afraid* forever.

"You'll raise the water bill," he murmurs, breath a low vibration on my neck.

"You can afford it," I shoot back, but my voice slips a little, words smeared by the way his palm pushes at my waist, angling me with a pressure that hovers just below pain.

His mouth ghosts the shell of my ear, lips wet and wicked. "What if I want you to owe me?"

I tilt my head so he can see my smile—a razor curve. "Then you'll have to collect."

He moves me, a hand at my throat, gentle but insistent, and I let him, let my head fall back against his shoulder. The spray beats at my collarbones, drumming a syncopation against my sternum. I can feel his cock, already hard, nudge against the small of my back.

I pivot, turning to face him. Water sluices down my body and spatters across his chest, beads tracking over the rise of his pecs, the column of his throat. He's beautiful—too much so, really, for a man who lives by only what he wants in that moment.

The only thing protective about Dante Valera is the way his hands cradle my jaw when he kisses me, as if I'm made of something that could break.

His mouth takes mine, lips parted to drag in my bottom lip. His tongue is back to searching, patiently. My hands skate down his chest, fingers catching on the faint scar that arcs under his ribs. I trace it, wishing I knew which fight it came from.

The contrast—heat and chill, the comfort of his body and the threat of his strength—is exquisite.

He kisses down my jaw, biting lightly at my pulse, then lower, tongue flicking at the water that beads between my breasts. His hands map my sides, thumbs dragging under the curve of my ribs, and it's all I can do not to arch into him, not to surrender an inch more than I mean to. He knows the game, knows it's about who takes and who allows, and he never pushes until I break.

I drag my nails down his shoulder blades, scoring pink lines that fade as quickly as they appear. He makes a noise, low and hungry, and lifts me—just enough that my back is flush to the wall, my feet off the ground. My legs circle his hips, and the position leaves me exposed, open, an offering I pretend isn't desperate.

He looks at me, eyes blown wide and predatory. "Tell me," he says.

"Do it," I whisper.

He lines himself up, presses in. It's slick, almost frictionless, but I still gasp at the intrusion, at the stretch that borders on hurt. He fills me in a way that I have become accustomed to and fear I can't live without. I grip his shoulders, every muscle strung tight. The heat between us is unreal, suffocating, the wet sounds echoing louder than the waterfall shower overhead.

Dante fucks me the way he does every time, with focus, with intent, every thrust a statement. He holds my jaw and makes me look at him, makes me see every ounce of hunger he usually hides behind those whiskey eyes. My own reflection—wild, untamed, pupils blown—wavers in the glass behind him. I wonder, briefly, if he likes the monster he's made of me, if he knows he's always been the only one who could do it.

He brings me to the edge very slowly and when I start to shudder, his teeth sink into the juncture of my neck and shoulder, grounding me, keeping me here instead of lost in some abyss of sensation. I lock my ankles around him, force him deeper, and the rhythm goes brutal, a mutual undoing. Every sound is swallowed by steam and the hiss of the jets.

I come with his name, not even bothering to stifle it, and he follows a second later, forehead pressed to mine, breathless, bodies shaking in sync. The aftermath is white hot, nerves shattered, my entire body singing with the aftershock. He holds me there, not letting me slide down, his arms trembling like he's the one who barely survived.

He smiles and nips my earlobe, and says, "You'll be the death of me."

I smile back. "Not if I get you first."

Eventually, he sets me down, careful like I'm fragile when he knows damn well I'm anything but. We rinse off.

He squeezes some shampoo in his hands. I do not like the smell of this one. I feel nauseous every time I smell it. I liked the old one but this one is a big no.

I wring out my hair and step out first, grabbing a towel, letting the droplets trace lines down my thighs. In the mirror, I watch him behind me—still hard, still watching, a man who knows what he wants and will never apologize for it.

I pull on soft black shorts and a sleep shirt that hits mid thigh. No bra. No makeup. Clean face, damp hair, bare feet.

He grabs his pants from the bedroom drawer. Black sweats, no shirt. Still damp around the collarbones, skin kissed pink by the shower.

We walk to the kitchen and I go straight to the fridge. "Sit," I say, not looking back.

He doesn't argue and sits on a barstool. I know he probably hasn't eaten. So, I cook for him. Something quick and easy since it's almost 2AM.

The scent that wafts from the kitchen is glorious. I make some for myself too.

"What is that?" He asks.

"Aglio e olio," I say, "but I always add some extra chilis."

He grunts, which I choose to interpret as approval.

I swirl the pasta straight from pot to pan, drag it through oil and garlic and brine. Pecorino, cracked pepper, a little pasta water to loosen the sauce.

Two bowls. I slide his in front of him and sit on the other side of the bar, watching him.

I twirl a forkful of pasta, and take a bite. He lifts his fork but doesn't eat right away.

Instead, he says, "You always cook like that?"

I glance up. "Like what?"

"Like it's the only part of the day you can just be yourself."

I pause, the fork halfway to my mouth. He's not wrong. I chew. Swallow. "It's normal," I say finally. "Food doesn't lie. If something's off, you can taste it. Unlike people who always lie."

He hums in agreement and finally takes a bite. "It's good."

"That sounded almost surprised."

"I'm used to being fed either the most expensive things or just whip something tasteless together so I can go to sleep," he says. "This tastes like something else."

I blink. "It's pasta, Dante."

"No." He sets his fork down. "It's care. You don't show people that side of you lightly."

I look down at my bowl. "I don't really... do this."

"What—cook?"

"No. Sit with someone. Eat. Talk." I shake my head,

laugh under my breath. "Feels like I'm playing house with a man who breaks ribs for a living."

He smiles at that. "You make it sound worse than it is."

"Is it?"

He shrugs, still watching me like I'm a puzzle he's just now realized he wants to keep. "I've had dinner with a lot of people. This is the only time it's ever felt real."

I don't know what to say to that.

So I eat. And so does he.

When we're done, I rinse the bowls in the sink, hands moving on muscle memory, but I feel him behind me again. He doesn't ask what I'm thinking. Doesn't press.

I dry my hands, and turn to face him.

"Come on," I say, ready to be done with this night. "Let's go to bed."

He nods once, and we walk down the hall. He listened to me without an argument. I don't make a production out of it. I don't dim the lights or fold the blankets just so. I pull back the covers like I do every night.

He hesitates just inside the doorway.

I slide into bed and pat the mattress beside me. "What? You think I'm gonna bite?"

He smirks faintly. "I was hoping."

He lies back, one arm behind his head, the other loose at his side.

I turn off the light.

And for the first time in years, I don't fall asleep with thoughts rushing through my ears.

I just fall asleep listening to *him*.

I wake to the blaring shriek of my phone ringing.

Disoriented, I reach blindly toward the nightstand, knocking into the lamp before my fingers find the screen. The caller ID glares bright in the dark room. Maris.

My heart kicks.

Behind me, the bed shifts. A low sound—Dante, dragging in a breath as he stirs. I glance over my shoulder. His arm is still stretched across the mattress where I was lying, hand open, fingers curled slightly like they'd been reaching in his sleep.

The phone is cold against my ear. "Maris?"

Her voice crackles. "We've been trying to reach you. You and Dante. No one's answering."

Beside me, Dante sits up, already alert. He doesn't ask what's wrong—just watches me, sharp eyed, completely awake.

"What's going on?" I ask, swinging my legs over the side of the bed.

"It's Michella," Maris says. "She's trying something. It's bad. She's come out of hiding. You need to get ahead of it."

A flush of cold floods my veins. "What kind of bad?"

"She's talking about you and your marriage. How it's a contract. Her and our mother released part of the contract that you apparently signed. Opal what is going on?"

Dante's voice cuts in, low and lethal. "Put it on speaker."

I do.

Maris doesn't skip a beat. "Stellan's already moving to contain fallout. But if she gets traction before we can step in—" Her voice breaks off. "—it could blow wide open."

I look at Dante. His jaw is set. His eyes are darker than before.

"We're coming in," I say.

"Good." Maris exhales shakily. "Just—move fast."

Twenty minutes later, we walk into Talia's office. Thankfully, the girls are at school, this is a part of this world that I don't want them anywhere near. Even if. it would be just playing in the corner or doing something nearby to occupy themselves.

Talia doesn't say anything when she slides the tablet across the table. She's handing me a live wire.

I don't flinch. I tap the screen. The headline loads in bold, blood red font.

VEGAS VULTURE EXCLUSIVE

"Shadow Wife?" The Truth Behind the Valera-Greer Marriage Contract

By now, we all know something strange happened behind the velvet curtain of Obsidian. Dante Valera—Vegas's most guarded kingpin—married Opal Greer in what sources initially called a "private agreement." But now? It looks more like a strategic acquisition made under threat.

This morning, two insiders went public.

Celestine Greer, estranged mother of the bride, and Michella Carr, former fiancée to Dante Valera, are claiming Opal Greer is not just a wife. She's a Shadow Bride.

Yes, those Shadow Brides—the ones whispered about in elite corridors, trained by the Society for high value placements, strategic marriages, and psychological compliance engineering.

According to Celestine:

"I didn't want to say anything. But I've seen the contract. She is the type who will jump on whatever so she can get ahead. She doesn't care who she hurts or destroys in the process."

Carr was more direct:

"Dante didn't choose this. She was assigned. And the contract proves it. He didn't fall for her—he fell into her. There's a difference. You can train a woman to seduce. To soothe. To pretend. But you can't fabricate gravity. Dante and I had that."

Leaked excerpts from the marriage contract were included in a sealed file sent to The Vulture overnight. Here's a redacted portion:

Society Placement: Bride #78

Subject: OPAL GREER

Assigned To: VALERA, DANTE

"The Assigned shall ensure emotional compliance and strategic assimilation within 12 months of cohabitation. Physical exclusivity required. Termination of contract by Assigned is permitted only upon loss of target control or emotional divergence."

If that's not enough to raise eyebrows, what about the signature line—where Dante Valera's name appears beneath a timestamp marked simply:

"SIGNED UNDER OBSERVATION."
That means that this whole arrangement—if that's what you can even call it—isn't voluntary, but forced.
So what does this mean for Obsidian's quiet queen?
According to our sources, Opal Greer has been operating under layers of surveillance, Society privilege, and untraceable authority. One Rothwell insider even claimed:
"She doesn't report to Dante. She reports to the ones watching him."
And Vegas wants answers.
Why is Dante letting this stand? Why hasn't he gone scorched earth? Or maybe... he's not allowed to. Maybe his first bride would have been better.
One thing is clear—the Shadow Bride program isn't a myth anymore. It's in the headlines. And Opal Greer is their proof of concept.
So we ask again: If this marriage is real... why does it read like a weapon?
More soon, darlings. You know we never sleep.
— The Vulture

The screen is still glowing when Dante mutters, "This isn't even true."

He paces the entire office. "Staged quotes. Leaked documents. They spun this. It's not even the contract we signed—look at the formatting. Look at the seal. It's doctored—"

But I'm not moving. Not blinking. Not breathing. Because something's *wrong*. Not with the article. Not with the press tactics or the carefully sharpened slander.

With the words.

First bride.

That phrase hits me like a switchblade between the ribs.

First.

There was a first.

That means I'm the second.

The room is buzzing.

Talia's pacing with a tablet in hand, muttering numbers and timelines. Stellan's jaw is locked, arms crossed as Beckett scrolls through server data on a separate screen. Maris is half on the phone, half listening. Frankie's leaning over the couch, whispering something into Beckett's ear.

No one notices I haven't moved. Not until I speak. "If I'm the second..."

Everyone turns.

I lift my chin, eyes locked on Dante. "Then who was the first Bride?"

CHAPTER TWENTY-THREE
Dante

Then who was the first Bride?

The room freezes. I don't have an answer.

I open my mouth—and close it again.

Because the truth is simple. And fucking annoying.

I don't know.

I don't know her name.

I don't know what happened to her.

I only know there *was* someone before Opal... briefly before Opal.

Mirelle called it a misalignment. "Not a fit," she said. "Don't worry about it."

So I didn't.

I didn't ask. Didn't push. Because by the time they brought Opal in front of me, nothing else existed.

I pull out my phone and scroll until I find Mirelle's name.

She answers too fast. "Dante—"

"This isn't just bad press," I cut in. "It's coordinated sabotage. And it goes back further than we thought."

Her silence confirms what I already know. "You told me the first bride wasn't a fit. That it was handled."

"She wasn't stable," Mirelle says tightly. "We cut her before it progressed."

"Why does the contract still exist?"

I know she is trying to find an answer. "She had to have a copy, Dante. She signed an NDA to keep it quiet."

"It wasn't kept quiet," I growl. "The Vulture got it from someone. It was leaked by someone! She's involved, Mirelle. Whoever she was, she's not gone. She's in this. The leaks, the rumors, Michella—it's all tied together. She's not some dismissed bride. She's active. She's playing a long game, and Opal became her new target."

I grip the edge of the table. "I need her name."

"Dante..."

"I need the fucking file."

She exhales. "I'll send it."

"Send it to Opal," I snap. "This isn't just about me anymore. She deserves to see the war someone declared on her."

Click. She hung up.

I stare at the phone. The first bride isn't just a name we forgot. She's the one who never let go.

The file hits the shared drive thirty minutes later. I watch Opal open it the second it pings.

CANDIDATE DOSSIER — CODE: 77-VALERA

NAME: Mallory Elise Mitchell

BRIDE ID: 77

ASSIGNED MATCH: Dante Alejandro Valera

DATE OF INTAKE: [REDACTED]

TRAINING FACILITY: Compound Vega—Shadow Brides Program

DURATION: 31 Days

STATUS: Rejected—Final Week Evaluation

LEGACY STATUS:

- Heir, Mitchell Vineyards (Liquidated)
- Socioeconomic Rating: Tier 2
- Aesthetic Compatibility Score: 91%
- Psychological Compliance Score: 86%
- Match Viability: *Conditional Approval*

TRAINING OVERVIEW:

Week 1-3: High marks in etiquette, presentation, and behavioral alignment. Strong verbal and social mimicry.

Week 4: Noticeable increase in emotional subjectivity during scenario simulations. Developed overly specific attachment to assigned match.

Peer interaction: Neutral. Candidate was compliant but emotionally isolated.

FINAL EVALUATION NOTES:

Candidate 77 exhibited a high degree of polish and poise throughout training. However, during final interviews and emotional resilience testing, evaluators noted a pattern of internalized fixation on assigned match. Responses indicated a **loss of** strategic objectivity—particularly when challenged with hypothetical rejection or match reassignment.

Direct quote during simulation: *"If he's broken, let me be the one who holds the pieces."*

Decision: Rejected. Emotional centering was deemed incompatible with the strategic detachment required for high risk placement (Valera).

Candidate was not flagged for active danger. Dismissed with exit protocol and monitoring waiver. No post release surveillance was recommended at the time.

ADDITIONAL NOTES:

- No history of disciplinary infractions.
- No flagged communications during training.
- Recommendation for future eligibility: None.

FILE CLOSED.

ACCESS LEVEL: INTERNAL SOCIETY ONLY

MODIFIED DATE: [REDACTED]

Mallory Mitchell.

My eyes still over the name.

Reese Vineyards. Owner and operator of a once prestigious label. Some of the best wine to come out of Nevada and one of the only vineyards that operated here.

On paper, she was a legacy heiress picking up her father's torch. In reality? She inherited a crumbling empire and lost it sip by sip.

"Mallory Mitchell." The name leaves a cold taste in my mouth. "I know her."

Talia looks up from her tablet. "How?"

I lean a hand on the desk, the words in my throat. "She ran Reese Vineyards. Her family supplied Obsidian for years."

I don't need to check the file again. The memories are forming in the outer recesses of my mind. "I remember when the wine started going bad. Not the taste, not at first—but the feel. Something was off. The barrels weren't aging right. Vintage slipped. Notes went flat. Clients noticed. Bottles from bottle service came back with barely a glass gone."

I glance at Talia. Her brow furrows. "Then came the Rothwell tasting. Private. High stakes. And the bottle she sent embarrassed the client in front of a boardroom full of legacy names."

Talia winces. "Shit. I remember that. I didn't realize it was the same vineyard."

"I cut the contract the next day," I say flatly. "Didn't even warn her. Just severed the line."

"And then?" Opal asks, more intrigue than anger.

"She vanished after Reese started bleeding money. Three other vendors dropped her. She lost everything. No noise, no fight—just silence."

I stare back at the screen. "Until now."

I tap the file again, my voice dropping.

"She was destroying me to save me," I mutter. "Trying to strip down the empire she thought was corrupt. And when they pulled her from the program, she must've snapped."

I look at Talia. "But the second Opal took that contract? Everything shifted."

"Because she wasn't just rejected," Talia says slowly. "She was replaced."

I nod once.

"She didn't want to ruin Obsidian anymore," I say. "She wanted to ruin Opal."

Opal doesn't just read the file. She works it.

Eyes scanning. One hand flipping back and forth between pages, the other tapping the edge of the tablet with a rhythm I've come to recognize—she's tracking something. Building a pattern. A web.

She mutters, "This doesn't make sense," almost absently.

I move closer. "What doesn't?"

"She owns Reese Vineyards, right?" She says without looking up. "But her name's Mallory Mitchell."

Talia frowns. "So?"

Opal shakes her head, still flipping. "Reese was her

father's surname. The vineyard was his. If she inherited it, why does she use a different surname name? People like her—legacy kids—they cling to that kind of history. It's part of the brand."

She minimizes the current page. Opens another Society packet. Cross references. Her fingers are flying now.

"Unless... she isn't the heir. What if the vineyard wasn't a family name, but was named after someone else?"

She pulls up a smaller, overlooked footnote from the personnel data. She stops typing for just a moment and stares at it.

"There," she says softly. "David Reese Mitchell." She turns the screen toward us. "Her brother."

The name settles in my chest like ice water.

Dave.

I know that name. That signature.

"Wait," I say, voice catching. "Dave handled the Obsidian orders. He was our logistics contact. Always signed with a smiley face. Reese's wine guy."

Opal nods. "Handled Rothwell orders, too. Never tripped a single flag. Always kind."

She's already digging deeper. She's logged into a restricted channel—one of her own design. Pulling up archived financial traces, side account routing logs.

And then she freezes.

OBITUARY – LAS VEGAS JOURNAL

David Reese Mitchell

Beloved Brother, Son, and Legacy Winemaker

David Reese Mitchell passed away unexpectedly at his family home in the Lasora Valley.

Raised among the vines of Reese Vineyards, David devoted his life to the land his family had cultivated for generations. Known for his quiet discipline, sharp palate, and deep loyalty, he was the heart of the operation long before his name ever appeared on the label.

After completing his education in viticulture, David returned home to steward the family legacy alongside his father, eventually assuming full responsibilities as his parents' health declined. He was joined in recent years by his sister, Mallory Mitchell, with whom he shared an unshakable bond—both professionally and personally.

David was a man of few words but lasting impressions. Those who knew him speak of his unwavering work ethic, his calm under pressure, and the kindness he offered freely and without need for recognition.

He is survived by his sister, Mallory. A private service was held at the family estate. The family has requested privacy.

She hasn't said a word in over a minute. That alone tells me something's wrong.

Her posture's off too. Her shoulders are tense and eyes fixed straight to the screen. She hasn't even blinked.

I know that look. She's thinking. She's trying to find something. Maybe something unfinished.

I shift slightly on the edge of the desk, watching her. "Opal."

No response. Her brow furrows like she's trying to file something away, but can't.

"Opal," I repeat, more gently this time. "What is it?"

She comes back to the room like she forgot I was here. "There's something off," she murmurs, eyes still on the screen.

"The obituary?"

She nods once. "No dates. No cause. Just 'passed away unexpectedly' like that explains anything."

"Maybe that's all the family wanted to share."

"Maybe." She doesn't believe what she is saying. "But then why is it gnawing at me?"

I lean forward, resting my elbows on my knees. "Because when something starts chewing at your gut like that, it's not just something that you can easily let go. It's a pattern of truth trying to claw its way out." Her jaw tightens. "You think she lost more than a vineyard."

"I think..." She trails off, tapping the edge of the screen. "I think her brother didn't just die."

"And you want to prove it."

"I need to."

I nod once. "Then start digging."

She doesn't speak when she finds it. Just goes very still—one hand hovering over the keyboard, the other pressed flat against the desk like her body needs anchoring.

"What is it?" Maris asks.

Her voice is barely above a breath. "A file attachment. On an old cloud backup tied to the vineyard's business license. It wasn't public. Just... buried."

She clicks. An email opens. Titled for M.

Mallory,

If you're reading this, it means I didn't make it. I'm sorry for that. I know this will ruin you in ways I can't fix. But I also know staying is ruining you worse.

I was the one who didn't clean the barrels correctly. I told you the readings were fine. I lied. And that shipment that got returned? That was on me. I couldn't face you after. I couldn't fix what I broke.

But it's more than that. I see you trying to hold everything up with bleeding hands. I see how much you gave up for this place. For Dad. For me. And now that it's all coming down, I know you think this is the end.

So I'm making room.

You deserve a chance to start over... without me holding you back.

Love you always,

Dave

She freezes mid scroll.

"Dante," Opal says quietly. "She found him. In the barrel room."

She scrolls once more, like she has to force herself to keep reading.

Subject discovered suspended from ceiling beam using industrial grade rope. No signs of forced entry. Time of death estimated during early morning hours.

Opal inhales sharply.

"She walked in thinking something was wrong with the lights," she says. "The report says the motion sensors tripped but there were no alarms. She followed the sound."

"What sound?" I ask, even though I already know.

"The rope," she whispers. "Swinging. Hitting the oak barrels."

I feel something cold slide down my spine.

"She didn't see his face at first," Opal continues. "Just his boots. Hanging inches above the concrete." Her voice cracks. "She thought it was a joke. Or a break in. She called his name." She swallows hard. "There are fingerprints on the ladder. Her hands. She climbed it."

My jaw locks.

"She tried to lift him," Opal says. "Tried to take the weight off his neck. The beam couldn't hold both of them. It snapped."

The room feels too small. Everything is closing in around us.

"She fell with him," Opal finishes. "He was already gone. She screamed until the workers came running. They had to sedate her. She kept saying his name like it would rewind time."

Opal finally looks at me. Her eyes are bright with tears.

"That's the moment she broke," she says. "Not when the vineyard failed. Not when you cut the contract."

I nod once. My throat is tight.

"She didn't just lose him," Opal continues. "She was trapped in that image. Over and over. And no one pulled her out."

I lean closer without touching her. "And now," I say quietly, "she wants to make sure no one else ever forgets what she saw."

Opal's jaw sets.

"She didn't want him to disappear quietly," she says.

"So she made sure everything after was loud. She blames you for his death."

Stellan's voice comes out of nowhere. "So what now?"

I barely get a breath in before my phone vibrates in my pocket. Lucrezia.

I step aside, answering as I watch Opal from the corner of my eye. She hasn't moved. Still locked in place. Still processing everything we've just uncovered.

"Lu," I say.

Her voice comes low and tight, coiled like wire. "You need to get to Obsidian. Now."

"Why? What's going on?"

"Colten Hadings," she snaps. "He's in the lounge causing a scene. Screaming about Alex. Says if his best friend doesn't show up, he's going public."

My jaw tightens. I don't speak, but I feel the shift with rage simmering under my restraint.

Alex Knight's face flashes behind my eyes. The way he tried to beg. The way his voice cracked when he realized there was no one left to call. I remember the sound his breath made when I cut him. The warmth on my hands. The way his body went heavy, useless, like a problem that had finally been solved.

I remember thinking how easy it was to end someone who'd spent his whole life hiding behind other men's names.

And now Colten is screaming for him. What he doesn't know is that Alex is not missing.

He's just past the point of being found.

"He knows something," Lucrezia adds, startling me

back to the present. "Or he thinks he does. Either way, you can't leave him out there like this. It's a fuse already lit."

I glance back at Opal—shoulders rigid, eyes far away. Still reeling. "I'm on my way."

I hang up.

Of course it's Colten.

I swear if it's not one thing, it's another.

I don't want anything else to happen. I just want it all over with.

CHAPTER TWENTY-FOUR

Opal

"Go," I tell him quietly. "We'll handle Mallory."

Dante hesitates. Just for a second. He steps close. Cupping the side of my face. And kisses me gently. "I'll be back," he murmurs against my lips.

"I know."

He pulls away slowly. Lingers for one more breath. Then turns and walks out. The door clicks shut behind him.

Stellan exhales and checks his watch. "I have to get to a meeting." He leans in, brushes a kiss against Talia's temple. "Call if it escalates," he says.

Talia nods without looking at him.

The front door shuts again.

It's only women left in the room. Me. Frankie. Talia. Maris.

"Oh my *God*," Frankie says, dragging out the words like she's biting into the juiciest gossip she's ever tasted.

"Did anyone else see that kiss? Because I think I just got secondhand intimacy whiplash."

"I saw it," Maris says, arms crossed, one eyebrow up. "That wasn't a kiss. That was a declaration of property."

Talia tilts her head. "You let him."

I blink. "What?"

"That kiss," she says, walking toward me with the slow, amused precision of a woman who's definitely about to start shit. "You didn't flinch. Didn't dodge. You leaned in."

"I didn't lean—"

"You *melted*," Frankie corrects, grinning. "Like some sad little spaghetti noodle."

"I am not spaghetti."

"You're married spaghetti," Maris deadpans.

Talia narrows her eyes and points at me like she's lining up a target. "You looked married."

"Like *actually* married," Frankie adds. "Not Shadow Bride technicality married. Married married. Emotionally compromised. Soft core domestic."

"Disgusting," Talia says, making a gagging noise. "I think I'm going to be sick."

Maris just smirks. "You gonna make him lunch again, wifey?"

"I hate all of you," I mutter, turning toward the hallway.

"Wait!" Frankie follows. "Can we at least talk about how your face went all soft when he said he'd be back? Like—soft soft. It was gross. Are you nesting?"

"I will stab you with a decorative fork," I call back.

"Can't wait," she sings.

I smirk—sort of. But it fades fast.

Something twists low in my stomach.

The floor tilts slightly. Cold sweats break over my spine, and my throat tightens with acid. I barely make it to the trash can before I'm retching.

"Opal?" Talia's voice is fluttering around the lack of my mind.

I wave a hand, trying to tell them not to come closer, but it's too late. Footsteps rush back in.

Frankie skids to a stop in the doorway. "Okay, what the hell—are you dying?"

"I'm fine," I manage, breathless.

"You're puking into a trash can, babe," Maris says, calm but pointed, already grabbing paper towels. "That's the opposite of fine."

Talia crouches down next to me, eyes narrowing. "Could be food poisoning. Or a stomach bug."

"When's the last time you had a full meal?" Maris asks, voice gently while someone hands me some water.

"Last night." My throat is rough.

She glances at Talia, who's watching me too closely.

"No, not that," Maris murmurs. "When's the last time you had your period?"

I freeze.

Frankie lets out a soft, stunned, "Ohhh shit."

"I—I don't know," I admit. "I haven't really been paying attention—"

"Dizziness?" Maris asks gently, but there's worry under it. "Smells bothering you? Random nausea in the mornings?"

My silence answers for me.

"And your boobs?" she adds with the kind of calm only someone who's done this before can manage. "Sore? Weirdly heavy?"

I close my eyes. "I thought it was stress."

"It could be," she says. "But I've been pregnant. You don't forget that particular cocktail."

Nope. I am absolutely not pregnant. This is not happening.

Frankie suddenly says, "I have a test."

All three of us look at her.

She shrugs. "What? Beckett and I are trying. I keep one in my bag. Just in case."

Talia raises an eyebrow. "No matter what it says... you're not alone, Opal."

I nod, barely.

Footsteps pat down the hall again—Frankie, carrying a small pink box. She holds it out for me to take. "It's one of the fast ones. Two minutes."

Talia opens the private bathroom door without a word.

Maris squeezes my shoulder. "Go. We'll be right here."

The bathroom smells like expensive hand soap and eucalyptus. All of which makes me want to puke all over again.

I take the test.

Then I wash my hands. My fingers tremble as I carry the indication of my future back to the room.

Maris takes the test and sets it gently on the table and

pulls out her phone. She puts it face down and starts a timer.

Talia pours more water into my glass. "Sip. Slowly. Don't think."

I take it, because it's easier than arguing.

Frankie leans against the edge of the desk. "You look like you just defused a bomb."

"That's what it feels like."

Maris snorts softly. "Oh honey. This is the easy part."

I glance up at her. "Easy?"

She lifts a brow. "The test is just an indication. It's not the answer. It's the question you're scared to ask."

Talia crosses her arms, studying me. "If it's positive... what do you want?"

I open my mouth. Close it. My pulse kicks up. I feel like I'm balancing on the edge of the precipice. On the edge of a giant cliff.

"But what if he doesn't want it?" I whisper. "This wasn't part of the contract. We're not even..."

Talia cocks her head. "Not even what?"

"Together," I admit, voice thinner now. "We're not real."

Frankie makes a low sound. "You think *that man* would look at you the way he does if this wasn't real?"

"I'm not saying it's fake," I murmur. "I'm saying... I don't know what it is."

Maris leans forward, putting her hand in mine. "Do you want it to be real?"

I don't answer. I can't. The truth is, I don't know. Not in a way I'm ready to admit out loud. I haven't even admitted it to myself yet.

I feel it... under the fear, beneath the static in my chest.

I do know.

Not the polished version. Not the fairy tale or the contract or the Society's stamped seal of approval.

But *our* version. The way he makes coffee exactly how I like it, even when I don't ask. The way he takes his time unbuttoning my clothes, like I'm the answer to all of his prayers. The way he puts me first, even when everything in his world is sweeping him away.

It's not black and white. It's not easy. But it's real.

And I want it. All of it. For the rest of my life. Even if I don't know what it becomes. Even if it terrifies me.

Frankie clears her throat again. "Okay, so, real talk—do we think Dante's going to faint? I'm just trying to mentally prepare for the comedy potential here. Should I record it? I should, right?"

I huff a breath that's almost a laugh. The pressure eases for half a second.

Maris smirks. "Let's be honest. I don't know Dante. But I know the type. I wouldn't be surprised if he cared more than anyone thinks. He may even lock you in the house.

"Terrifying," Talia says dryly.

"Honestly kind of hot," Frankie adds.

"I'm sitting right here," I mutter.

They all smile like that's the point. Also trying to take my mind off the test and if he wants me. This.

Beep.

Maris reaches for the test. I try to calm my racing heart.

She studies the window for a beat too long. Then looks at me. She flips the test around and sets it on the table.

Two pink lines.

Positive.

The breath I've been holding escapes in a slow, shaky exhale. The kind that makes my chest ache.

No one speaks.

Talia moves first, dragging the chair behind me gently, like she knows I won't sit unless someone tells me to.

I lower myself down.

Frankie breaks the silence. "Well... damn."

Maris sits across from me, elbows on her knees. "How do you feel?"

I try to answer. Try to form anything resembling a sentence. But all I can manage is a half laugh, half sob that feels like it comes from somewhere deep. "I don't know."

Maris watches me for a long moment.

"You're allowed to feel everything at once, you know," she says quietly.

Talia leans against the desk, arms crossed. "You don't have to decide anything tonight."

"We've got you, okay?" Frankie adds, her voice gentler than usual. Her usual teasing demeanor is gone.

I manage a small smile and nod. Maris' phone buzzes against the table.

She glances down, frowns, and picks it up. "Hang on," she says, stepping toward the corner. "Hey, Rena. What's up?"

A pause. Her body stiffens. "Wait—what?"

Frankie straightens. Talia is already pushing off the desk.

Maris' voice drops lower, tighter. "You went to the school and they weren't there?"

My stomach twists.

"They weren't there?" I repeat, barely breathing, already rising to my feet.

Maris turns slowly, one hand pressed against her temple. "And no one saw them leave?"

Another pause. Her jaw locks. "Okay. Lock the doors. Stay put. I'm going to call the police."

She hangs up.

Maris faces me, her voice hard, but she's trying to stay strong. "The girls are missing."

My breath vanishes and my soul drops out from under me.

Talia blinks once, then steps forward, toward Maris. "Define 'missing.'"

"The school released them to someone on the approved list," Maris says, but her voice isn't just clipped now, it's cracking along the edges of despair. "But not Dante's driver. Not anyone from the detail." She runs a hand through her hair, the motion jerky. Her eyes are wild. "Someone got to the list. Someone took my girls."

Dante's driver. I didn't know he had him picking the girls up. I'm glad he did. At least that made them safe for a time being.

"How the hell does that happen?" Frankie demands. She's already halfway to the door like she can physically will them back.

"It's Fletcher," I say. The name comes out like poison. "It has to be. I knew he wasn't done."

Talia looks at me. "You have something?"

"Not yet." I push past her, already moving. "But I will."

I drop to the floor in front of the files spread across the desk, yanking open folders, digging through records. The sounds behind me blur into one, phones buzzing, someone swearing, the scratch of panic just beneath the surface.

Frankie crouches beside me. "You need to breathe."

"No time."

"Opal, you are pregnant," Talia says, stepping closer. "You just found out. You cannot throw yourself into this like it's any other op."

I stop. Only for a second. Then I flip another file. "They're my family too," I say. "I'm not sitting on the sidelines."

"Let us call Dante," Talia says. "He'll go. He'll bring hell with him."

"If you call him, he'll try to stop me." I stand, one paper in my hand shaking. A lease. A payment record. A debt notice. "And we won't have time. He owed someone something."

Frankie frowns, reading over my shoulder. "Who owed who?"

"Fletcher owed money. A lot of it. This name... he's tied to the pickup location. A warehouse." I tap the page. "I've seen this name before in the files I kept after the custody hearing. From his attorney and everything."

Talia steps in front of me. "You go out there and something happens—that baby, your life—it all shifts."

I know Talia knows what she is talking about. I know what she went through with her own pregnancy.

"And if I wait, they die." I stare at her. "You think I don't know the risk? I've lived inside risk since the day I learned what heartbreak and manipulation really were."

Maris gently grabs my wrist. "We can handle it."

"You're the mother," I whisper. "You can't be the soldier today."

That hits her right in the heart. She lets go.

Frankie tries once more, softer now. "What about you?"

I breathe hard, eyes already scanning for keys, routes, entry points. "I'm the one who can make it hurt."

"Opal—no." Frankie steps into my path like a wall blocking me from the door. "You're not thinking straight. This isn't a hit. It's a recovery."

"I don't need to think straight," I snap. "I need to think fast."

Maris shakes her head, voice breaking again. "They're *my* kids."

"And that's why you can't go," I say, gentler. "You're not objective. You're not trained. I am."

"You're pregnant." It comes from Talia this time. She lowers her phone, her expression steel. "You're pregnant, and reckless, and if Dante finds out—"

"He won't." I'm already moving. I duck around Frankie, snatch the keys off the table, and head for the door.

"Opal—" Three voices say my name at once.

"I'm not asking permission," I say, gripping the doorknob. "You want them back? Let me do what I'm good at."

Talia tries again. "Just wait—he'll be here any second—"

I twist the knob. "The girls might not have seconds."

And then I'm gone.

CHAPTER TWENTY-FIVE

Dante

The second I walk into Obsidian's lounge, I know it's already too late to de-escalate.

Colten Hadings is pacing like a wolf in a cage, jaw tight, fists clenched, eyes red rimmed with sleepless rage. The moment he sees me, everything in him snaps to attention—like he's been waiting for a target.

"There he is," he spits, voice echoing off marble and glass. "The man with all the answers."

He storms forward two steps, all adrenaline and accusation, chest puffed like he's gearing up for a brawl. "You've been dodging me, Valera. Hiding. Like a goddamn coward."

Lucrezia shifts by the bar, calm as ever, but her fingers twitch like she's one breath away from drawing blood.

"Where is he?" Colten demands, eyes wild. "Where the fuck is Alex?"

He's not asking. He's accusing.

"Where's Alex?" Colten demands again before I'm

even close enough to assess the situation. "Don't give me that neutral bullshit either, Valera. I know he was here. Everyone knows."

He steps forward. I step closer.

"Step back," Lucrezia warns.

Colten glares at her, but obeys.

"You're running out of time to explain why my best friend vanished the same night you ran off with the Bianchis," he spits. "Seems convenient, don't you think?"

I keep my voice flat. "You're talking about theories. I deal in facts. If you had one, you'd have led with it."

He barks a hollow laugh. "Oh, that's cute." He doesn't stop. "Girls like Sofia," he sneers. "Pretty little things you keep off the books—bought, passed around, vanished. You think no one notices, but some of us remember."

My blood ices. Sofia isn't just a rumor. She is a girl we failed. This bastard just used her name like it's a punchline. She was never and will never be for sale.

I move before I think. One step, then another, and my fist connects with his jaw so hard his skull ricochets off the mirrored wall behind him. The crack echoes. He crumples. I don't wait for him to speak again—I press in close, low and lethal. "Say another name," I murmur. "And I will end you right here."

Colten eyes her, then me. I can see it now—he doesn't have proof that anything happened to Alex.

Manny leans in close, murmurs, "We're seeing chatter spike again. Vulture might be prepping another drop. Rothwell will handle it unless you want me to suppress it."

Colten is up, muttering and pacing back and forth. I can't hear exactly what he's saying. He's lost his fucking mind. Lucrezia catches it too. Her gaze flicks toward me.

"Bride games, contracts, missing witnesses," Colten is saying. "And you think people won't put the dots together? That we don't know what this is?"

He's half right. Which makes him dangerous.

"You know what I think?" he continues. "I think you made a deal, and Alex found out. I think your little killer wife silenced him before he could tell anyone."

Lucrezia moves in before I can say anything else to him. "This conversation is over."

Colten sneers. "Oh, I bet it is. But I'm not leaving until someone gives me—"

He doesn't finish.

Because I move first.

A shift, half a breath, and I've got him by the collar, slammed against the mirrored wall again so fast the entire room takes one giant step back.

Colten chokes, staring at me—eyes wild, all his bravado leaking out like air from a slashed tire.

"You want answers?" I murmur. "Here's one. Alex Knight isn't your problem anymore."

He tries to struggle. I tighten my grip.

"Here's another," I continue, voice like ice. "Mention my wife again, and I will make sure the only thing anyone remembers about you is how you disappeared in a puddle of your own piss."

Lucrezia doesn't flinch. Manny doesn't blink. I release him with a hard shove against the mirrors again.

He stumbles, coughing, red faced and shaking, but he knows better than to throw another word.

"You're done here," Lucrezia says, stepping forward. "Permanently. You show up again, scream again, breathe too loud—your name vanishes from every ledger in this city. Understood?"

Colten doesn't respond. He just backs away like a man who's finally seen the monster under the bed and realized it's not afraid of him.

Manny opens the front door. Colten walks through it.

He's out. Out of Obsidian. Out of our world.

For good.

The second the door clicks shut, Lucrezia turns to me. "You want him watched?"

"Not necessary," I say. "He won't risk coming back. Not after today."

I barely finish my sentence before my phone buzzes again. Talia's name on the screen. She wouldn't call me unless it's necessary.

I answer without hesitation. "What?"

Her voice is clipped, shaky. Not the usual tone of Talia Rothwell. "Dante... Maris' girls are missing."

My heart stops. "What do you mean, missing?"

I signal to Lucrezia and Manny to come close, and put the phone on speaker.

"They were signed out of school early," Talia says, breath hitching. "Someone with approved credentials. Not the sitter. Not the driver. Not anyone that we have on record. Opal traced the sign out code. It came from a warehouse whoever Fletcher owes is linked to."

My grip tightens on the phone. "Where?"

"East Industrial. A dead zone."

I exhale. "Tell Opal—"

Her breath hitches, tight.

"Dante... she already knows where they are."

My mind is pulsing with all the thoughts running through my head. Her voice comes back in a way where she feels like she is telling me something she shouldn't be.

"And Dante..." My breath staggers over itself. "...she's pregnant."

She's pregnant.

I can't even process what is going on.

It doesn't compute.

"She's pregnant," I repeat. "I didn't fucking know. Didn't even really think about it."

She's carrying something I didn't even think I could have. I never thought it was in my cards.

I'm not ready. But that doesn't matter now. Because she's mine. And someone just tried to rip a piece of her world away.

My jaw locks. I can feel my pulse like a warning in my neck.

I bring the phone back to my ear. "Where is she?"

"Already gone," Talia says. "She wouldn't listen. We tried—Dante, she—"

I cut her off. "I'll handle it."

"Dante—"

"Tell Maris I'll bring them home." I lower the phone.

Lucrezia is already watching me. "Orders?"

My voice is low. "Gear up. We're going after them. Call Massimo and Alessio. We could use all the help we can get."

It's war.

Whoever thought they could touch her—hurt her family—while she's carrying mine?

They're already fucking dead.

The thought doesn't fade... it digs itself deeper with every turn we take toward East Industrial.

Behind me, the others fall into formation. Alessio and Massimo arrive in one of the black SUVs, stepping out without a word. I know they're pissed. Opal is family to them, too.

Manny checks something on his phone, then nods once, already confirming where she is. Opal may think she's smart. But she's neglected one thing—I know her better than anyone.

Lucrezia scans the perimeter, one hand resting on her gun that people forget she carries everywhere.

Alessio tracks her movements as he falls into step beside her. "You shouldn't be here, love."

She keeps her gaze forward, lips twitching. "If I were you, I wouldn't tell me what to do... or I'll make our wedding 80's themed," she says with a smirk, not even bothering to look at him.

Massimo lets out a short laugh, head shaking. "You two stress me out."

"We're engaged," Lucrezia replies without missing a beat, dry as she can make it. "This is just the beginning of the stress you're about to feel."

Two sets of eyes look at me.

"Don't look at me," I say, trying not to chuckle. "She's always like this. Your problem now."

That earns me a mock glare from Lucrezia.

Alessio exhales in complete exasperation. He has been doing this since he was in diapers. One of the many reasons why I do not envy Alessio Bianchi. "Fine. Just don't get too much blood on you. I'm not buying you another pair of boots. I just got these. You're getting the next ones."

She doesn't respond. She only raises a brow. Alessio takes a step back. Best not to make Lucrezia mad with a loaded firearm in reach. Not like she needs it. She could just as easily punch you in the face.

Stellan and Beckett pull up right next to us.

I narrow my eyes as they both hop out of the suv. "What the hell are you doing here?"

"Did you really think we wouldn't show up?" Stellan sounds offended that I would even ask. "Talia called me, and Beckett got a call from Frankie. We know everything. They're worried about her. We heard her leave my office."

"We're here for you," Beckett adds, shifting from one hip to another. "And Opal."

They must have been informed. I know all about what happened to Stellan and Talia. She's worried because she doesn't want what happened to her for Opal to feel as well. "You know?"

Stellan nods once, watching me closely. "Yeah. We know. You gonna act surprised, or just tell us how deep in it she is?"

I huff out a breath that comes out dry and humorless.

"It's Opal," I say. "What do you think?"

No one answers, because a gunshot cracks through the air. It's close to us. Inside of the building.

I'm already moving.

Gravel skids under my boots as I break into a run, pulse roaring loud enough to drown out everything else. There's no space for strategy now, no room for backup or caution. Just the image of Opal in my head and the sick certainty that if someone touched her...

I don't finish the thought.

I refuse to. I need to keep my mind focused.

Whatever's waiting inside that warehouse made a mistake the moment they pulled the trigger. When I reach her, they're going to understand exactly how much that mistake is going to cost them.

The warehouse door buckles under my boot with a shuddering crash.

Dust flies through the air and the hinges crack right off sending the door flying into the room.

I see Opal, pacing with a gun in her hand. Four men are tied to chairs, spread out next to each other in a half moon shape. One already bleeding from the thigh—gasping, pale, slumped against his restraints.

She doesn't look at me.

"He'll bleed out nice and slow," she says to one of the men in the chair, emotionless. "That's what you deserve for what you did to my nieces."

Behind me, boots scrape against concrete. Alessio enters first, flanked by Massimo, both guns drawn, eyes sweeping the scene and freezing suddenly.

"Shit," Massimo mutters, lowering his weapon slightly. "That's Barone muscle."

Alessio's jaw tightens. "Not just muscle. That's Elio Vescari's crew."

I glance back. "You sure?"

"Positive," he says, getting closer to the men to double check. "I've seen them at his table. Enforcers. Loan men. The kind who make people disappear in the desert until payment is complete."

Massimo crosses to the side, surveying the bleeding one. "What the fuck are they doing here? Barone territory doesn't cross state lines."

"They do if someone pays them," Alessio says darkly.

That changes everything. This is a message. Someone just used the Barones to send it.

I approach her slowly.

Her back is to me, but her shoulders are trembling. The gun in her hand is trembling. I know that she's holding herself together with sheer force of will.

The man slumped in the chair moans again, blood pooling under him. The other three are silent now. They're not scared. They think she is crazy. How can they get out of this without dying? That is what they are thinking.

I step into her line of sight. "Opal."

She doesn't look at me. Her eyes are locked on the man in front of her like he's the only thing anchoring her to this reality.

"It's okay," I say softly. "I'm here now."

"You weren't there," she whispers, barely holding back the shake in her voice. "They took them, Dante. They took them, and I—I didn't even *know*. Not until Maris got the call. I was tracking them. I should have realized the possibility of this happening."

"I know."

"I should've known. I should've—" Her voice cracks. She takes her hands and starts slamming them against her temples, gun still in one hand.

I reach for her.

She jerks away, gun raised toward the ceiling.

"Don't," she chokes out. "Don't act like you get it."

"I *do* get it," I say, stepping closer. "Because you're not the only one who would do anything to protect the people we love."

She looks at me and something flickers behind her eyes.

Her mouth opens, but no sound comes at first. "What?"

I take a step closer, voice low but steady. "I know that you're pregnant."

She looks at me like I've smacked her clean across the face.

"It's yours," she says, automatically. She's taking her anger out on me. Because I'm stopping her from continuing to take her anger out on these guys.

"I know it's mine," I snap, more insulted than I mean to sound.

Her eyes widen. I can see the fear and surprise in them.

"I'm not some idiot who'd question that," I add. I try to brush off the lingering sting of it all. "Don't do that. Don't throw walls where they don't belong."

She exhales, shaky. "I just—"

"I know you," I cut in gently. "And I also know that you are not someone who kills when angry."

She makes a broken sound in her throat that sounds

like a sob and backs into the wall like she's trying to pull herself into it.

"I didn't—I wasn't trying to keep it from you. I didn't even know if I wanted—" Her knees buckle. "This wasn't supposed to happen."

I catch her before she hits the ground.

"I can't do this, Dante," she whispers, breath hitching. "I can't lose them, I can't—"

"You're not going to lose them," I murmur, pressing my hand to her back, grounding her. "You already saved them. You did that."

"But I'm not okay," she says into my shirt. "I haven't been okay in a long time."

"I know."

I hold her tighter.

Behind her, I tip my chin once.

That's all it takes.

Alessio and Massimo move first, boots echoing as they cross the concrete toward the men still tied to the chairs. Manny follows, already pulling gloves from his pocket. Lucrezia has the girls outside of the warehouse and safely in the car.

Opal knows what's going on. "No," she says, twisting against me. "No—Dante."

I tighten my grip, one arm locked around her back, the other braced at her shoulder.

"I'm not leaving," she screams, voice breaking open now. "Not until they're dead. Not until I see it. You don't get to take this from me—"

"I'm not," I say into her hair. This is not like her. Or maybe it is. Maybe she trusts me enough to show me her vulnerabilities. "I'm carrying it for you. I won't let this be the thing that stays with you. Not when you're carrying something that deserves better."

She snaps. Back to the Opal I know. The one that shoves everything away. The eyes that once held so much emotion empty and turn black.

"You don't get to decide that!" she screams, twisting in my arms.

Before I can brace, she shoves me hard. My back hits the wall, breath punching out of my lungs.

She doesn't hesitate. Palms flat to my chest, body close, she pins me there like she's trying to get me to listen to her, not just hear her.

"Don't you dare act like this is protection! They're *mine.* They *touched* what's *mine,* and you want me to walk away?"

Her voice cracks.

"I should be the one to end them," she spits, each word like a loaded round. "*I* should be the last thing they see."

I know what it feels like to need to do something. I get her. "Then we do this together."

I reach for her hand with the gun and hold it.

If she is pulling the trigger, I'll be right by her side when she does.

CHAPTER TWENTY-SIX

Opal

He understands. He knows what I need to do.

"Everyone clear out," he says. "Opal and I only."

Boots shuffle until they are all gone. It's just us now. Me. Him. And the four men who took my nieces.

I stop in front of the first man. His head lifts sluggishly, one eye swollen shut, the other bloodshot and glassy. He doesn't look scared yet.

That bothers me.

Behind me, Dante shifts close to me. He speaks quietly. "I'm right here if you need anything."

"Rhea cried for her shoes," I say, calm as anything. "Pink ones with stars on the side. She didn't want to leave them behind."

I lift the gun. The shot tears through his thigh, splintering bone. His scream comes high pitched and fast, choking off into a garbled wheeze. I don't give him time to catch his breath before I shoot again. In the lower stomach this time. He jerks forward, blood soaking into his shirt, mouth stretching wide in agony. The third bullet lands in the center of his chest. The fourth finishes it.

I step over the blood. Move to the next.

"Lenore counted every turn the car made," I say, walking slow, circling him like a predator finding her prey. "She thought if she remembered the roads, she could find her way home."

He's crying now. Shoulders shaking. Mouth moving in silent apologies that mean nothing to me. I shoot him in the foot. The crack of bone echoes against the walls. When he lurches forward, I put one in the other foot. He screams, a raw, broken thing that shreds the air around us.

I walk behind him, press the barrel to the base of his skull, and pull the trigger. His body goes limp.

The third tries to talk. Something about getting me later. His voice cracks around the word like he's always had his way with intimation and fear before.

"Rhea stopped crying first," I say, crouching so we're eye to eye. "She realized no one was coming."

I rise and shoot him in the shoulder. He rocks sideways, choking on his own spit. The next bullet slams into his knee, dropping his body like a sack of meat. He starts to sob—ugly, wet sounds that stick in his throat. One more through the forehead, and he finally goes still.

The last one looks at me like he already knows what's coming.

"Lenore didn't stop," I say, quiet now. "She waited. She waited the whole time."

I don't blink when I shoot him through the thigh,

then the side. Blood spills fast and hot, painting the floor in dark streaks. He tries to move. Like that could ever matter.

I step closer, lift the gun beneath his chin, and end it.

It's done.

Dante steps in beside me.

The gun's still in my hand. My breathing hasn't leveled out. Adrenaline is still at an all time high.

Dante steps in front of me. His hand closes gently over mine. The one still clutching the gun. Fingers firm.

"I've got it," he says softly.

I don't let go immediately. But eventually, I release the gun.

His other arm wraps around me at the same time—pulling me in, anchoring me with a grip that makes me feel safe now.

"I'm right here," he murmurs into my hair. "Let's go home."

I nod, because there's nothing left here.

No more monsters to unmask. No more questions I'm willing to ask.

He wraps an arm around my back as we leave the warehouse, the air thick with blood and the kind of vengeance that doesn't let you breathe until it's over.

As soon as I see the girls—Rhea and Lenore wrapped in Lucrezia's arms, their tiny faces blotchy with tears and relief—I feel something snap and realign all at once.

They're okay. They're safe.

"Aunty Opal," Rhea says. "The bad man was talking to daddy on the phone. Said that if he didn't pay them, then they were going to kill us."

Those words echo in my head the entire drive back. There is a giant knot in my chest that never went away.

Not even when we pull up in front of Rothwell Strategic and I see them.

Maris is already outside, arms wrapped tight around both girls as soon as they jump out of the car. Lenore clings to her like a lifeline, her little face buried in her mother's neck. Rhea's quieter, blinking up at the building like she's still catching up to the fact that the danger is gone.

They're okay.

They're safe.

I keep repeating it. That mantra is the only thing holding me back from tearing someone apart.

Then I see *him*.

Fletcher.

Standing just behind Maris. Arms crossed. Face hard. Posture like this whole thing was someone else's fault. Like he wasn't the one who caused this. Like he wasn't the one who spoke on the phone to the people that took my nieces.

I walk towards him, fury building with each step. He straightens as I approach, eyes flicking from me to Dante behind me and then back again.

"You don't want to do this now," he says, menacingly.

"Oh, you do *not* want to say that to my wife," Dante murmurs to him.

Maris turns, sees me, and immediately pulls me into the hug like I'm another one of her girls. The girls reach for me too. Rhea's small hand fisting in my coat, Lenore whispering my name so soft it nearly breaks me.

I hug them.

Then I look back at Fletcher. The voice that tears out of me is one that even I don't recognize. "You did this."

Fletcher straightens, like he's surprised I'd say it out loud. Like he thought he could stand here—smug, intact—while I hug the girls he put in danger.

"I don't know what you think—" he starts.

"You sold them," I snap. "Your debts. Your refusal to help them or even find them. With whatever handshake you made thinking no one would trace it back to you."

His mouth opens. Closes. "That's not—"

"Rhea said the man who took them was talking to *Daddy.*" My voice cracks with fury so loud it drowns out the world. "She said he was on the phone. Said if you didn't *pay up,* they'd never come back."

His face drains of color.

"You think I wouldn't put it together?" I press in. "The offshore transactions. The pressure on your attorney. The quiet cleanups after your fuckups. You were bleeding money, and instead of asking for help you used your *own daughters* as a way out."

I'm not done. I take another step forward. "You didn't think I'd make it in time. Didn't think I'd find them. You thought you could clean it all up before anyone noticed, before Maris noticed."

That's when *she* moves. "Take them inside." Maris says, pushing the girls back in Lucrezia's arms.

The look of fury on her face is something that I've never seen in all of my years knowing her, it's something that can only be described as a primal rage. "You used our children?"

Fletcher opens his mouth. But no sound comes out.

"You told me you were changing your ways," Maris says, blinking like she's seeing him for the first time. "You told me you had everything under control. You told me to *trust you.*"

"They were never supposed to be hurt," he says, weak. "I didn't know it would go that far—"

"You *let them go,*" she hisses. "You let someone *take them.*"

"Maris, please—" He's pathetic, fucking pathetic. But I do hope he keeps begging.

"No," she says.

He flinches.

"You're done," she says. "Do you hear me, Fletcher? You are *done.* I'll make sure the police and social services pulls your name from every document, every file, every report. You'll be a ghost in your own children's lives. They deserve better than you. We all do."

Fletcher looks at me like he might say something else.

I don't let him.

I meet his gaze. "You better hope," I murmur, "that you never see me again."

Fletcher doesn't argue. He steps back, right into Manny's waiting grip.

"No sudden moves," Manny says, grabbing his shoulder. "Unless you want to find out how fast I can erase your face."

Fletcher stiffens. He knows better. Manny steers him toward the car.

I barely watch. The moment he's gone, Dante steps forward.

"Maris," he says, not unkindly.

She doesn't look at him. She's still staring at the space Fletcher just left, like if she blinks, she might break completely.

"You need to get out of town."

Her head snaps toward him. "What?"

"Tonight," he says. "Pack a bag. Take the girls. Go."

Maris straightens, shoulders taut with pride and defiance. "I'm not running."

"It's not running," Dante replies, calm but relentless. "It's starting over. Do it before someone decides Fletcher's debt is now your problem."

"You think I haven't been trying?" she snaps. "You think I haven't *already* started over a hundred times?"

"I think you're tired of fighting for scraps." He pulls a card from his jacket. It's black with a silver seal. "The Society owes you for how much you've helped me. And Stellan. Take this. Call the number. Tell them your name."

Maris doesn't take it right away.

"What is this?" She asks warily.

Dante's eyes soften. His tone changes from something stiff to something more comforting. Or as comforting as he can get. "It's your turn to find something real."

I want to believe he is talking about us.

Maris hugs me one more time before taking the girls. He nods his head at Manny to go with them. We get into another car and go back to the apartment.

We need to talk. About everything. It is important.

We're silent when we get in the apartment. We're not

avoiding each other anymore. The apartment looks like the two of us and not the shell of emptiness that I first moved into.

I head inside first, but I don't go far. I feel... unsteady. There is an awareness now. Change is happening. I hate when things feel like they are out of my control.

I've never been nervous with him. Not really. But now? I don't know how to start this. How to say what's sitting as the giant fucking elephant in the room.

Dante locks the door behind us and I rub my palm over my lower stomach without thinking. The motion feels foreign. I'm trying to smooth something I can't see yet. I feel it though.

I try to calculate when it happened. It had to be the first time. God. Of course it was that night.

I don't know if I want to laugh or break.

Dante looks at me and says nothing. So I break the uncomfortable silence first.

"We need to talk," I say, fraying slightly at the edges. "About everything."

We walk to the bathroom and he turns on the shower. A lot different circumstances than the last time. We get in unceremoniously.

He grabs the shampoo bottle. I try not to gag at the smell of it.

Fuck. Well I should've known I was pregnant when the smell made me sick the last time.

He begins to wash my hair and I forget about everything as he massages my scalp. I almost melt into his arms.

Once we're settled back in the living room, trying to act like any of this is normal.

"I didn't think it was possible," I say, quietly. "I mean... statistically, it shouldn't have happened that fast."

He smirks, but there's something serious under it. "We're not exactly built for halfway, Opal."

"No," I murmur. "We're not."

"Does it feel real yet?" He asks.

I breathe in slowly. "It didn't. Not at first. It was just... shock. But now? I feel different. Like my body knows before my mind can catch up."

He nods like he understands that in a way I don't expect.

"I keep thinking," I admit, "how fast everything changed. One second I'm hunting the truth, and the next—"

My hand drifts to my stomach again without finishing that sentence.

"I don't know how to do this," I say. "Any of it." I look away. "You've never said you wanted this. A family. A future. With me."

There I said it. What I was dreading. That I will be doing this alone along with everything else in my life. That he doesn't want kids. Or me.

"I didn't think I did," he says. "Not until recently. Not until... you."

I turn back to him slowly, something in my chest breaking open.

He closes the distance this time. One step. His hand lifts to my jaw. Fingers gentle, his thumb brushing my cheek like I'm something sacred.

"I didn't want anything," he says, voice raw. "Not until you."

"You love me," I say. It's not a question. I'm not asking anymore.

His answer comes quickly. He didn't flinch. "Yeah," he says. "I do."

I look at him, and the ache in my chest shifts into something more.

Something blooming in my lungs and spreading through my limbs. Something nerve wracking. Something that feels a hell of a lot like falling.

He sees it. I know he does. Because it flickers across his expression too. Something fragile and ferocious all at once.

I take one step forward. He meets me halfway.

His lips brush mine. I press in—deeper, hungrier, fingers knotting in the front of his shirt. The kiss turns messy fast. Like we've been fighting each other to *feel* this fully.

He groans low in his throat as my hands slip under the hem of his shirt. His mouth breaks from mine, just long enough to yank it over his head. Then he's pulling me with him—walking backward down the hall like he knows I'll follow.

I stumble once. He catches me with one hand on my hip, the other slipping beneath my jaw, tilting my face up to kiss me again. Slower this time. A little worship. A little war.

I don't know when my shirt disappears, only that it's gone. I don't know when his hand finds the bare skin above my waistband, but it sears when it does. He guides me around the corner, our bodies colliding with the wall outside the bedroom. His palm braces beside my head as he kisses me harder, deeper, like he can't get close enough.

"Opal," he murmurs against my mouth. Like my name's a confession.

I hook my fingers in his belt loops, dragging him the last few steps. The bedroom door is open. He kicks it shut behind us without looking.

I walk him back this time.

He lets me push him.

When the backs of his knees hit the bed, I apply more pressure, pressing him down with a hand to his chest. His eyes darken as he looks up at me, breath ragged, chest rising in short bursts. I crawl into his lap, and the moment stretches just long enough to register the way his hands settle on my thighs.

I kiss him again.

He flips us in one movement.

Now I'm beneath him.

And everything else melts away.

The weight of the day. The blood on my hands. The evil that surrounds us in this world. None of it follows us here.

Here, there's only his mouth on my throat. My fingers in his hair. Our bodies moving like they're remembering something sacred.

I don't want easy or simple. I don't want promises.

I want *him*.

And he gives me everything.

CHAPTER TWENTY-SEVEN

Opal

A month is both everything and nothing at all.

That's what I keep thinking as I slip my hand over the curve of my stomach in the back of the car, watching the city blur past. I'm showing now. Just enough that it isn't a secret anymore, not enough to feel real to anyone else.

I miss Maris. I wish she was here for this part. She went into the training program as soon as she applied. She is about to get her arrangement. We text here and there. I just miss having her around.

I miss my nieces too. Maris wrote into her contract that they go with her. She will probably never let them out of her sight again after what they've gone through. I can't blame her. I would do the same with my child.

Through hell and high water, I would do anything to protect them.

I'm scrolling through my phone until I see it.

VEGAS VULTURE EXCLUSIVE

The House Always Wins—And Opal Greer Just Changed the Odds

Well, well, well. Looks like the marriage wasn't just for headlines or for show.

Late last night, Rothwell Strategic dropped the kind of statement that sends publicists scrambling and insiders scrambling harder:

Opal and Dante Valera are expecting their first child.

"The couple remains united and private as they prepare to welcome the next generation. We ask for discretion and respect during this time."

— Rothwell Strategic

And just like that, the game flipped.

Vegas didn't expect her to last. They didn't expect her to matter.

But here she is—pregnant, married, and more unbothered than ever.

And for the first time since Michella Carr set fire to the gala guest list, the city doesn't seem so sure of its favorite villain narrative.

Because maybe Greer isn't a placeholder.

Maybe she's the plan.

Carr had elegance.

Greer has an edge. And Dante Valera made his choice.

Carr left behind curated photos and silent tears. Greer leaves blood in the water and the city still asking—how did she do it?

Sources confirm the couple will appear together at the Foundation Noriel Gala—a second annual event that typically avoids scandal, which makes their attendance all the more telling.

"Opal Greer may have come in as the storm," one donor says, "but she looks a lot like the new sky."

No press appearances. No rebuttals. No apologies.

Just a power moves in designer silk, wrapped around a future no one saw coming.

And this time, no one's betting against her.

More soon, darlings—you know we never sleep.

—The Vulture

The gala is tonight. This makes me laugh.

Not because it's funny. But because *this*—the article I'm scrolling through on my phone—is supposed to be a glowing decree to me.

The Vulture tried to spin it like they didn't try to create a giant scandal to begin with.

Dante glances over. "What are you laughing at?"

I tilt my phone toward him, thumb still scrolling. "The Vulture tried to celebrate us. Ended up writing our wedding vows."

He hums, one brow lifting. "What'd they say?"

"That I have an edge. That they thought we were faking it, but now they're basically eating their words since it looks like we're actually a real married couple."

I grin. "Which they should because they were the ones who listened to Michella to begin with."

"They're right about one thing," he murmurs, voice low against my ear. "We already won."

The car slows to a stop.

Outside, light explodes—camera flashes strobing

through tinted glass, a frenzy of reporters and celebrity watchers pressed against velvet ropes. The Foundation Noirel Gala has always been the city's most exclusive performance. But tonight? We're the headliners.

Dante exits first, buttoning his jacket as he turns, hand extended into the car like he's reaching for something priceless.

Which just so happens to be me.

I take it. The moment I step out, the world stops moving. It's suddenly just Dante and I.

Flashes go off like thunderclaps.

We don't hide it anymore. His hand is on my lower back and my hand is resting on my slight baby bump.

Tonight, the world is watching.

The cameras are already behind us. The doors ahead gleam gold and glass, polished to reflect every angle of power.

Inside this gala—beneath the Society's quiet approval and the press's carefully filtered glances—a trap is waiting to be sprung. Mirelle's art. Talia's intel. The Society's consent. All of it designed to catch one woman in the act.

Mallory Mitchell won't be able to help herself. She thinks I took everything from her. Her future. Her legacy. Her place beside Dante. But she stops trying to ruin me tonight.

We step through the doors. Dante's hand finds mine again.

I glance up at him. He doesn't look at anyone else. Neither do I.

Let Mallory come find us.

We don't get ten steps inside before I see Michella Carr. She is doing whatever she can to remain relevant apparently. While the trap wasn't for her, I'm not exactly surprised she came.

There's a twitch in her posture. A fraying edge in her laugh. She's holding on too tight. Gripping too hard. A woman who knows the rope is slipping through her fingers and still pretends she's the one pulling the strings.

She's not alone.

Mallory Mitchell lingers near the eastern arch, half hidden behind the Murano sculpture centerpiece. Her dress is red. Crimson silk that clings like it's trying too hard to seduce, with a neckline low enough to threaten and heels just high enough to weaponize. Interesting since Dante wants me in red. I predicted this. Which is why I'm in cream.

Her dark blonde hair is curled within an inch of its life, lacquered into glossy waves that don't move when she turns her head. Her eyes are icy blue and they scan the room with the desire to blend in with the rich and famous.

I lean in toward Dante, keeping my voice low. "She came."

"We knew she would," he murmurs. "Pride makes people predictable."

I glance back at Mallory. She's alone, but not for long. Michella drifts in her direction, glass in hand, mask of confidence slipping for just a second as their eyes meet.

"Time to play," I whisper in Dante's ear.

His smile doesn't reach his eyes, but his hand tightens at my waist.

We separate like we rehearsed. Him toward Mirelle and the Society delegates and me toward the gallery's northern wing. The crowd parts for us like we are some of the richest and most famous people here. Richest, yes. But famous... absolutely not.

Mallory is still near the arch, sipping champagne she didn't pay for. Michella stands beside her, wearing a smug half smile and a silk gown two sizes too small for her self respect. They're laughing at something, heads tilted close like old friends on the winning side.

Mallory's gaze skips over me before her brain catches up with Michella.

Her spine stiffens. Mouth twitches. She masks it with a sip, but her fingers are white on the stem of the glass.

I walk straight toward them. Slowly in a way where it can come off as a threat to the right people.

Michella sees me second, and her expression flickers. Then hardens into something brittle.

"Well," she says, loud enough to draw a few curious glances. "If it isn't the dethroned analyst darling."

I tilt my head. "Funny. I thought I was still on the throne."

"You weren't even invited until you married into it."

"And yet here I am," I say coolly, "pregnant with the next Valera heir."

Michella flushes, steps back. But Mallory–she doesn't move.

So I step closer.

"Hello, Author," I say.

Her eyes widen just enough for me to know she wasn't

ready. Not for that name. Not in public. Not with cameras and high society ears nearby. Around us, the gallery hushes like someone pulled the power from the room.

She opens her mouth.

Michella's voice breaks through, nervous now. "What are you talking about?"

But Mallory already knows exactly who I am talking about. "I'm sorry," she says, eyes wide, lips curving into practiced innocence. "Author of what?"

Her voice is smooth but her pulse is visible now, fluttering at her neck. I don't give her an inch to be the victim any longer.

"You tell me," I reply, voice honeyed with a bit of an edge. "You've written so many stories lately, maybe you forgot which ones are lies."

Michella glances between us, stiffening up. "Mallory, what the hell is she talking about?"

"She's mistaken," Mallory says quickly, eyes still locked on mine. "I think the stress is getting to her. First trimester can be so... destabilizing."

I smile at her. The most unnerving one I could possibly think of. "Oh, you want to talk about destabilizing?" I say, just loud enough for the room to catch it. "Let's talk about the vineyard you ran into the ground. The suicide you turned into a pawn. The family you used as revenge. Or wait—should we talk about the contract that didn't stick?"

Mallory's mask cracks just a tiny flicker but it's enough. "I don't know what you think you have—" she starts.

Oh looks like little Ms. Mallory Mitchell made a mistake. "Oh, honey. I have *everything*."

Her breath stutters but I catch it.

"I have the plan I created," I say. "Every step, every misdirection. And guess what? You're in it. You're *all over* it."

A tremor flickers through her jaw. "I have your Bride file. Unredacted. Bride 77… remember her?" I lean in just a hair. "You were dismissed for being too emotionally volatile. Too subjective. Too *obsessed*."

Michella stiffens beside her, shifting uncomfortably.

"I know about the shell company that owned the house I was put in after the Rothwell incident. That's right. You owned it, Mallory. Me, inside your walls. You planted me in your own trap and didn't even realize it."

She swallows hard. Her eyes dart past me, scanning for an escape that doesn't exist. "And your connection to Dante? That's the best part. Your *brother* was the reason your wine turned sour. He was the one tampering with the barrels."

Mallory flinches like I slapped her. I don't stop. "See, he thought he was helping you. Thought if he destroyed your reputation just enough, the Society would see you as a savior when you brought it all back from the brink. Turns out you were so upset that you were willing to fake a suicide as what… justification? Or pettiness?"

"Stop it." Her voice is tight now, trembling. "You don't know what you're talking about."

"Oh, but I do," I say, louder. "I know that when you found out *he* was the one who ruined the barrels, the one who made Rothwell drop you... you didn't fix it. You used it."

"Stop."

The room stills. All eyes on her now. I tilt my head. "Except here's the thing, Mallory. He didn't kill himself, did he?"

Her pupils blow wide.

Because she knows what I'm about to say.

I step closer. "You found out he was the one who tampered with the barrels. You blamed him. And when he wouldn't play your game anymore... you made sure he couldn't talk."

Mallory lunges. Security moves fast. But not before the scream leaves her mouth—raw, broken, unhinged. "Don't talk about him! *You don't get to talk about him!*"

Security closes in, hands already outstretched, but Mallory is wild with grief and fury now—her limbs jerking like she can tear the truth out of the air if she moves fast enough.

"He was *my* brother," she spits, struggling against the guards now gripping her arms. "He *loved* me!"

"I know," I say. "That's why it worked."

Her breath shudders. Her body slumps in the hands holding her. But her eyes—her eyes are still bleeding rage and something uglier. Evil to her core. The kind that rots from the inside.

"You let him die with that guilt," I continue, quieter now, but no less brutal. "He wrote that letter thinking *he* ruined you. That *he* lost everything. And you let him believe it because it was easier than facing what you'd become."

"I didn't kill him," she hisses.

"But you did," I say. "He was drugged and pulled up that beam. You did that."

Mallory jerks again but the fight is gone from her bones.

Now the crowd knows.

Now they see her.

Not as the woman in the red dress sipping champagne like she still belongs.

But as the desperate sister who orchestrated her brother's suicide and tried to frame it as a tragedy instead of the stepping stone it was.

The Society will make the rest of her disappear.

But I make sure Mallory sees me before she's dragged out of the light.

"I was your plan," I say. "But you were never a part of his."

Mallory's still clawing for ground when the Society agents step in—Mirelle among them, face unreadable, voice crisp as she gives the order. "Take her."

Mallory screams something unintelligible, rage strangling the words as two agents flank her, locking her wrists behind her back in one smooth motion. Her red dress crumples at the edges, glamour giving way to chaos. They cuff her with efficiency.

Michella moves next. She starts to run, too fast. Like she thinks she still has time to escape. Like money, influence, or history might still be enough.

She doesn't get far.

Lucrezia steps into her path before the second heel even hits the marble, one hand on her hip, the other raised with an arrest order she's clearly been waiting to use. Cops standing next to her.

"Michella Carr," an officer says. "You are under arrest for aggravated stalking, electronic surveillance, and unlawful data mining with intent to intimidate."

"Who is blaming me for this? Who is framing me?"

"I accuse you, but no framing is involved," I say aloud, eyes never leaving Michella's. "We found enough documentation to bury you in court records for a decade."

Michella's mouth drops. "That's insane—"

"It's documented," Lucrezia snaps. "You made it easy. Private investigators. Voice activated taps. A fucking drone at their balcony, Michella? What exactly were you hoping to catch?"

Dante's voice cuts in behind her. "Me. She was hoping to catch me."

Michella pales, eyes darting from him to me.

"She's lying," she says, desperate now. "I was just concerned. You can't arrest me for caring—"

"You can," Mirelle says, arriving just in time to finish the circle, "when you weaponize that care to harass a member of the Society and her unborn child."

Michella doesn't scream like Mallory. She crumbles. Right there. Right on the marble floor, like something fragile that finally understood it was never as important as it thought. She realized in this moment what the society is capable of.

They cuff her, too.

Mallory snarls as she's dragged past me. "This isn't over."

I tilt my head, meeting her with a calm she'll never understand. "It is for you."

They're dragged out under flashing cameras and a Society that doesn't clean up messes like normal. The crowd parts silent and wide eyed, watching the fall of two women who once thought they were untouchable.

Dante appears at my side again, his hand brushing mine.

"They won't come back from this," he says quietly.

I nod once. "Good."

Because some stories need an ending.

And this... this is the last page they'll ever write in mine.

Epilogue
CLAUDE

If I had a glass in my hand, I'd be swirling it. Something dramatic and vintage, aged to perfection—just like my patience.

But alas, I'm empty handed. And cornered.

"I'm forty two," I say flatly, staring across Elias's study like the walls might shift and let me out. "Surely that exempts me from whatever matrimonial nonsense you're all plotting."

"You'd think," Elias replies, deadpan. "But apparently not."

He's leaned back in one of those monstrous leather chairs, the ones that practically demand ancient regrets and a whiskey decanter. Amara perches beside him, calm and terrifying in equal measure, flipping through a folder like it's not about to ruin my life.

"Gerard Montcroix couldn't inherit a paper cut," I say. "Yet here we are."

"Looks like he's about to get what's yours," Elias says, mouth twitching. "Bit of a downgrade, isn't it?"

"Bit of—? He imports flavored absinthe and sleeps in silk pajamas with his initials embroidered on the chest. The man once sent a woman perfume samples as an apology for forgetting her name." I throw my hands up. "What in God's name does being married have to do with any of this?"

"It's about legacy optics," Amara says coolly. "They want a Montcroix heir who looks like he's settled. Predictable. Respectable. Married. With another heir on the way."

"And who, pray tell, is responsible for lighting this particular fire under the board's ass?"

Elias slides a thin folder across the table. A glossy headshot peeks out. Elegant. Blond. Grinning like the cat that buried the canary in diamonds.

I freeze. "Is that—?"

"Josephine Duclare," Amara confirms. "She's been petitioning the board to declare you 'unfit for succession.' Citing erratic lifestyle, unstable investments, and"—she actually air quotes—"a 'persistent bachelor identity unbecoming of the Montcroix legacy.'"

"She's trying to *force me into marrying her*, isn't she?"

"She's betting you'll do anything to keep the estate."

"Then she clearly hasn't met me."

"You're right," Amara says, not missing a beat. "She hasn't."

I narrow my eyes.

I exhale through my nose. Suddenly I'm more exasperated than when I arrived. "So your brilliant solution to this—this Montcroix monarchy speedrun—is what? Toss me to the wolves? Line up a desperate heiress with a tasteful veil and a hidden prenup?"

Elias lifts an eyebrow. "No. She lined up something better."

That's when Amara closes the folder and meets my eyes. "I got you a Shadow Bride."

I do not like the sound of this at all.

"You... what?" I say, choking on air.

"She needs protection from her ex husband," Amara says in a way where she is trying not to get annoyed. "And you need a wife."

"No," I say immediately, standing. "Absolutely not. I am not marrying a stranger in some shadow laced transactional charade—"

"She's perfect," Amara cuts in. "Smart. Steady. Two daughters. She doesn't want love, Claude. She wants safety. A new start. You want your legacy. It's mutually beneficial. It's only for a year."

I stare at her like she's grown another head. Elias just watches me with that barely contained amusement he saves for when I'm about to lose a game I didn't know I was playing.

"I thought you liked dramatic entrances," Amara says mildly. "She arrives next week."

"Then what?" I ask, incredulous. "I just say 'I do' and hope she doesn't kill me in my sleep?"

Amara smirks. "Only if you deserve it."

Elias lifts his glass at me like a toast. "Get your affairs in order, Montcroix."

I sink back into the chair, rubbing a hand over my face. "I don't even know her name."

Amara smiles. One of her smirks that says that she got her way even though we all knew she would. She always does.

"You'll find out at the wedding."

"The future Mrs. Montcroix," I echo. My lips spread into a twisted smile. "Poor girl."

Author Note

This book was a labor of love. Dante and Opal held pieces of my heart from the moment they existed on the page, long before I knew how their story would unfold.

Since book one, I knew this was the story I wanted to tell. I carried it with me through every outline, every draft, every decision. What I didn't realize was what they would become to me once I finally sat down to write it.

I thought I understood these characters. I thought I knew their ending. But the closer I got, the more the story resisted being contained by the version I had planned. The heart of the book moved somewhere more vulnerable than I expected, and I had to choose whether to force it back into shape or follow where it was leading me.

Following it meant confronting things I thought I had already resolved in my own life. It meant admitting that some wounds don't disappear just because time passes, and that growth isn't always empowering. Sometimes it's uncomfortable. Sometimes it looks like standing still long enough to recognize what still hurts.

Writing Opal taught me that setting boundaries with yourself can be harder than setting them with others. It's easy to draw a line for someone else. It's much harder to stop yourself from stepping back over it out of habit, guilt, or longing for something different. Whether it is different choices, people, or an outcome to a situation.

She taught me that it's okay to tell people to screw off. She also taught me that it's okay to admit that sometimes, you don't ever fully escape the people who destroyed you. Their voices linger. Their influence echoes like a ghost of your past. And acknowledging that doesn't make you weak. It makes you honest with yourself.

Dante taught me that wanting something doesn't make me selfish. That desire doesn't need to be justified to be valid.

There are people I have cut out of my life who still feel like they hold strings. For a long time, I believed that meant they still had power over me. Writing this book made me realize something harder to accept. I am the one holding those strings. I am the one letting *them* borrow them.

That realization didn't come with relief. It came with grief. Grief for the time I lost, the energy I gave away, and the version of myself who thought endurance was the same thing as strength.

But grief also made room for clarity.

I don't owe those people my strings.

I don't owe them a piece of my heart.

I don't owe them anything at all.

I owe myself peace.

I owe myself control over my own life.

I owe myself the kindness I kept reserving for everyone else.

And if you saw yourself anywhere in this story, if something here felt uncomfortably familiar or achingly close, I hope you know this wasn't written to expose you. It was written to remind you that you are allowed to let go of what hurts you, even if it once felt impossible to do so.

Thank you for trusting me with this story. Thank you for staying with Dante and Opal until the end. And thank you, most of all, for choosing yourself every time you close a book and carry its truth with you.

I owe myself everything.

I hope you do too.

Want more of Dante and Opal?

See how they celebrate Christmas... with their little surprise coming.

Read it here: https://dl.bookfunnel.com/eq9eay605j

Up Next

Coming Soon in the Shadow Brides Series

Opal Greer and Dante Valera found their version of forever.

Now it's Maris's turn.

A woman who ran.

A mother with two daughters and no margin for mistakes.

A husband who refuses to stay gone.

So she disappears.

A new town.

New rules.

And a choice no one should have to make.

The Society of Shadow Brides offers protection.

The price is marriage.

The match is made. The paperwork is ready. All that's left is her signature.

Welcome to Thronwick.

Try not to lose your soul.

Coming Soon.

Up Next in the Devil's Bargain Series

He's never been in a hurry for anything.

She's spent her whole life giving too much to everyone else.

But Sloth isn't about to wait.

He's about to take his time... because he refuses to destroy something beautiful.

Enemies will return. The world is about to fracture.

Coming March 2026

Also By

The Devil's Bargain

Wicked Union– A prequel novella (Liora and Evander's Story)

The Devil's Canvas

Gilded Lies

Unholy Vows (Selene and Theron's Story)

The Shadow Brides

Veil of Fire

Wildflowers & Whiskey (Frankie and Beckett's Story)

The Damaged Bride

The Huntington Brothers Series

Destined for Love

Tangled Hearts

Promises to Keep

Standalone Novels

The Keeper's Secret

Love on the Edge

Anthologies

Head in the Clouds: A Romantic Comedy Anthology

ALSO BY

Desperate: A Deadly Thriller Anthology

Did you love *The Damaged Bride*? If you enjoyed the story, I would be so grateful if you took a moment to leave a quick review. Thank you for reading, for your support, and for spending time with these characters. I can't wait for you to see what happens next!

About the Author

Sara McClaflin writes romance with feelings, flaws, and just the right amount of emotional damage. Her stories are character-driven, morally gray, and often ask one very important question: what if love was a little dangerous—and we liked it that way? After years of reading and reviewing books with too much angst, she finally started writing her own.

She lives on the West Coast with her husband, their chaotic dog, and more book boyfriends than she's willing to admit. Her TBR pile is a cry for help, her playlists are 80% heartbreak, and she's always chasing the next character who'll ruin her in the best way.

Newsletter Sign-Up

https://subscribepage.io/saranewsletter

Amazon Author Page

https://www.amazon.com/stores/Sara-McClaflin/author/B0CR8VHBHJ

Instagram

https://www.instagram.com/authorsaramcclaflin

Facebook

https://www.facebook.com/profile.php?id=61551822185090

TikTok

https://www.tiktok.com/@sara.mcclaflin

Goodreads

https://www.goodreads.com/author/show/47632250.Sara_McClaflin

Threads

https://www.threads.com/@authorsaramcclaflin

Content Warning List

- Off page rape/sexual assault (involving a side character, not the FMC)
- Off page suicide and suicide ideation
- Child endangerment and kidnapping
- Parental emotional abuse and toxic family dynamics
- Morally gray/black main characters
- Power imbalance in romantic and family relationships
- Arranged marriage (non-cultural, strategic/forced context)
- Themes of manipulation, gaslighting, and betrayal by friends/family
- Power play and control dynamics (emotional, romantic, and organizational)
- Active criminal investigations, cybercrime, corruption, and coverups
- Blackmail, coercion, threats of violence
- Gun violence and execution style scenes
- Profanity/strong language throughout
- Pregnancy, labor, and birth scenes (some intense)

Emotional trauma and PTSD like behavior

www.ingramcontent.com/pod-product-compliance
Lightning Source LLC
La Vergne TN
LVHW100503110826
845146LV00002B/499

* 9 7 9 8 9 9 9 1 7 7 8 2 7 *